I0606509

Wolf Creek was a place where people looked out for each other—until the summer of 2013, when a serial killer stalked the town, and I realized I might be the next victim…

"Did you see that?" I asked, afraid to look away from the spot for fear I'd lose it.

Riff glanced at the trees, then looked back at me. "See what?"

I pointed. "There."

"Dude, all I see is trees."

The bushes rustled crazily. Then a scary-looking Mr. Anderson stumbled out of the woods. The knees of his Wranglers were torn, one of the sleeves of his Levi jacket was missing, and his flannel shirt was untucked on the right side. His face was splattered with dark, gooey spots, and he peered compulsively over his shoulder like something was chasing him.

"Whoa." Riff took a step back. "Freaky."

I ran toward the man. "My God, Mr. Anderson. What happened? Are you okay?"

He stared at me with haunted, unseeing eyes, and babbled incoherently as he pointed back into the woods.

"Thing—eat—kill—" he sobbed hysterically and collapsed.

"It's okay. Everything's going to be okay. Nothing's going to hurt you."

He continued to snivel, but calmed a bit, and pulled his head out from under his Levi jacket collar.

"It's okay," I told him. "You're safe now."

But I wasn't so sure. I needed to get home and tell Beth what happened, so we could talk about what to do next. I figured we had until the next full moon before someone else was murdered.

The nightmare of Wolf Creek starts the night of the last full moon in the summer of 2013, and the close-knit little community will never be the same again. Someone—or something—is murdering the townspeople during each month's full moon. Incredibly, no one connects the murders to the cycle of the moon. At least, not until fourteen-year-old James Manarro is confronted by his eleven-year-old cousin Beth Ann with her suspicions about the identity of the killer. A werewolf. At first, James just laughs it off, but with each vicious murder, he's forced to admit that Beth may be right…and one, or both, of them might be its next victim.

KUDOS for *Moonspell*

In *Moonspell* by Lisanne Harrington, James "Jaime" Manarro is a fourteen-year-old boy whose town is experiencing a series of brutal murders. James and his cousin Beth think the culprit is a werewolf, and they think they know who it is, but how to prove it? Especially when no one believes them because they're just kids? As the bodies mount and the town panics, James and Beth decide to take matters into their own hands, making themselves unwitting targets for the killer's wrath. Can they survive long enough to make someone listen, or will the killing continue with each new full moon? It's an intriguing story, a little dark for YA, but that is part of its appeal. Once they pick it up they won't be able to put it down until they finish. ~ *Taylor Jones, Reviewer*

Moonspell by Lisanne Harrington is a story of the horror visited on a small town in Southern California when a vicious serial killer tears apart its victims. The town is in an uproar while a teenager and his young cousin try to solve the murders and end up on the killer's hit list. Our hero, James Manarro, is fourteen years old, and when his cousin Beth, who is just eleven, tells him she saw the killer who murdered her father and it's a werewolf, James laughs—at first. As more and more people get torn to shreds, James is forced to admit that his cousin might be right. But what to do about it? The sheriff seems to believe them, but he's not about to announce his suspicions to the public. They'd laugh him out of town. The deputy sheriff has it in for James, so he's no help either. And James's parents still insist on calling him Jaime, his childhood nickname, so they obviously won't take him seriously. As the adults turn their backs on James and

Beth, the two decide to go after the killer themselves. With the help of the only adult who believes them, these unlikely heroes set about trapping a monster, only to discover that monsters aren't as easy to take down as they might think. *Moonspell* is a dark fantasy that explores both sides of bravery—courage and fear—and what it's like to know the truth when no one believes you so you have to watch the worst happen, knowing you can't stop it. It's an exciting, terrifying, and suspense-filled tale that should appeal to young adults, new adults, and older adults alike. ~ *Regan Murphy, Reviewer*

ACKNOWLEDGMENTS

First and foremost, thanks go to my family for putting up with my weirdness as I set out on this journey to my life-long dream of writing for a living. To my precious first-born, Jennifer, my harshest critic and biggest cheerleader. To Erin, my lovely youngest, who keeps me sane and grounded and in touch with my feelings. To Tod, my Beloved husband, who doesn't really understand what I do but supports me with all his heart anyway. I love you guys.

To my friend and mentor, Bonnie Hearn Hill, who taught me how to craft a story and has inspired and encouraged me all these years. To Carol Davis Luce, who gave me additional tools that enabled me to grow in my writing.

A special thanks to Black Opal Books and Lauri Wellington for taking a chance on me, and to my wonderful editors, Shannon and Faith, for fine-tuning my writing and making *Moonspell* what it is today. And I couldn't forget Jack, who created an awesome cover that was just what I wanted.

And thanks to you, the reader. I hope you enjoy my story.

Moonspell

Book 1 of the
Wolf Creek Mysteries

Lisanne Harrington

A Black Opal Books Publication

DEDICATION

For Dad
We did it!

Tuesday, August 20, 2013

BLUE MOON

Third of four full moons of the season,
rather than the usual three
100% visible

Chapter 1

Wolf Creek's nightmare started during the last full moon of the summer, leaving the close-knit town forever changed.

Two days before New Student Orientation at the middle school, Martha Sommes, the Language Arts teacher, was on her way home. She'd spent the better part of the afternoon and early evening preparing her homeroom for the influx of new seventh graders. They would fill her days with their constant chatter, squirrelly activity, and the electronic toys they secretly used while she attempted to teach them how to write an essay and use vocabulary beyond OMG, BFF and TTFN. God, how she hated texting. And don't even get her started on twerking.

That year, the hot Santa Ana winds started early and chased Mrs. Sommes home as she stopped at the market for a can of dog food for Bitsy, her Cocker Spaniel, best friend and only companion. The hot, dry winds made her hair stand on end and her skin itch as though a posse of fire ants marched across her body. They also made her nerves jump, and she glanced over her shoulder several times to make sure she wasn't being followed.

Today, she'd lost track of the time and hadn't left school until nearly dark. She regretted her mistake because it meant she would be walking the last few blocks home from the market in nothing more than moonlight. And the odd light of the Blue Moon to boot. Lord, how she hated the dark.

It was all that moron, Arnie Kaczynski's, fault—a city employee whose only real responsibilities consisted of planning the annual Labor Day Festival and changing the bulbs on the light standards whenever they burned out. Or when some middle-school hoodlums broke them. She was sure he'd neglected the lights all over town for the past month because he was so busy making sure there were enough weenies to be bought by hungry picnickers. After all, he had the brains of a sea sponge with the attention span to match. On her way to school just that afternoon, she counted no less than five broken lights and called Gus Ingstrom, the City Manager, to complain.

"Fat lot of good that did."

Laziness infuriated her, and it came as no surprise that Arnie grew into a larger version of the slothful teen who had taken up space in her classroom years before.

No one but me cares about this town any more. The lazy kids she'd taught her first few years had grown into parents, who passed their apathy and lack of ambition on to their own kids, which were now her current crop of students. Thank God Arnie never managed to father a child. A least not yet. Picturing a second generation of Arnies wasting her time caused Mrs. Sommes to shudder.

She shifted her handbag to her other shoulder. As she did so, she thought she heard footsteps behind her. It was hard to tell, because the winds picked up again, growling as they blasted in from the desert. A lone tumbleweed careened crazily toward her and narrowly missed knocking her off-balance before it hurled itself against the door of The Quiet Riot, the nasty country bar run by Donna Glass. Donna had been one of Mrs. Sommes's more promising students. True potential unfulfilled.

"Who's there?" Mrs. Sommes demanded in her strict teacher's voice, turning to face whoever was behind her.

She hoped she sounded more confident than she felt. The angry wind whipped her hair into her eyes, and she brushed it impatiently away. She peered over the top of her glasses into the darkness, but couldn't see anything. She hurried on.

The wind screeched its high-pitched warning and exploded past her. The teacher dodged another tumbleweed and was nearly knocked ass-over-teakettle in the process.

"Heavens," she exclaimed, clutching the front of her blouse and trying to catch her breath. She leaned against the door of the First Edition Bookstore and fished in her purse for her asthma inhaler. Grasping it in both hands, she winced at the pain that flared in her arthritic knuckles as she brought it to her lips and puffed. As she sucked in the foul-tasting medicine, another big gust of wind blasted her in the face. She almost lost her glasses. While trying to hold on to them, she heard something growl behind her.

Fear strangled her. She couldn't catch her breath, in spite of repeated pulls on the inhaler. The shadows moved and darkened. Something was coming for her. She tried to scream, but nothing came out. Not even when she heard the howl of the wind and underneath it, the sound of something razor-sharp as it sliced through the air. There was a brief flash of pain, then nothing.

The nightmare was unleashed.

Wednesday, August 21, 2013

FULL MOON

Second day of lunar cycle
100% Visible

Chapter 2

Mrs. Sommes had threatened for years to retire to Florida or some other old-people place, so no one thought anything about her disappearance. Not at the time.

Not even when Principal McFadden found a hastily scrawled note, supposedly from her, on his desk. Any one of her former students could've told him that Mrs. Sommes wouldn't be caught dead writing anything that messy. Most people had trouble writing on a blackboard in a straight line, but not Mrs. Sommes. Her writing was always tiny and perfectly formed. She had even fought against dropping penmanship from the curriculum, knowing full well it was a losing battle.

Wolf Creek was a small town in rural Southern California, where everyone knew everyone else, or at least everyone else's business. It was a town where people looked out for each other, where they cared about their neighbors, but acted like they couldn't stand them. It was all very Homer Simpson.

At least, that's how it was before the summer of 2013. I was fourteen years old that year, and my cousin, Beth, was eleven.

Thursday, August 22, 2013

WANING GIBBOUS

Old moon
Growing smaller
97% visible

Chapter 3

Our house was nothing fancy—two bedrooms, kitchen, living room and a full bathroom. Currently, it was a little crowded because Aunt Judy and my cousin were now living with us. On the way home from work one night, Uncle Fred had a heart attack and crashed his car, and there wasn't enough money for them to live on their own. Uncle Fred had been a pretty cool dude. When I was a kid, he used to grab me under the arms and throw me in the air. He smelled like stale coffee and Old Spice. On holidays, he always gave me a quarter, pretending to pull it out from behind my ear. Last Christmas, when I was thirteen and too old for magic tricks, he snorted as he did the old quarter thing, even though I wasn't a kid any more. Since I liked Uncle Fred, I laughed too. I missed him.

I didn't mind them being there, mostly, even when Mom made me give up my room and sleep on the couch. What pissed me off was her insisting I make it "girl-friendly" and take down my poster of the Kardashian sisters in white bikinis.

My cousin Beth could be a real pain in the neck, always following me around and stating her baby opinions. But she was kind of cute with her thick brown hair in braids that stuck out at odd angles, and all those freckles dotting her nose and cheeks. I used to tease her by asking her to get me a pen so I could connect the dots. Her tagging along everywhere I went wasn't cool, but she was fun, and, most of the time, we got along. Not that I'd ever admit it to anyone, but I didn't mind having her around.

They'd lived with us for about a month when Labor Day weekend came. That weekend brought a terrifying nightmare to Wolf Creek, one the town would never forget.

I know I never will.

☽

Our new living arrangements went pretty much as expected. It was crowded, but Mom always said an ounce of blood was worth a pound of friendship so I had to get used to them staying.

From the beginning, when my aunt and cousin showed up, lugging everything they owned in three huge suitcases and Beth's school backpack, I could tell something was wrong. It was there in Beth's pinched face and unusual frown, not to mention the careful distance she kept from her mom.

I picked up the two largest suitcases and couldn't believe how heavy they were. What, did they have a dead body in there? Tucking the smallest one under my arm, I shoved one of the backpack straps into my mouth and followed the women inside. Setting the luggage down just inside the door, I watched Beth stand uncertainly in the middle of the floor. She scowled so hard it gave her a unibrow.

Aunt Judy went to kiss her on the forehead, but Beth flinched and took a step back. Aunt Judy frowned and shook her head slightly. "Sweetie, you go on with Jaime, now. Get situated. I'll be in the kitchen if you need me."

Beth glared at her. What was that look about? Was she mad at Aunt Judy about something? Beth was so quiet it was kind of creepy. Usually, she wouldn't shut up. Maybe it was because of what happened to her dad? Or maybe she was just being a girl. Who knew? But I made it my mission to get her to laugh again soon.

Picking up her overstuffed suitcase in one hand, I reached for her hand with my other. "Come on, kiddo. Let's get you unpacked."

Silently, she picked up her backpack and glanced at me before looking back at her feet. Looking at them, too, I wondered what was so interesting down there. We went into my room and I tossed the suitcase on my bed. Without a word, she did the same with her backpack then climbed on the bed and unzipped the suitcase. I sat on the edge of the bed and watched as she flipped open the top and took out a few things.

She fingered a couple of T-shirts then looked at me. This time she didn't look away. Her eyes were beginning to tear up. "I miss him so much," she whispered. It was the first thing she'd said since she arrived.

Before I could say anything, she bolted to her knees and hurled into my chest, sobbing so hard it nearly broke my heart. Crying girls made me squirm. I never knew what to say. On account of she was my cousin, this was even worse.

Shifting a little, I put my arm around her. Not being a nurturing kind of guy, I didn't know what else to do. So first I patted then rubbed her shoulder. Couldn't think of anything to say, so I sat there and let her cry, hoping she would stop soon.

After what seemed like forever, her sobs slowed, and she lifted the edge of her shirt to try and wipe the snot and tears off her face. Instead she managed to smear most of it onto the end of her freckled nose and chubby cheeks.

I crossed to my desk and grabbed a couple of tissues. "Here." I handed them to her. "You missed a spot."

She took the tissues and folded them in half. "Where?"

I grinned. "Well, everywhere."

She did her best to get it all, then waded the tissues and tossed them into the trash basket.

"You okay, Bethie?"

"Yeah, I'm all right. Sorry about that."

"No problem." I opened my arms as wide as possible. "Welcome to my crib."

She smiled and scratched her cheek. "Sorry about taking over your room." She rubbed one wet eye while taking in the rest of the room. "Where will you sleep?"

I gestured toward the living room. "My kingdom awaits."

"You have to sleep on the couch because of me?"

"It's actually more comfy than this lumpy old bed, what with the big hole in the middle. Better watch out, or it'll swallow you in a single bite."

"Liar." She giggled, then picked up the clothes that fell on the floor while she was crying. She sat there a minute, staring at her hands, and then took a deep breath. "Thanks, Jaime. I wasn't sure about coming here. I mean, it was bad enough when Daddy died, but then when Mom said we had to leave home and move in with you guys, I thought…"

"You thought what? That I wouldn't want you here?"

"Well…" she mumbled.

"Don't be stupid, cuz." I scootched over, threw my arm around her shoulders again, and squeezed. "Not want you here? Puh-leaze."

I planted a big, wet raspberry on her cheek.

She giggled again and pushed me away. Then, without warning, she lunged forward and hugged me so tight I was afraid she would bust my ribs if she didn't stop.

"You're awesome, you know that?" She pulled back and tucked a strand of hair behind her ear. "Now, where can I put my things?"

Monday, September 2, 2013
Labor Day

WANING CRESCENT

Old moon
Growing smaller
9% Visible

Chapter 4

Labor Day was hot and dry. The Santa Ana winds, what my uncle called devil winds, had blown in for over a week. With gusts up to forty miles an hour, it was a pain just walking across the street. Bits of paper clung to the bushes, and piles of dirt lined the gutters and dotted the sidewalks like paint ball splatters. Dead twigs were scattered everywhere.

Beth and I braved the winds and went down to the park right after breakfast. We were supposed to meet my best friend, Riff. Beth didn't like him because he usually picked on her, but if they wanted to hang out with me, they needed to learn to get along. Or I would kill them both.

There were a lot of other people already there. Riff would be late as usual, so we sat on the bandstand and watched folks apply last-minute touches to the carnival booths. At one booth, some guy put up a hand-painted sign saying they were giving away free samples of homemade cookies. At another, hot dogs were a dollar and canned sodas were seventy-five cents. Multi-colored crepe paper was twisted around the poles holding the booths together. Tables and chairs were set up for picnickers. One Direction blasted from one of the booths, but couldn't drown out the noise of the drills and hammers.

After a few minutes, a short, loud whistle caught our attention. It was Riff. He raced across the greenbelt, trying not to spill his usual Big Gulp filled with Mountain Dew. It seemed to be a losing battle. How could he stand that stuff? He was never without it, drank gallons every day.

"Hey, dude," I said in greeting. "What's up?"

"Dude," he got out between labored pants. "I ran—all the way here—as soon as—I heard."

Beth and I exchanged looks. "Heard what?" I asked.

Riff was so random, you could never be sure what he would say or do.

"They found Mrs. Sommes." He took a deep breath. "Or at least what was left of her."

"Wait—what?"

"In the field by the train tracks. That kid you were in Boy Scouts with? Mark…what's-his-name? He's the one who found her."

"You mean Mark Richards?" I couldn't believe it. I hadn't spoken to Mark since I left Scouts in the fourth grade. "No way."

"Way." Riff nodded, his eyes wide. "They said he was out collecting rocks to earn some loser merit badge he was working on. When he reached down to pick one up, his hand brushed against something."

"What was it?" Beth piped up.

I wasn't sure I wanted to know.

"A severed foot. Dude." He paused, no doubt for effect. "It was still wearing a ladies' shoe. Like the kind your mom wears."

"Oh, my God." My stomach rolled and bitter acid rose to the back of my throat. I couldn't imagine what Mrs. Sommes went through, or what happened to the rest of her. I didn't want to know. "How do they know it was Mrs. Sommes's foot?"

"It had a tattoo of a wolf's head on the ankle. Just like Sommes's."

Freaked out by what Riff told us, Beth and I ran home to tell our parents, but they already heard. They were in the living room, the TV on low, when we flew through the front door.

"Mom, Dad," I yelled, stopping so suddenly Beth bumped into me. I hardly noticed. "You'll never guess what Riff told me."

"Shh." Dad pointed at the television. The news was on, and they were talking about finding Mrs. Sommes's body.

"…the fifty-four-year-old school teacher taught Language Arts at Wolf Creek Middle School for the past thirty years. She will be missed. This is Dawn Summers, Channel Ten news. Back to you, Jim."

Dad clicked the remote. The TV went off. At first, no one said anything.

"Did they say anything about—" I wanted to ask about Mark, but Mom cut me off.

"Who would've thought something like that could happen here?" She and Dad exchanged glances.

"God," Aunt Judy pitched in. "Let's hope it was just a one-time thing and never happens again."

Beth snorted and we all turned to her.

Aunt Judy narrowed her eyes. "You got something to say, little missy?"

"No. Mother."

Beth's empty voice caused my mom to frown, and my dad tilted his head as if trying to figure out what was wrong. I just stared at her. She ignored all of us. "I'm going to my room."

When she slammed the door, Mom turned to my

aunt. "What in the world was that all about?"

"I don't know. She's been acting weird ever since Fred died. I'll tell you what, I've had just about all I can take." Aunt Judy stood, her fists clenched tighter than the lid on a pickle jar.

"Maybe its puberty," Dad suggested.

Mom shot him a scowl, then reached out and took hold of Aunt Judy's arm.

"Come on, sis," she coaxed. "Just let her be. Help me make some sandwiches for lunch."

They headed into the kitchen, and I plopped down next to Dad. He flipped the TV back on and channel surfed until he got to the SyFy channel. There was an old *Twilight Zone* marathon on, which was one of the few things we both enjoyed, so we sat there, pretending to watch until Mom called us for lunch.

Beth refused to come eat, so after devouring two ham and cheese on rye and one chicken salad sandwich, I slapped together a PB and J. Jamming it and a bag of Chili Cheese Fritos into a lunch sack, I went and knocked on her door.

"What?"

She was still pissed, all right.

"Beth, it's me."

"What do you want?"

Geez, what a diva.

"We never did find out about the concert. Let's go back and see when it starts. Want to?"

Silence.

"I got your favorite here." I held up the sack, as if she could see through the door. Wiggling it back and forth, I hoped she would hear it and come out. "PB and J. With apricot 'J.' Nice and thick, just the way you like it."

About to give up and turn away, I heard scraping noises, and then she opened the door. "Show me."

I opened the sack so she could look inside. While she inspected the contents, I peered around her and saw my desk chair sitting in the middle of the room. "Did you barricade the door?"

"What?" With the sandwich hanging out of her mouth, she turned around and seemed surprised to see the chair there. "Oh, yeah. Let me put it back."

That was weird, barricading the door, but I didn't ask her about it because with girls, who knew?

"Hey, you know what?" I snapped my fingers as if I'd just thought of something. "How's about we go back to the park? Hang out a while. What do you say?"

"'Kay."

By the time we got to the park she'd finished her sandwich and was munching on the Fritos. Riff was still there, sitting on a bench, drinking his never-ending soda and watching a girl in a tank top and shorts attempt to attach a sign to the top of her booth. She was about three inches too short, and her belly ring, shaped like a dragon-fly, dangled against her skin.

"Hey, dude," I called. "S'up?"

"Dude." He motioned to the girl with his cup. "Nice."

I watched the girl, too. "Yeah."

"Creeps," Beth muttered.

Riff didn't take his eyes off the girl. "Babysitting again?"

"Knock it off, Riff," I warned, knowing he could push Beth back into her weird mood. "Just shut up, will you? I'm sick and tired of you ragging on her all the time."

"Oh, yeah?" he retorted. "And what if I'm sick and tired of her always hanging around?"

"Then I guess you don't have to hang out with me, do you?"

He sucked angrily on his straw and glared at me over the top of the cup. "Fine."

I raised my left eyebrow just to annoy him. As soon as he saw that, he jammed his free hand into a pocket, turned on his heels, and stomped back the way he'd come.

I watched him until he turned around to glare at us, which I knew he would do. "Fine." Then I turned very deliberately to Beth. "Real mature."

Crossing my eyes and sticking out my tongue, I got a snort from her and grinned. As expected, Riff saw this and left the park.

She watched him stomp away, and her big green eyes filled with sadness. "Sorry you guys had a fight over me."

"Pfftt." I scratched behind my ear. "Don't worry about Riff. He'll get over it. He's always pissed off about something or other, but it never lasts long. Besides, how do you think he got the name 'Riff' in the first place? Think he'd rather be called Harold?"

"Harold? That's his name? Really?" She chortled so hard I thought she would pee her pants. "You're kidding, right?"

"Nope. Now let's go see about that concert."

I chuckled as we headed over to the Information Booth. Riff would be so pissed when he found out I told her his real name. But the pay-off would be awesome, because, knowing Beth, she'd find a way to get back at him someday and use it when it would embarrass him the most. Part of me hoped it would be today, because that would get her mind off Uncle Fred's death for sure.

There were flyers pinned up all over the park. I grabbed one off a pole and found the concert started at four.

"Hey, cuz." I turned, but she'd vanished. "Now

where'd she go?" I muttered, looking around. She was on the other side of the park, hunkered down in the middle of some trees, peering between a couple of low branches. There was no telling what she was doing. I strolled over to her. "What are you gawking at?"

"Shh." She didn't so much as glance at me. "Look."

She pointed in between the trees into the clearing. I crouched next to her and looked where she pointed.

Arnie, the guy who did a great job planning the Labor Day picnic every year, was waving his arms all over the place, yelling at Mary Fitzpatrick. Mary, three years older than me, was crying.

"I don't care what you say." Arnie looked like he swallowed a bug. "It ain't mine."

"Arnie, how can you say that?" Mary sobbed. "I love you."

"Love me? You don't even know me."

"Yes, I do. You—you're the only one I've ever been with…you know…that way."

"Who're you trying to kid? I know for a fact you've screwed half the boys in the senior class. Probably the entire football team, too."

"That's not true," she hollered. Her face was so red, I thought she might have a stroke. "I've never been with anyone but you."

"Look, you little ho. I'm sorry you got yourself knocked up, but I'm not the father. You ain't going to trap me with your lies."

He turned to go, and Mary grabbed his arm, jerking him back.

He glared at her with unfettered hostility.

"What am I going to do, Arnie?" Mary's voice was so quiet we could barely hear her. "I can't tell my parents. You've got to help me."

"Let go." Arnie's voice turned icy.

She hesitated then released her grip.

He shook his arm like she had cooties.

"Arnie?"

He got right in her face and poked her shoulder with his index finger, hard enough that she took a step backward.

"Listen up, you little bitch, and listen good. For the last time, it's not my baby. And if you tell anyone it is, you'll be very, very sorry." He punctuated every few words with a step and a jab.

She could do nothing but back up every time he poked her.

"But—"

"Leave. Me. Alone." He turned and disappeared into the trees on the other side of the clearing. Mary crumpled to the ground.

Beth and I gaped at each other. Even if Mary was lying, and I seriously doubted she was, Arnie didn't have to leave her in a weeping heap on the ground.

"She's having a baby?" Beth whispered.

"Yeah, I think so."

Beth forced her way through the underbrush, ignoring the stickers. I grabbed her arm. "Where do you think you're going?"

"She's crying, you big dope. We have to help her." She wrenched her arm away and stomped her foot. It would've been funny, if she hadn't been so mad.

On second thought, it was funny, and I laughed.

"Oooh, so serious."

Instead of making her giggle, my teasing made her madder. "Screw you." She pushed the branches aside and marched straight into the clearing.

Mary's plaid skirt had ridden up on her hip, exposing her white panties, now grass-stained and dirty. I never really noticed her before, but if it weren't for the smudges on her cheeks and the snot bubble threatening to drip off her left nostril, she might have been kind of pretty. In a plain sort of way.

Beth knelt and touched her shoulder. "Hey, you okay?"

Mary sniffed and wiped the snot off her face with her sleeve. She looked up and caught me watching her. Then she grabbed the hem of her skirt and daintily smoothed it down over her legs.

"I—I'm all right," she stammered, pulling her blouse out of the waistband of her skirt and using the end of it to dab her eyes.

Beth sat back on her haunches and tucked her hair behind her ear. "We heard what you told Arnie."

I elbowed her roughly in a vain attempt to shut her up. It wasn't any of our business what happened between them. When she turned around to glare at me, I furrowed my eyebrows right back and held my finger to my lips.

She didn't back down. "What? We were standing right there."

Sometimes, I wished she was older so she could understand things like discretion and tact. Hopefully she would learn soon, preferably before her mouth got us into big trouble.

Mary scrambled to her feet. "I don't know what you're talking about."

Beth turned from me and focused on Mary. "We just want to help."

"Well, I don't need any help, thank you very much."

She tucked her blouse back into her skirt with such force I thought she might tear a hole in it.

Mary was smart enough to know about DNA and stuff, but I decided to bring up the obvious, just in case she hadn't thought about it. "You know, they have tests they can do to prove who the father is."

Mary brushed grass off the back of her skirt. It was short and showed her chunky legs. Her hand moved almost too fast to follow. "You guys need to mind your own business."

Beth picked invisible lint off her shirt. "I was only trying to help."

"I don't need your help, you stupid little creep," Mary snapped. "I don't need anyone's help. Just leave me alone." Bursting into tears again, she turned and ran away.

Beth sniffed then peered up at me with red-rimmed eyes. "Guess you were right, huh? We should have left her alone."

I slung my arm across her thin shoulders and gave her a squeeze. "What am I going to do with you?"

She made a small noise deep in her throat, and her face turned white. She made that same rumbling noise again, and it started to freak me out.

"Are you…growling?"

"Look." She pointed across the park. "It's my mom. Let's get out of here." She ran across the grass and ducked behind the stage.

"Hey, wait up." I ran after her. "What's the matter?" When I caught up to her, I grabbed her arm and spun her around. "What's your problem?"

She gave me that standard-Beth-one-shoulder shrug. "My mom's here."

"So?"

"So, I don't want to see her."

"Why not?" My eyes narrowed land I frowned. "Why're you so pissed off at her, anyway?"

"You wouldn't understand."

That made me roll my eyes. Drama mama.

She peeked out from behind the stage. "Good. She's gone." She gave me her lopsided grin. "Let's go see who's in the dunk tank now. Want to?"

"Yeah." What was going on with this chick? I sighed. "Sure."

We headed back toward the carnival booths. She threw her leg up behind her and kicked me in the butt.

"Hey, no fair." I kicked her back. We both laughed, and I was glad she seemed to have forgotten all about Mary.

Neither one of us would think about her again until the next full moon.

$$\mathbb{D}$$

"Jaime, take out the garbage, will you?"

I sighed heavily. For years I tried to get my parents to call me James, or even Jim, anything but Jaime. It was a stupid baby name, and I couldn't stand it. Since fifth grade the kids at school called me James, mostly because if they didn't, I threatened to beat them up. Not something I could do with my family, though. For some reason I never figured out, the 'rents ignored my repeated requests. Finally, I just gave up.

"I'll do it later."

"You'll do it now, young man." She gave me the "mom" look. You know the one.

"Fine." I yanked the trashcan from under the sink, took out the bag, and began twisting it shut while they talked like I wasn't even there.

"I just don't know what to do about her." Aunt Judy pulled a tissue out of the waistband of her shorts and dabbed gently at her nose. "You've seen her. She hardly eats, and she almost never says anything to me anymore. When she does, it's usually snotty or outright angry."

Mom reached across the table and patted Auntie's

hand. "Give her some time, Jude. She just misses Fred, that's all."

"I don't know. I think it's more than that. I think she blames me, somehow, for his death." She turned to me. "What do you think, Jaime?"

These days Beth was always pissed around her mother, but how could she blame her for her father's death? She hadn't been driving the car. I shrugged. "Beats me."

"Well, has she said anything to you at all?"

"About what?"

"Jaime," my mother scolded. "Pay attention. Has Beth said anything to you about blaming Judy for Fred's death?"

"No." I shook my head. "Nothing."

Even if she had, I'd never rat her out. Besides, Aunt Judy told us a massive heart attack made Uncle Fred lose control of his car and plow into the huge oak tree. How could that be anyone's fault?

☽

Mom's so full of it. Beth lay in Jaime's bed. *She killed Daddy, and she's lying about how he died.* She picked at the fuzz on the nose of her stuffed Elmo. Her constant companion when she was little, she'd told her mom she could donate him to charity, but grabbed him back out of the cardboard box at the last minute. Something told her she would need him again soon. Two weeks later, her father was dead.

She rolled on her side and buried her face in Elmo's soft red fur. "Oh, Momo." It was her special nickname for the toy. "It's just not fair."

There was a knock and the door opened. She quickly

swiped her eyes, not wanting anyone, especially her mother, to see her crying. She wished she remembered to barricade the door.

"Can I come in, sweetie?"

It was her aunt, not her mom. Beth sighed with relief and rubbed her face against Elmo to get rid of the last of her tears. "Sure."

Aunt Annette walked over and sat down on the edge of the bed. She stroked Beth's hair. "Honey, are you okay?"

"Yeah, I'm fine. Just tired. Busy day, I guess."

Her aunt gently took hold of her chin and made Beth look directly at her. "You sure that's what's wrong?"

Beth hesitated only a fraction of a second before she nodded, but she could tell her aunt didn't believe her by the way she tilted her head and squinted her eyes and studied her. Beth almost broke down and spilled everything, but then Jaime stuck his head in the door. "Hey, is this a girlie party, or can anyone come in?"

"I was just tucking in our little angel, here." Aunt Annette brushed Beth's bangs off her forehead and kissed her cheek. Then she whispered into her ear, "I'm here if you need me, sweetie."

Beth smiled, but decided not to say anything. Her aunt grinned back, tweaking Elmo's nose. She got up from the bed and walked slowly toward Jaime. She placed her hand on his arm and whispered something to him. He nodded and waited for her to leave the room before he came and sat next to Beth.

She gestured toward the door, her head tilted. "What was that all about?"

"What? Mom?"

She nodded and hugged Elmo a little tighter.

"Oh, you know. She's worried about you. Everyone is."

"Yeah, I know. Poor little Beth," she said, mimicking her mom. "I just don't know what to do about her." She rolled her eyes. "Yeah, right. Like she doesn't know exactly what's going on."

He cocked his head, a peculiar expression on his face, the same one Uncle Robbie sometimes wore.

She realized what he was about to say, and held up her hand to stop him before he said a word.

"Don't ask. Even if I did tell you what's really going on, you wouldn't believe me."

"What are you talking about?"

"Nothing. Just forget it." Tucking Elmo under her arm, she rolled away from him. "I'm tired. Shut off the light."

When he stood up, the bed jiggled. She could feel him watching her. Finally, he flicked off the light and left without saying another word. She'd hurt his feelings, and she was sad about not being honest with him about how her father really died, but she wasn't sure she could trust him. After all, she'd had a hard time believing it herself. How could she possibly make him understand something so scary and unreal? What could she say to make him believe her?

It took her a long time to fall asleep. When she finally did, she dreamed of her father being killed by a monster. Then the monster chased her and tried to kill her, too.

When she woke up the next morning, she knew time was running out, and that she needed to come clean to her cousin about how her father had died.

And who had killed him.

Tuesday, September 17, 2013

WAXING GIBBOUS

Young moon
Growing larger
95% Visible

Chapter 5

I really miss you, Momma."

Eleven-year-old Lindy St. George studied the picture in the heart-shaped locket her mother had given her. It was a tradition started by her great-grandmother. Every girl got it on her eighth birthday. There was a teeny picture of her mother on one side and one of Lindy on the other. It was Lindy's favorite possession. She looked inside it often.

"Dishes won't wash themselves," her father called to her from the living room, where he drank his dinner. Again.

She turned on the faucet and squirted some Palmolive into the sink. "I'm filling the sink now."

"Well, hurry up. Then go to bed."

She didn't understand why her father hated her. He never used to. When Momma was still alive, Lindy would run to him every night when he came home from work, and he would take her in his arms and throw her up in the air. Up, down. Up, down. Then they'd twirl around the living room until they were both so dizzy they fell onto the couch in a heap and giggled until they couldn't breathe. Once, she loved her father and he loved her. Now, she only wanted to stay out of his way.

She gazed out the kitchen window at what used to be her mother's flower garden. The two of them had planted everything from pansies and Johnny Jump Ups in the fall, to agapanthus and daylilies in the summertime. Her mother loved pansies, but to Lindy, the magenta daylilies were the prettiest. Momma said they reminded her of little pink stars.

But when she died, Lindy didn't have the heart to tend the garden, and now it was all weeds and dead plants. The hot Santa Ana winds had blown everything all over the place, and it had become an unloved patch of dirt.

Something tickled her arm, and she was surprised to find the sink so full the soap suds were about to spill onto the floor. While she quickly turned off the water, she checked over her shoulder to make sure her father was still in his chair, drinking his Coors and blissfully unaware of his daughter's near mistake. She piled the dirty dinner dishes into the suds.

As she reached for the knife she used to cut the chicken before frying it, she heard something rustling around in the back yard, somewhere beyond the lifeless garden. She strained to hear over the roar of her father's television set. She couldn't be sure, but…Yeah, there it was again. She distinctly heard something growling out there. It sounded like a big dog, maybe a Rottweiler or even a Mastiff. But not exactly. Something was different about the sound. It was deeper, angrier, somehow.

Cranking open the window over the sink, she peered outside and squinted in an attempt to make out anything through the twilight gloom. Everything was murky, and she wished the wind would die down so she could hear what was out there. She also wished it would stop blowing clouds across the moon so she could see into the shadows surrounding her father's dilapidated tool shed.

Whatever it was, she wasn't about to go out there and investigate. Better to simply finish the dishes and go to bed. The last of the silverware was in the drainer, so she wiped her hands on the ragged dishtowel and hung it neatly over the oven door handle. Then she stuck her head in the doorway between the kitchen and the living room and watched her father as he sat in a stupor, mouth slack and his hand jammed down the front of his pants. She took a deep breath and pasted her best smile on her face. "Night, Daddy."

No response. She hadn't really expected one. Sighing heavily, she went into her room and closed the door softly behind her. As she got undressed, she thought about the sounds she heard coming from the back yard. She could have flipped on the outside light and flooded the yard, but she wasn't sure she really wanted to see what was out there. It scared her. She wasn't sure why. It was probably nothing, just a dumb old dog. But what if it wasn't?

She crawled into bed and pulled the sheet over her head. Was she safe here in her room, all alone? At least she had her mother's picture on the nightstand. Momma was there to chase away the bad dreams.

Lindy looked around for her teddy bear, the one she sprayed with her mother's perfume. If she held Teddy to her nose, she could pretend her mom was right there with her.

She snatched the bear off the floor and wrapped her arms around him. The sounds were getting stronger. There were no such things as boogeymen or monsters. She knew that. But that growling scared her, even more than her father scared her, and she wasn't going to take any chances. Besides, her mother was up in heaven watching down on her, and Momma wouldn't let anything bad happen to her.

Would she?

☽

Great kid. Homer St. George listened to the sounds of his daughter cleaning the kitchen. After he took a swig of brew, he burped loudly, wiped his mouth on his sleeve, and turned back to the boob tube. One of those lame commercials with a couple on a park bench eating ice cream was on. The voice-over was supposed to be the old woman, saying something about never being apart a single night in all the forty-some-odd years they'd been together.

Tears welled in his eyes. It wasn't fair. They were supposed to be together forever. His beloved Elizabeth wasn't supposed to die so young. Even after the doctors told them there was nothing else they could do, he held out hope until the very end. Cancer had eaten her alive, from the inside out, until the day she finally gave up and left him.

Since then, it hurt to even be around their daughter. She reminded him so much of her mother. Every time she smiled, it was Elizabeth's face he saw. When she laughed, it was the same musical sound his wife had made. Her mother was the only woman who ever really loved him, and now she was gone. He couldn't stand it, so he started drinking, even though it wouldn't numb the pain forever. At first, it felt good to forget about her.

But he had to drink more and more in order to get to the point where he could forget, and that pissed him off. He tossed another can on the mound piled in the corner then examined the shabby living room. Before it was always spotless. Now, he couldn't seem to get Lindy to keep it clean.

Why was it so hard for her to toss out the trash and run the vacuum once in a while?

"Lindy," he shouted. Damn kid was probably wasting time reading or something equally stupid. He would have to teach her a lesson, whether she liked it or not.

Even if it killed him.

Thursday, September 19, 2013

HARVEST MOON

Full moon closest
to the autumnal equinox
99% Visible

Chapter 6

Mary Fitzpatrick sat on the edge of her bed and picked at the yellow daisies embroidered into the coverlet by her mother. The baby was beginning to show. It wouldn't be long before she'd have to confess everything to her parents. The kids at school were sure to talk about it behind her back soon, if they hadn't already. She could already feel their stares.

She'd called Arnie at work and left several voice mails, but he hadn't returned any of them. Finally, she confronted him at the Labor Day picnic, only to panic when those kids tried to help. She was ashamed of yelling at them, particularly that little girl.

But Mary had more to worry about than some kid's feelings. Her life was over. Arnie had lied when he told her he loved her. Only now did she realize that he would have said anything to get into her panties. He'd even promised to divorce his wife and marry her. She was such a dumbass to believe him. And so, here she was, with only one thing left to do.

A soggy paper cup, half-full of Diet Pepsi and melted ice, sat on the nightstand next to her bed. She'd chewed the straw most of the way through. The tiny white tablets she stole from her father's pharmacy were laid out next to her soda. She grabbed them and spread them out on her bed. Twenty-five ought to do the trick. As a pharmacist's daughter, she knew what kind of pills to use, although it hadn't made choosing them any easier. Usually, she tuned her father out whenever he started talking about how he hoped she would join the family business when she graduated from college. As a good daughter who loved her parents and couldn't bear the thought of disappointing them, she'd never quite found the guts to tell him that all she ever wanted to be was a mother. But not now. Not this way.

"Well," she said. "Now I won't have to tell him anything. I'll just go to sleep and then nothing'll matter anymore."

Choking back a sob, she grabbed the first pill and placed it on the tip of her tongue, and immediately grimaced. It tasted gross.

Taking a deep breath, she fidgeted with the tiny crucifix she wore on a silver chain around her neck. As she reached for another pill, she stopped suddenly and cocked her head. Outside, the Santa Ana winds blew like crazy, but she thought she heard something else, something underneath the screech of the wind. It was getting dark, but the harvest moon was high in the night sky, illuminating everything with its eerie yellow glow. She peered between two slats on her blinds. Her mother's rose bushes waved back and forth in the wind, and the McGovern's palm tree lost one of its fronds. It bounced off their son's Chevy Nova, illegally parked with two tires up on the curb, but there wasn't anything out of the ordinary.

She sighed and turned back to the business at hand. "Stop wasting time. If you're going to do this, just do it already."

Perched on the edge of the bed, she scooped up the rest of the pills and poured them into her mouth. After gagging a few times, she managed to swallow several sips of soda, then closed her eyes. Suicide was wrong, but she couldn't have stopped herself even if she'd wanted to.

She settled into her pillow and waited for the pills to take effect.

☽

The werewolf sniffed the air. It was full of the girl's scent. The still-human part understood that the girl deserved to die. While human, it'd heard the girl tell the man in the park that she was with child. Since she was throwing her life away anyway, the human buried under the fur figured, by killing the girl, it was actually saving her from going to hell for committing suicide.

Besides, it was so hungry, the beast could hardly stand it. It was impossible to think about anything else but filling its belly. It crept along the side of the house. When it came to a window, it stopped. The scent was strongest here, and it rose up on two legs and put its huge front paws on the window ledge. Its jagged claws scratched lightly against the glass. Something moved inside, and the werewolf retreated quickly. It crouched in the bushes and waited, listening to see if anyone had heard it. It didn't want to be discovered, not yet anyway. It could wait, for a little while, at least. But soon, the urge would become uncontrollable. Before long, it would have to satisfy its hunger for human flesh.

☽

Mary drifted along in that dark state somewhere between wide-awake and sound asleep. Images floated through her mind, happy pictures of times spent with her parents, playing Monopoly and Scrabble, taking long drives up to the mountains or down along the coast, watching TV and gorging on popcorn. She loved her parents and they were going to be very disappointed in her. But she just couldn't face them.

Dark images abruptly replaced thoughts of happier times. Rotting fetuses, their not-quite-human features scary and full of blame, sneering at her. The flames of hell scorched her flesh as she cried out for salvation. Her parents' faces, horrified and disgusted, melted off their skulls. A snarling demon, looking suspiciously like Arnie, came at her, jaws wide and claws ready to rip her apart.

Her eyes flew open. Disoriented, she tumbled off the bed and landed on the carpet, scraping her elbow and giving herself a huge rug burn.

"Ow," she mumbled. Struggling to pull herself into a sitting position, she grabbed big wads of the coverlet to do it. Nausea threatened to bring up the pills. She leaned against the bed and waited for it to subside. Dimly, she heard something scratch at her window.

Her head weighed a ton, and she grunted in a vain attempt to focus. A shadow appeared in her window, or at least she thought it was a shadow. She blinked several times, trying to see who was prowling around outside. *Arnie, that you?*

Mary tried to walk over to the window to let him in, but couldn't figure out how to make her legs work. The shadow moved, flickered, then disappeared altogether. She didn't understand what was happening, exactly, but she couldn't let Arnie go.

"Arrr," she called, trying to get his attention. The shadow reappeared, larger and darker than ever. It wavered a little, and even through the fog in her head, something didn't seem quite right. *Wha—Wait—*

Something growled a nanosecond before the window exploded, raining shards of glass all over her. The shadow loomed inside the splintered window frame, filling her with a terrifying darkness.

Mary tried to scream, but it came out as a thick, phlegmy screech. She struggled to stand, to run. The stench of rotten, maggot-infested meat assaulted her nostrils. Revulsion filled her throat with bile and she gagged. Claws, ragged and filthy, slashed, gouging bloody furrows into her neck and stomach. She tried to scream again and crab-walked to get away. She was cold, so cold. Hadn't the sweltering devil winds blown through her room all day? It might have been hot in her room, but she couldn't quite remember.

The next thing she knew, she was floating along the ceiling. It was pleasant there. Warm. She glanced down and saw herself being thrown all around the room. Watched as her life force poured out of her body with each splash of blood pulsing from her neck and belly. But it didn't matter. Nothing mattered any more. Not the baby, not her parents. Not even being condemned to hell for committing suicide.

She floated away.

☽

In the city maintenance engineer's back room, Arnie Kaczynski rearranged a deck of cards in his favor. He was in a hurry for his weekly poker game to begin. Every Monday night, holiday or not, four or five of the city employees got together to enjoy a friendly penny ante game. Sid Weinstein was a much better poker player than Arnie, but after all, neither one of them was really there for cards. For the past four or five months, he and Sid were the last to leave. Arnie knew he wasn't the sharpest tool in the shed, but even he was smart enough to know that kiddie porn wasn't for everyone. He and Sid indulged only after the others went home. Sid got off on pre-teen boys, but Arnie preferred girls between nine and eleven. It was his love of little girls that led him to sleep with that whore, Mary Fitzpatrick, in the first place. After all, she was built like a nine-year-old, chest like two raisins on a breadboard and almost no hair down there. Who did she think she was, getting herself knocked up and then trying to force him to claim it as his? She'd threatened to tell his wife, too. Even if it was true, even if the kid was his, he sure wasn't about to leave his wife for that slut or the bun in her oven. Nancy may not be anything special, but at least she earned a steady paycheck and left him alone to do whatever he wanted. He wasn't about to lose his security over some lying little bitch who was trying to trap him.

He grabbed a magazine out of his desk drawer and put his cigar down on the edge of the desk. While studying one particularly sweet young thing, he thought he heard something out in the hall.

"Who's there?" he called out. "Sid? Harry? That you, guys?"

No answer. *Must be hearing things*. He went back to his fantasy. He sure wanted to get him some of that.

The scratching sound came again, louder this time, and he couldn't ignore it. Reluctantly, he tossed his magazine in the top drawer of his desk and snuck over to the door. When a shadow passed behind the half-window, he threw himself back against the wall.

"What in the hell's going on here?" he mumbled.

If the guys were trying to pull a fast one on him, he'd show them a thing or two. The wind howled like a banshee, and it creeped him out.

He needed to get a grip and turn the tables on those morons.

"One," he whispered. "Two." Before he got to three, Arnie threw open the door and jumped through it, sure that the guys were lurking in the hallway. Thought they could scare him, did they? But no one was there. Confused, he scratched his head and scanned the hall. He squinted and tried to see into the farthest, darkest corners. Maybe they were hiding down there somewhere.

"Okay, you jerks." He hiked up his pants and sniffed. "You've had your fun. Now, can we play some cards, or are you gonna stand around in the dark and act like pussies all night?"

When there was no response, he turned and slowly walked back into the janitor's room to discover that his smoke had rolled off the desk and burned a small hole in the floor. Now they'd done it. He'd catch it for sure. That cow, the mayor, was always on his back about something, and he had no intention of giving her anything else to bitch at him about. He picked the cigar up and took a long drag to steady his nerves.

As he sat down, he had a sudden nearly uncontrollable urge to get the hell out of there, to flee some unseen terror. Something breathed raggedly behind him. He turned around slowly. Hundreds of teeth, razor sharp and dripping with sizzling hot foam, bit into his neck. He screamed. Struggled to get away. As he pulled back, his arm was ripped from his body. Blood poured out of his wounds. He stared at the bloody stump that had been his arm and whimpered. Scrambling back until the wall stopped him, he slid along it until he found the doorknob. He latched onto it with his one remaining hand. Almost safe. His blood-slicked fingers slid off the handle. Frantic, he finally managed to turn the knob. Teeth sank deep into his shoulder, jagged claws hooked in, dragging him back and slamming him into the wall. He hung there for an instant before crumpling to the floor.

He moaned. Every ounce of him was on fire. A crushing weight on his chest kept him from getting up. He opened his eyes. There it sat, seeming to leer. He wanted to ask the monster what it wanted. But the words came out as a gurgle. *God help me*. Then the beast leaned forward and sank its teeth into his jugular.

Friday, September 20, 2013

WANING GIBBOUS

Old moon
Getting smaller
99% Visible

Chapter 7

Evan Fitzpatrick, Mary's father, sat on the back bumper of the paramedic's truck in complete and utter shock. His sweet, loving daughter had been ripped apart as if by some sort of wild animal. Her blood drenched the floor and saturated her bed and the pink coverlet with the dainty yellow flowers her mother made for her. Even the walls across the room where he found her mutilated body were sprayed with her blood. He was devastated, and Margaret, Mary's mother, would be too when she found out what had happened.

"Oh, God," he cried wearily. "How will I tell her mother about this?"

He put his head in his hands and wept. There was the shuffling sound of footsteps on asphalt. A shadow fell across him, and Sheriff Brazelton put his arm stiffly across his shoulders.

"There, there." The officer patted him roughly on the back. "We'll send someone over to tell her. Where is she right now?"

"Li—li—library," was all he could manage.

"Okay," Sheriff Brazelton told him. "I'll see to it that she's notified as soon as possible."

Evan grabbed the officer by the sleeve. "No!" he

shouted. Then he licked his lips and tried to compose himself. "Please." He stared down at his stocking feet instead of at the other man's face. The situation was difficult enough, and Evan didn't want his wife to be told by strangers what had happened to their daughter. "I have to tell her myself."

"Do you think that's such a good idea?"

"You don't understand." He dug his fingers into the sheriff's arm and pulled him close. "My wife is frail. News like this could kill her if not handled right."

He could feel Sheriff Brazelton studying his face, and Evan jammed his knuckles into the corners of his sore eyes. He used the heel of his left hand to wipe his nose. When he felt more in control of himself, he rubbed his eyes one more time and then silently pleaded with the sheriff. He wasn't going to take no for an answer.

"All right, Evan." The sheriff nodded. "I'll have a deputy take you to Margaret and then drive you both back here. Why don't you let me have one of my deputies grab you some shoes?"

"Thanks, Sheriff." Evan gestured with his head. "They're in the bedroom closet. Down the hall, first door on the left."

He watched the sheriff whisper something to his deputy, who then disappeared inside the house. Evan wondered how he would break the murder of their only child to his wife.

Saturday, September 21, 2013

WANING GIBBOUS

Old moon
Growing smaller
95% Visible

Chapter 8

Two days after the murders of Mary Fitzpatrick and Arnie Kaczynski, Beth and I sat at the counter of PJ's Diner enjoying the unexpected reprieve from school, which had been cancelled for the rest of the week on account of the three murders. All the flags around town flew at half-mast. We sipped on root beer floats and shared a side of fries while having fun eavesdropping on other people's conversations. It was lunchtime, and the diner was full of office workers on their lunch break, all trying to get their orders at once so they could get back to their desks on time. The place hummed with gossip about the murders.

Diane, the server, carried two platters heaped to overflowing with thick pastrami sandwiches, homemade potato salad the diner was famous for, and extra pickles to the table where two local men sat. She plopped the plates down and leaned one hand on the table.

"If you ask me." She paused to make sure she had their attention.

The two men didn't even look up, intently manhandling their sandwiches. She glanced over her shoulder, probably checking to make sure PJ couldn't see her chatting up the customers during the noon rush.

"Yeah?" The tall one encouraged from around his sandwich.

"If you ask me," she repeated. "I think they were part of a love triangle. You guys know what a sleaze Arnie was."

The men put down their sandwiches and focused on Diane. Their nosiness spurred her on.

"Well." She glanced toward the kitchen again. "My friend Regina told me, about a month ago, that her daughter told her that her boyfriend's older brother, the one who works as a part-time janitor at City Hall? She said he told them he'd seen that creep take that little girl into one of the back rooms. He said that before the door closed all the way he saw Arnie unbutton Mary's blouse. He also told them—"

"You going to stand there yakking all day long, or are you going to actually get back to work sometime this century?" PJ yelled at Diane from behind the grill.

The strawberry birthmark on PJ's forehead stood out like a splotch of paint on a blank canvas.

Rolling her eyes at the lunchtime patrons, Diane grabbed her order pad and pencil out of her apron pocket and pretended to take their order.

"Can't you see I'm taking their dessert order, PJ? Gawd," she shot back.

"Well, be quick about it then."

"Yeah, yeah." She turned back to the table. "Tell you the rest later." She flashed her gap-toothed, horsey smile and moved behind the counter.

Sheriff Brazelton and Deputy Riggs sat at the table directly behind us. As I watched them in the mirror behind the counter, it seemed like Riggs wanted to say something, but the sheriff held his index finger to his lips to shut him up. I nearly missed Riggs nodding before he turned back to demolishing his corned beef on rye. I had no idea he was smart enough to pick up on things like that. The sheriff blew on a spoonful of beef barley soup. He didn't seem interested in it.

As soon as Diane was out of earshot, Riggs leaned forward and spoke quietly to the sheriff. "Did you know that scum bucket was screwing a kid?"

"Have some respect, Riggs," the sheriff snapped. "That little girl is dead."

"Sorry, Sheriff." Riggs fiddled with his tie. "But did you know?"

"No, I didn't." After a surreptitious glance around, he leaned forward and pointed at Riggs. "But I intend to find out who else he was screwing around with, and whether or not his wife knew anything about it."

The sheriff reached into his wallet, withdrew a twenty, and walked over to the register.

Diane scurried over to ring him up. She took the money from his outstretched hand. "Everything okay, Sheriff?"

He flashed what my mom called his "public service" smile and tipped his hat. "Fine and dandy, Diane. You have a great day now, okay? Oh, and keep the change."

"Thanks." She tossed the change into her pocket. "You, too."

We listened to every word said. It amazed me how invisible kids were to adults. Once the cops were gone, Beth turned back to me. "They're never going to figure out who did it."

"What?" I folded a ketchup-stained French fry into my mouth. "You going to tell me you know who did?"

"Maybe." She spun around on her stool a few times. If she was trying to bug me, she was doing a great job.

"Oh, give me a break, Beth. How can you possibly know that?"

"Never mind. God." She turned back to her float and

worked the ice cream out of the bottom of the glass.

"No," I persisted. "You're not getting out of it that easy. What's up with you, anyway?"

For a second at least it looked like she might actually answer me. Then she jumped off her stool and ran out the door.

"Beth," I called after her. "Where you going? Wait up!" I pulled some waded up bills out of my pocket and tossed them next to the register.

"Kids," I told Diane as I headed after Beth. "Got to go."

"Take care, Jim." Diane waved. At least she paid enough attention to not call me "Jaime."

I'd been coming into PJ's for root beer floats ever since I was little, and Diane was always there to fix them for me. She made the best floats around.

☽

I eyeballed the street for Beth. I wasn't going to run after the twerp. Chances were she was playing some sort of joke on me. But after I went about two blocks and still hadn't found her, I started to worry. As I passed a store window, I peered inside. I didn't see her until it was too late.

"Boo!" She jumped from behind the open door to Anderson's Hardware. Mr. Anderson was a cheapskate who didn't believe in air conditioning, and customers were always leaving the door open to try and cool the place down.

"Ha, ha, very funny." I tried not to let her see how much she startled me.

That wouldn't be cool.

She giggled and reached behind the door to pull another girl out onto the sidewalk in front of me. "Look who I found."

"Hey, Lindy, how you doing?" Lindy St. George was Beth's age, maybe a little younger. She had short, spiky hair and never seemed to say much. At least, not to me.

Lindy contemplated her feet. "Hey."

"We're going to walk Lindy home, okay?"

"Sure."

Beth grabbed Lindy's hand, and off they skipped. I walked far enough behind them so they could forget I was there, but close enough to listen to what they said. Most of it was little girl prattle, but then Lindy said something that pricked my ears and I listened.

"I've been hearing some weird sounds from behind my house," she started. The St. Georges lived four houses down from Mary Fitzpatrick and her family.

"Yeah?" Beth glanced back at me, clearly puzzled, her forehead wrinkled and one side of her lip upturned, but when she turned back to Lindy, she just looked curious. "Like what?"

"Well." Lindy hesitated and peeked over her shoulder at me. Quickly turning my head, I pretended to be interested in the orange tabby sunning itself on the sidewalk across the street.

"Growling, kind of."

"What kind of growling?" I couldn't resist asking. Things were starting to get interesting. Beth ran back and punched me for interrupting, and it actually hurt. I rubbed it. "Ow. What was that for?"

"You just better stop it right now."

"Stop what?"

"Stop making fun of her, you moron."

"I'm not making fun of her." I turned to Lindy. "I'm not making fun of you. Honest."

"Are you sure?" Beth sounded skeptical.

"Scout's honor." I held my fingers together in the Boy Scout salute.

"Well, okay." Beth grabbed Lindy's hand again.

"So." I turned back to Lindy. "What kind of growling was it?"

"Well, like a big mean dog or something, but not exactly."

"What do you mean, not exactly?"

"I don't know. It's hard to explain."

"Can you growl like it?"

"Maybe." She tried, but it sounded more like a purr than an actual growl. "Oh, forget it."

"No, that's okay." I tried to reassure her. Maybe it was how white her face was, or how tightly she was hugging herself, or maybe it was the way her eyes shifted from side to side every few seconds as if she expected something to happen. Whatever it was, she was serious. This was no joke. "Try again."

It didn't really sound like a growl, more like a snarl, but it creeped me out anyway. The way Lindy acted, it wasn't like one of those baby fears, either. Not like the boogeyman that lived under the bed, or yellow-eyed closet monsters. Not even like a nightmare. More like a real, honest to God fear. Something maybe we should all be scared of.

☽

To Beth, Lindy seemed scared, really scared. Her eyes were huge, and her face was pale. She looked like she wanted to cry, and Beth had an urge to run away as fast as she had run last fall when she won all the races at school. Instead, she slung her arm around her friend's shoulders, pulled her close, and kissed her on the cheek.

"It's okay." Lame, but she didn't know what else to say. Or do. She was scared, too. Real scared. Maybe her mother had been lurking in Lindy's yard. If so, did that mean her suspicions were true, and not imagined? Had her mother actually killed her father, then started killing others?

"It'll be okay." It had to be, but unable to fight the fear she turned back to her cousin for reassurance. "Won't it, Jaime?"

"Sure," he answered. "Come on. It's getting late. We'd better get going."

They continued to walk slowly toward Lindy's house. The girls wrapped their arms around each other's waists. Beth took comfort in their friendship. As they approached the house, Lindy's steps slowed until she finally stopped. The devil winds had calmed to a heavy breeze, and even though the temperature was in the low nineties, goose bumps lined Beth's arms and legs. Lindy watched her house intently, and Beth wondered what she was thinking about. "Lindy?"

"Mmm?"

Beth shook her friend gently. "Lindy."

Lindy blinked rapidly several times, then seemed to come out of her trance. "What? Oh, sorry."

Jaime rubbed his eye with his index finger. "So, where did the growls come from, anyway?"

Unable to believe he was still harping on that, Beth punched him again.

"Dude, take a chill pill, will you?" She smirked when he rubbed his arm again. "Why don't you just leave her alone?"

"Because I want to see if there's maybe a logical explanation. Lindy, show me where the growls came from."

"I don't want to. I'm scared to go back there."

"Come on," he insisted. "It'll be okay. I promise."

"Well…"

Beth grabbed her hand and squeezed. "Don't worry. We'll be right here with you."

"Well, okay." Lindy took a deep breath, then plunged off the curb and trotted across the street.

Beth let herself be dragged along. Whatever it took to make her friend feel better. When they got to the sidewalk in front of her house, Lindy hopped delicately onto the curb and continued to pull Beth along until they got to the narrow side yard. Lindy stopped so suddenly that Beth nearly crashed into her. It was so fast that Jaime stepped on her foot before he could stop.

"Ow. Watch it."

"Sorry."

She thought she saw him smirk but couldn't be sure and decided to let it go. This time.

The three of them crept across the dirt and somehow managed to avoid the bags of garbage piled high along the wooden fence between Lindy's house and the next-door neighbor's. The fence was in shambles and listed so far into Lindy's yard it laid almost flat. Several of the boards were split apart, and they reminded Beth of the wooden stakes used in the movies to kill vampires. Considering her suspicions, maybe vampires were real too?

"Watch out for the nails," Lindy warned. Beth barely managed to move her arm before one of the rusty things scratched her. She loved to play outside, so she always had bruises and scratches, especially lately, since she felt safer outside and never worried about getting hurt. She was glad she missed being raked by the nails in Lindy's fence, though, because rusty things were dangerous and could make you really sick. If you got scratched by some rusty something or other, you ended up at the hospital, getting a nasty Tetanus shot. A few summers ago Jaime stepped on a rusty nail and had to have one. He said the shot hurt worse than the nail going through his foot. Beth hated shots, and she didn't trust doctors, either. Especially after what happened to her dad. Thinking about him these days caused a huge lump in her throat, and she struggled to keep from crying like a baby. Again.

Besides, Lindy had something important to show her, and she was eager to see it.

Even if she was a little scared.

$$\newcommand{\moon}{☽}\moon$$

Lindy trudged along the narrow side yard while Beth and her cousin followed. Flies buzzed everywhere. She stepped over the maggots crawling on the trash bags. In the heat, the smell was awful. She held her nose and tried not to puke.

When they finally reached the tool shed, she couldn't believe what she saw. The door was flung open and hung on by part of the one remaining hinge. The roof was caved in and the window blown out. It looked like some-one—or something—had torn through it like a tornado, except there weren't any tornados in Wolf Creek. At least, not any she ever heard of before.

Not only was the shed a disaster, but deep gouges scored the trunk of the jacaranda tree next to it, while some of the splintered wood from the fence held what looked like teeth marks. Maybe it hadn't been a night-mare after all.

"Lindy!" her father screamed, drunk again. And pissed off. So what else was new?

Her first instinct was to stay still and hope he would forget about her. She put a finger to her lips and motioned for her friends to be quiet. Her father leaned precariously against the torn screen. *Please let him fall down the stairs and break his neck.* She immediately regretted the thought. Her father was all she had left. What would happen to her if he died?

He took a long draw from his beer can and, unsurprisingly, spilled some on his stained undershirt. She cringed when he scratched his balls and hoped Beth hadn't seen him do that. After he sniffed his fingers, he wiped his mouth with the back of his forearm. Ashamed at what her father had become, Lindy closed her eyes and tried not to cry.

"Where the hell is that little ho?" he muttered.

Lindy's eyes flew open in horror and she looked at Beth, who wore an understanding smile on her face. So did James. Thank God they weren't laughing at her. It was nice to know they really were her friends.

She stepped out where he could see her. "Yes, Daddy?"

"Girl, get your butt in here and get me another sixer."

"But, Daddy, Beth's here. I'm just showing her—"

"I don't give a shit if Jesus Christ hisself is here. I said, get your butt in here and grab me some more beer."

"Why can't you get it yourself?" Lindy mumbled, and then turned to her friends. "Guess I'd better go in and do what he wants. See you guys later?"

Beth reached over and gave her a quick hug. "It'll be okay, Lind. You'll see."

Lindy forced a smile. "Hope so. Bye."

She ran up the porch steps and squeezed past her father. As she went by, he shoved her. She stumbled and nearly fell, but after more than a year of abuse, her sense of balance and reflexes were sharp. She quickly picked herself up, scurried into the kitchen, and over to the refrigerator to do as she was told. Long ago she learned the best thing, the thing least likely to get her smacked around, was to do whatever her father said. Still, learning how much beer Homer needed to pass out before he got angry enough to knock her around was like walking a tightrope.

Reaching inside the ancient side-by-side, she hooked her finger around the plastic six-pack holder. As she backed up to close the door, something grabbed her around the neck and yanked her off her feet.

"Whaddaya think you're doin'?"

Homer wore a wicked sneer and there was a gleam in his eyes that worried her. The sour stink of stale beer colored his breath, and she fought the urge to barf. Summoning every ounce of courage she could from deep inside, she went into survival mode and beamed at her father, hoping he wouldn't see her fear underneath.

"Daddy," she started in her "I love you best" voice. "Here's your sixer. Want me to fix you a sandwich? Or how about some peanuts? You like peanuts, don't you, Daddy?"

Struggling to remain calm, she managed not to wince at the tremendous pain in her neck. Instead, she tried to judge how far the drop would be when he finally let go and she tumbled to the floor. Maybe four or five inches? Not too bad. She steeled herself for the certain pain if she didn't land on her feet correctly. Time to risk another question and hope he wouldn't change his mind and decide she needed to learn how to "respect" him. "Daddy? I think there's another rerun of *Walker, Texas Ranger* coming on cable in a few minutes. You like that show, remember, Daddy? Want me to put it on for you?"

"What?"

His rheumy eyes blinked rapidly. He shook his head as if to clear his sight and reached for the Coors she managed to hang on to through this familiar ordeal. She handed it over, and closed her eyes. A tiny sigh of relief escaped, and she stole a peek at her father to see if he heard. Nope. Good. *It'll be over soon. Just hold on.*

Sure enough, he released his vise grip on her neck and she fell to the floor in a heap. This time he hadn't held her high enough to do any real damage when he let her go. Nevertheless, she would have an awful bruise on her neck in the morning and maybe one on her hip where she hit the floor when he'd pushed her down. Sitting on the cool linoleum, she tried to catch her breath as she listened to the sounds of her father lumbering back to his easy chair. She heard his "oof" when he lowered himself into the leather chair and his grunt when he pulled the lever to raise his feet. So used to his different noises, when he farted, she barely noticed. Instead, she waited a few more seconds, then sighed with relief when the TV came on.

Good, let him find his own damn rerun. I'm going to fix him a sandwich and hope he chokes on it. The spurt of anger gave her enough strength to get up.

She tried not to wobble as she slowly stood and rubbed the back of her neck again. She better take some ibuprofen to ward off the pain that was sure to hit in about an hour. For the hundredth time that week, she wished her mother were still alive.

"Where's my sammich?" Homer yelled, and she scrambled over to the fridge and took out what she needed.

"Be right there."

All thoughts of her mother and how happy they used to be were put aside. *No sense wishing for the impossible.* She hurried to finish before her father got mad again.

☽

Lindy's dad is so mean to her. He never used to be

that way. Beth could remember many summertime slumber parties where Mr. St. George rented Lindy's favorite movie, *Beauty and the Beast*, popped lots and lots of popcorn, and let them stay up all night and make as much noise as they wanted. And he never told them to be quiet.

But that was before Mrs. St. George got sick and died. Beth was a little sad about Lindy's mom, but she never understood why Lindy still missed her so much. Not until her own father was killed. Then she got it.

The monster who wrecked Mr. St. George's tool shed was the same one who murdered her father. The same one who tore Mary Fitzpatrick and Mr. Kaczynski to pieces. She was sure of it. But she was also sure that if she wasn't careful, it would be the same thing that got her, too.

Sunday, September 22, 2013

WANING GIBBOUS

Old moon
Growing smaller
90% Visible

Chapter 9

Beth and I sat on the couch in the living room, vegging in front of the TV. The folks were doing their thing in the kitchen, sipping Earl Grey and talking to Aunt Judy. As usual Dad was planning out her life for her. He was always doing that. Mine had been mapped out since I was five. If he got his way, I would be "something special." Which meant I should either be a doctor or a lawyer. Someone who made a ton of money and people looked up to.

Personally I couldn't stand either choice. No, thank you. If I had anything to say about it, I would be a writer. I had four years of high school to plan how to break it to Dad. Mom already knew, but trying to get her to help was out of the question. She'd no more go against my father's wishes than a wolf could resist howling at the full moon. Nor would she want to.

Beth had been quiet that morning at church. Maybe she was nervous about Lindy's monster. Everyone was a little spooked, what with the murders and those damn constantly blowing winds. It was really bad this summer. People still got a little jumpy during fire season after the huge Freeway Complex fire back when I was eight or nine. Three big fires had merged to become one monster inferno. Forty-some-odd thousand people were evacuated and over thirty thousand acres had burned. It took nearly two weeks to put it out. Hot spots popped up for several more days before the firefighters took care of it completely. For years after, the whole hillside was a charred mess, and the dry riverbed that ran along the south side of town looked like something out of a sci-fi movie about some alien world. They said sunny Southern California was paradise, but between the fires, the earthquakes, and now these murders so close to home, I wasn't so sure about that.

Anyway, back home after church, we sat on the couch, sipping root beer and staring at the TV. I snuck a peek at Beth. She was slumped over the arm of the couch, slowly picking at a tiny hole in the ugly paisley upholstery.

I took a sip of root beer. "If you keep worrying over that thing, it'll grow and grow, and keep growing until it's big enough to swallow you whole."

She shook her head. "You and your starving furniture. First the bed, now the couch. Is there anything in this house that's not waiting to gobble me up?"

Pursing my lips, I studied the room. "Well, I think that lamp over there has already eaten today."

"Cute."

I smirked and she grinned back. All too soon, though, her face slipped back into a serious expression. She frowned, knitting her eyebrows together so hard they turned into that dorky unibrow again.

"Now what's wrong?" Was this one of those girl things, flipping from one emotion to another, over and over again, or was there something really wrong this time? I scratched my head and waited for her response.

"Nothing." She turned her attention back to the dirty brown stuffing she pulled out of the couch.

"Come on, Beth," I urged, leaning toward her. "Something's going on up there in that frizz-covered head of yours. I can tell."

"Yeah, how?"

"Because you stop your baby babble and get real quiet, that's how."

"Oh." She kept scratching at the hole, which grew from the size of a pea to something Optimus Prime could get lost in. But that was all she said.

"You know," I remarked. "Mom's going to get mad at you if you don't stop picking at that thing."

She immediately stopped and gaped at the hole as if she had no idea it was there. Then she looked at me. "Oh, shit."

"Don't worry." I skootched over and patted her leg. "We'll tuck it all back in and no one will ever know." Leaning across her, I stuck two fingers into the middle of the foam and shoved it back into the arm. "There. Good as new."

"M'kay."

Still, she wouldn't talk about what was wrong. It was probably a good thing, because at this point, I wasn't sure I was ready to hear it.

$$\mathbb{D}$$

Beth wished Jaime would go away and leave her alone. She wasn't ready to tell him what was up, no matter how much he bugged her about it. Sooner or later, she'd have to tell him what she suspected—no, what she *knew*—but not now. Now, she was too tired to get into it. Besides, he wouldn't believe her anyway. No one would. It was crazy. She might only be eleven, but she was old enough to know that.

There was only one thing she could think of to get him off her back—the thing with Lindy and the tool shed. "What do you think's going on with Lindy?" She watched him carefully, testing the waters. "Can you believe she thinks there's a monster or something running around?"

He watched her for a moment before he spoke, almost as if he knew that wasn't what was really on her mind. "Yeaaah." He drew the word out so it sounded like air being let out from one of her bicycle tires. "Pretty jacked up."

"Yeah, jacked."

He got up on his knees, leaned over, and wiggled his fingers high over her head.

"No, Jaime. Not now."

He grinned and wiggled his fingers again.

"Stop it. I'm not in the mood."

That's when he dive-bombed her, digging his fingers into her waist. It tickled, and she screamed in mock horror. It was the first time she'd attempted more than a giggle since her father had been killed. She laughed so hard she got a headache. Rolling back and forth, she tried to get out of his reach, but no luck.

"Ve have our vays." His Russian accent was horrible. His knees pinned her arms to her body, and even though she tried hard to knock him onto the floor, she couldn't budge. "Ve vill get ze information out of you before ve kill you."

"Hey, what's going on in there?" Uncle Robbie leaned against the doorjamb, his legs casually crossed, while he held a partially unwrapped package of Sno-Balls. He peeled one off the cardboard backing and popped the whole thing into his mouth. His cheeks puffed out like a chipmunk storing nuts.

The cousins stopped in mid-tickle. Beth craned her

neck back over the arm of the couch. Her uncle appeared upside down, and she giggled again.

"Why are you standing on your head, Uncle Robbie?"

He made a big show out of swallowing the huge piece of coconut-covered cake. "Ha, ha. Very funny." Some of the Sno-Ball tried to escape his mouth and he pushed it back inside. "Just keep it down, will you?"

He gestured over his shoulder with his thumb, emphasizing the point by jerking his head in the same direction. Then he rolled his eyes and turned back to the women gabbing in the kitchen, licking his fingers to get every last crumb.

Jaime turned his head away, squinted one eye, then backed off and sat on the arm of the couch. "Don't zink you have gotten avay," he told her. "Ve alvays get vhat ve vant." He reached over and tugged on one of her braids. "So, 'fess up, girlie." He turned serious. "What's really wrong?"

"Girlie?" She secretly loved when he called her that, but she wouldn't let him know that.

"Yeah, girlie." He held up his fists like a boxer. "Want to make something of it?"

She tugged on the ragged edge of her Levi shorts and bit her lip until it hurt. Glancing into the kitchen, she decided there was no time like the present. Something her father used to say. It was time to tell Jaime the truth about what was going on, and why people were suddenly being murdered in a town where, up until two months ago, the worst crimes were teenagers drag racing down Wolf Creek Road, or a break-in at the local Circle K. She wasn't sure he'd listen to her, but she had to give it her best shot.

No matter what.

☽

Something was definitely wrong with Beth. Something besides her father dying. But what? We'd always been close, and I intended to find out what it was she was hiding. I'd get it out of her one way or another.

After Dad went back to the kitchen table to pretend interest in the lives of the neighbors Mom and Aunt Judy were gossiping about, I reached over and tugged on one of Beth's thick braids again.

"Okay," I said. "You've avoided my question long enough. What's up with you, anyway?"

She seemed to struggle with herself for a second, biting her lip and getting all serious. She snuck a peek into the kitchen, probably checking where the parental units were, then grabbed my wrist and practically dragged me off the couch.

"Come on," she whispered.

"Where we going?"

"Just come on, will you?" She led me out the front door and down the street. At the end of the street there was a walkway leading to the kiddie park, and another one would take us to the baseball field. We could hear the racket the neighbor kids made on the playground as they ran around the monkey bars and slid down the slide. She hesitated a second then chose the path to the field.

Weeds had hijacked the baselines of the baseball diamond. A crater the size of Riff's ego covered home plate, thanks to the water that collected there when the sprinklers were on. Luckily, the pitcher's mound was almost visible beneath the ragged grass. She plopped her butt down in the middle of it and crossed her legs. Her knees bounced up and down. She was pretty upset about something.

I knelt beside her and put my hand on her shoulder. Then I sat back on my haunches and scratched behind an ear. "So, what's up?"

"You promise not to laugh at me?"

For the first time, I noticed the huge bags under her eyes. They were the color of a bruised strawberry, a red and purple so dark it was practically black. How long had they been there? I wasn't sure, but the way she was acting freaked me out. Deciding to go for the laugh, I drew a large X on my chest. "Cross my heart, hope to die, stick a fork in my eye." I mimicked sticking something in my eye, swirling my hand around to indicate I was pulling my eye out of its socket, then gave a mock flick, sending my imaginary eyeball off the end of the fork and into her lap. "He shoots, he scores."

She shot me *that* look. You know, the one all girls use. "I'm serious," she whispered.

"Hey, I'm sorry." I sat in the dirt and scooted forward until my knees touched hers. Taking hold of her hands, I ran my thumbs across her middle knuckles. It was supposed to calm her down, but since she pulled them away and folded them in her lap, I was pretty certain it didn't work. "What is it? What's wrong? You can tell me."

She took a deep breath, looked me square in the eye, and launched into the most bizarre, jacked-up story I ever heard.

Thursday, April 25, 2013

FULL MOON

100% Visible

Chapter 10

"It was the day before my birthday," Beth began and then told Jaime everything…

Every year, she looked forward to the tradition she shared with her dad. He would pick her up at school the day before her birthday and they would go to a matinee. They filled up on popcorn, bonbons, and Coke—lots of Coke. She always got to pick the movie, something her mother never let her do. When the movie was over, they'd grab cheeseburgers, fries and more Coke before going home. Beth could never figure out why this pissed her mom off. That night, her parents had a major argument. About what, she had no idea.

Her mom started in on her dad as soon as he and Beth walked in the door laughing and having fun. Beth hated it when they argued. It was usually about money and how they never seemed to have any anymore. Her father had been fired from his job as one of the CSI guys for the state. It had something to do with some lady named Tina, but Beth wasn't sure of the details. All she knew was that her mother was pissed at her dad because he'd lost such a good job, and Mom had no intention of ever letting him forget it.

Beth crawled into bed and yanked the covers over

her head, trying not to listen as her parents argued. Their voices rose and fell in a sort of rhythm that reminded her of something her old piano teacher would make her bang out on the keyboard. Their voices got louder, but she still couldn't make out what they were saying because everything was jumbled. Huddled under the covers, she squeezed Elmo to her chest and prayed.

"God? If you're there and can hear me, could you make it so that they stop fighting all the time? And maybe Dad could get his job back, the good one, not the mall security guard one he has now. Okay? Amen."

She rolled on her tummy and started to cry. "And God? Maybe they can remember that they really do love each other. Amen again."

She pulled her pillow over her head and held it tightly against her ears in an attempt to drown out the angry voices. She fell asleep cuddled up to her stuffed toy, feeling like he was her only friend in the world.

Later that night, she woke suddenly. She was scared, but didn't know why. Something out of the ordinary jolted her out of a deep sleep. At first all she could see were deep shadows and the red numbers of her clock. Waiting until her eyes adjusted to the darkness, she wondered what woke her up.

From somewhere outside—the front yard, maybe— came a low rumble. *Was it an earthquake?* It didn't feel like one. Her bed didn't shake. Nothing rattled on the walls. The windows were still. *There it was again.* It was definitely no earthquake. She got out of bed, pulled on her pink Harry Styles sweatshirt and fuzzy slippers, and then went to her window and looked outside. The noise came again. This time, it reminded her of her dad's chainsaw starting up. The sound started at her feet, bounced off her bones, and left out the top of her head. Even her teeth rattled.

She squinted in an attempt to see what was out there. When something moved out of the corner of her eye, she turned toward it. The full moon hid behind an angry group of clouds and she tried to see beyond the murkiness. Goose bumps rose on her arms and she could feel her heartbeat in her fingertips. That weird feeling of being watched made her tummy do flip flops like that time she ate four hot dogs and then went on a super-fast roller coaster at the fair. Whatever was out there, she hoped it went away soon, or at least stayed outside.

She had decided to go back to bed when the moonlight split open the clouds. The shadow of one of the trees moved, and she gasped. Her hand flew up to cover her mouth, holding the sound inside.

Fear held her in place, unable to move as two angry red eyes appeared in the darkness. The rest of the creature took shape as it stepped out of the shadows. Backlit by moonlight, she couldn't see anything but its silhouette. But it was the biggest, blackest, most ginormous thing she'd ever seen.

Then it saw her. It drew its lips back in a horrible snarl, and the eyes glowed. It growled, a strange, frightening sound. Then it turned and disappeared back into the shadows. Much later, she swore the eyes were level with hers as they peered into her bedroom window.

On the second floor.

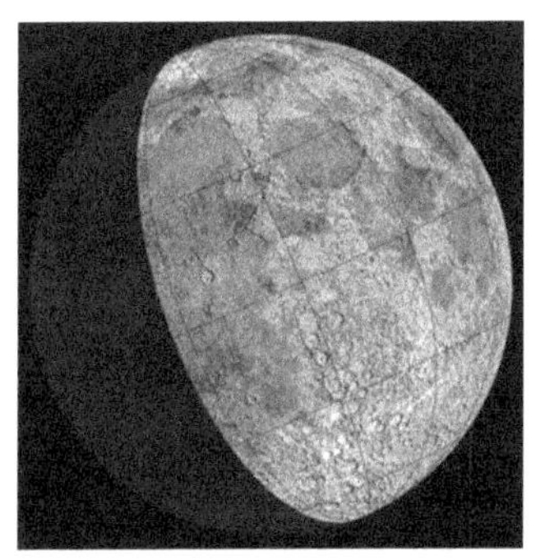

Sunday, September 15, 2013

WAXING GIBBOUS

Young moon
Growing bigger
80% Visible

Chapter 11

I couldn't help my laugh. It started as a snort, became a giggle, and then before I could stop myself, I'd thrown myself on the dirt and hooted until my sides hurt. The dirt on the pitcher's mound floated lazily up and made me sneeze. I should have known. Beth was such a brat. This time she managed to pull my leg hard and keep me going there for a while.

At least until she threw a handful of dirt and rocks at my head.

"Ow." I stopped laughing and rubbed the spot where the biggest rock thumped me.

She stood up, brushed off the seat of her shorts and glared down at me. "I knew you'd laugh. I thought maybe, just maybe, I could count on you, but I should've known better. You're just like everyone else."

She turned, marched off the mound and across the field.

I scrambled up and trotted after her, still rubbing my head.

"Hey," I called. "Wait up."

"No." The kid was most of the way through the field and practically to the street, but she didn't even turn around.

"Aw. Come. On." I gasped for air. She sure could run fast when she wanted to. Catching up, I grabbed her elbow and spun her around. "I'm sorry. I shouldn't have laughed."

I let go and bent over, hands on my knees, trying to catch my breath. Actually, my breathing was practically back to normal, but it was a good excuse to figure out what to say to calm her down. She was more pissed than I'd ever seen her. If she wasn't kidding, if she was serious about what she saw, then what did she think I could do about it? And how was it connected to Uncle Fred's death?

"Are you sure that's what you saw?"

Definitely the wrong thing to say, because she started to stomp off again.

"Hold on." I grabbed her arm. "It's a fair question. And you have to admit, this whole thing's a little bit, well, freaky."

"Tell me about it," she said. "By the next morning, it seemed more like a dream than anything else. Like a movie, you know? But I couldn't stop thinking about it, and the more I did, the more I was sure it really happened."

"So, what do you think it was?"

She studied me for a minute, her mouth twisted in thought. Then she hit me with the kicker. "I know exactly what it was."

"What?"

"A werewolf."

Monday, September 16, 2013

WAXING GIBBOUS

Young moon
Growing bigger
89% Visible

Chapter 12

The next morning, Beth didn't say one thing to me all through breakfast and most of the way to school. No wonder, what with the bombshell she'd dropped on me. Was she serious? A werewolf? And not just any werewolf, but one that could watch her through a second story window?

It was enough to blow your mind.

I needed to talk to her about it some more, but couldn't face it first thing in the morning. I hadn't reacted well to what she told me. I hurt her feelings, but jeez. Could she blame me? Could anyone?

She had to be wrong. Everyone knew there was no such things as werewolves. Even if there were, how could they be that tall? I hadn't been to her house up north since I was seven or eight, so I couldn't be sure, but it seemed to me there was an ivy-covered trellis right outside her bedroom window.

If she really did see something and not dreamed it, whatever it was probably climbed the latticework to peer into her window.

I shook my head. She almost had me believing her story.

"Hey, bozo."

I looked up to see Riff, a can of Mountain Dew in his hand, backpack slung over one shoulder.

"Butt wipe. How's it going?" Our standard greetings.

"What're you shaking your head at?" He snickered. "Talking to yourself again?"

"No, I heard the weirdest thing last night." I glanced over at Beth and saw the waterworks were starting again. Man, what was it with girls and crying? She gazed up at me with those big green eyes of hers and silently pleaded with me to keep quiet. I winked and turned back to Riff. "Someone told me you were a big fat weenie."

There was a moment of complete silence. Then Beth giggled. Riff's face turned bright red.

"Shut up, you little maggot." He pushed her and turned toward me. "And you can just drop dead."

"Lighten up." Dude could dish it out, but never could take it. "Geez."

We walked along in silence for a while, until we caught up with Lindy. Beth ran over to her and hugged her fiercely. Lindy giggled and returned the hug enthusiastically. They immediately started whispering their little girl chitchat. Beth watched me as Riff and I walked past. I winked in an attempt to reassure her that her secret was safe, but I wasn't sure she caught it.

Before long, Riff stopped. The girls passed by, totally oblivious to us, off in their girl world somewhere. Riff swung his backpack off his shoulder and rifled through it.

When he couldn't immediately find whatever it was that he was looking for, he slammed the backpack onto the sidewalk, and then dumped everything out.

Anything could be in that pack of his. I crossed my arms and bent over, trying to figure it out. "What are you looking for?"

"Wait."

I did, impatiently. The girls were getting too far

ahead and then I couldn't see them anymore. "For Christ's sake, hurry up, will you?"

He ignored me. After a mound of junk was piled on the ground, which included his green iPod with its matching sock, his TV remote, and three cans of Dew, he finally found what he'd been searching for.

"Here." He tossed something silver at me.

I caught it and shook my head. "Pop-Tarts?"

"Breakfast of champions." He also pulled out a second Mountain Dew. "But only with a Dew."

"Dude, how can you drink that junk?"

Instead of saying anything, he popped the top and guzzled it. Then he wiped his mouth on his sleeve and burped half the alphabet.

"Come on." I shook my head. "We're going be late."

He shouldered his pack and we headed down the street. About a block away the girls were sitting on the curb. When they saw us, they stood and picked up their backpacks. Beth plunged her arms through the straps, then adopted her typical "mad" stance with her hands on her waist and one hip cocked.

I scratched the back of my neck and arched my eyebrows at her. "What's with you?"

She stomped her foot. Just like a baby. "Where've you been?"

"What's your problem? We were behind you the whole time."

"Yeah, and we'll probably be late because of you slow pokes."

"So just go on without us."

Her glare intensified. "Fine. We will. We don't need you to walk with us anyway."

"Good." Crossing my arms, I glanced over at Riff and chuckled. "I'm tired of babysitting you all the time."

She pursed her lips and glared at me for an uncomfortably long time then turned and tugged Lindy's sleeve. "Come on, let's go."

They set off down the street and onto the electric company easement that went over the hill and into the field of the Wolf Creek elementary school. I was glad they were gone. "God, she can be such a pain."

"Dude." Riff snorted. "That's what I'm talking about. If you're going to have to play babysitter all the time, you should at least get paid for it."

"Yeah, right," I scoffed. "Like they'd ever pay me. As if."

"Hey," Riff said. "I'm just saying."

We munched our Pop Tarts and headed on to school.

☽

Beth hated when Jaime bossed her around, like he did on the way to school this morning. He liked to tell her what to do, like he thought he was her keeper or something. She sat at the lunch table and munched on the peanut butter and apricot jam sandwich her aunt made her. At least Aunt Annette still loved her. Her mother never did anything for her anymore.

She wished Lindy would get out of class already. *Wonder what Lindy's class did wrong this time?* Lindy said that Ms. Hanshaw was always pissed off about something.

They had crossed their fingers and hoped to be in the same class, but Lindy got stuck with Ms. Hanshaw, while Beth was lucky and got Mrs. Williams. She was a lot easier than Ms. Hanshaw, but Beth would have been willing to have her if it meant being in the same class with her friend. Lindy tossed her lunch on the table, narrowly missing Beth's carton of milk. "Hey."

Beth smiled in relief that she was finally there. "Hey," she replied. "How's it going?"

"Oh, man, Horrid Hanshaw's really pissed today." Lindy shook her head, but her spiked hair didn't move an inch. "God, and we've only been in school a couple of weeks."

"What's her boggle?"

Lindy shrugged and tore open her Doritos bag. "Who cares? All's I know is, if this is how she's going to be from now on, it's going to be a very long year." She pulled out a couple of chips and shoved them into her mouth.

"Yeah," Beth agreed. "I'll bet."

Neither one of them said much while they ate. Most of the other kids were already finished and on the playground. She watched a game of kickball start. It looked like fun. Maybe they'd go see if they could play.

"Beth?"

"Hmm?"

When Lindy didn't say anything else, Beth turned and looked at her. Something was up. She didn't know what, or even how she knew, but there was definitely something wrong. "What is it? You can tell me." She tapped her palm lightly on the points of her friend's hair because it made Lindy laugh. Except not this time.

"I know. It's just that..."

"What?"

Lindy turned and met her eyes. "Those growls I heard? The ones in the shed? I think it's a monster."

Yeah, a big old hairy werewolf. But she wasn't about to say that again any time soon. If she couldn't trust her own cousin to believe her, how could she expect anyone else to—even her best friend? Better not risk it.

"Did you hear that growling again?"

"Yeah, only louder this time. Scarier."

"You think it's some kind of monster?"

"Yeah, I do." Lindy took a deep breath. A single tear rolled from the corner of her eye. When it reached her lips, she licked it off and uttered a tiny whimper. "And I think it's coming to get me."

☽

That night, Beth wondered if she should have risked telling Lindy about what happened right before her father died. About the werewolf, and how she was afraid it was her mother. *After all, Lindy had been honest about what she'd heard coming from Mr. St. George's shed.*

But Beth couldn't do it. Thinking you heard some sort of monster, late at night, when you were tired and alone was one thing. But claiming there was an honest-to-God werewolf running around killing people? That could get you sent to the funny farm, or at least laughed out of school. She'd just die if Lindy laughed.

Her mother was a monster, a real live werewolf, with fangs and hair and glowing red eyes. Beth couldn't prove it, not yet anyway, but she'd figure something out. She had to, before somebody else got killed.

She couldn't turn off her brain. Her thoughts spun out of control: from her parents' fights, to her father's death, to Jaime making fun of her. That last one hurt almost as much as finding out her mother killed her father.

It took her forever to fall asleep. And when she finally did, the werewolf invaded her dreams…

☽

It was early morning, and Beth was back at her desk, bent over her math homework. She couldn't sleep because she'd forgotten all about the fifteen word problems Mr. Addams assigned. She was concentrating on trying to figure out how many patients Dr. Harris treated each week if he treated a total of 1,404 all year.

"Take fifty-two weeks and make them go into one thousand, four hundred and four patients," she mumbled. "Um, carry the one..."

A faint rumble came through the window. The rattling floorboards made her bare feet tingle a second before the noise reached her ears. Pausing with her pencil hovering above her assignment, she cocked her head and listened. When she didn't hear anything else, she shook her head. Her father always said she'd do anything to keep from doing her homework, and she guessed that meant pretending to hear things, too. God, she hated math.

She returned to her multiplication when the floorboards rattled again. The spare pencils she sharpened and put at the edge of her math book bounced to the floor as the desk shook. The sound kept getting louder.

She stole over to the window and peeked through the curtains. The walls shook so hard, the photos her father took and framed began flying off the walls. The hair on her arms stood straight up and she started to tremble. Something was wrong, really wrong.

Something was coming for her.

Even though there was a full moon, it was foggy outside. She strained to see through the thick soup. The rumbling was louder now, and she could hardly believe what it was. Footsteps. Gigantic footsteps. Coming closer, coming to get her. Her heart beat so hard she was afraid it would explode. She couldn't stop panting.

Outside the window, the fog cleared and two red and angry eyes stared at her. She tried to scream, but a furry paw, huge with ragged black claws, broke through the window and grabbed her by the throat. She couldn't move. Couldn't breathe. She was helpless. Hot, smelly breath invaded her nose and made her gag. She opened one eye and saw the scariest face she'd ever seen. Hairy all over, its eyes glowed and its teeth, its wickedly sharp teeth, were close enough to bite her face off. The monster's spit was incredibly hot, and she could smell her flesh burning. She tried to scream again, but the monster crushed her throat and no sound came out.

In her head, she could hear it laughing. When she opened her eyes, she could have sworn it was her mother's face she looked into. The monster opened its mouth to eat her—

☽

Beth jerked awake, sweat pouring off her face. Her breath came in harsh, ragged gasps. She sat up quickly and looked around the room, confused and disoriented. There was a strange blue light splashing across her bed coming from outside her door. After a second or two, she realized what it was, and sighed. Her stupid cousin must have fallen asleep with the TV on again. She wiped her face with the edge of her sheet. Somehow, that flickering light made her feel better. Jaime might never be able to protect her from the monster, not when it finally decided to come after her for real, but he would try. She was sure of it.

She was also sure the werewolf would come for her. And soon.

Wednesday, September 18, 2013

HARVEST MOON

Full moon closest
to the autumnal equinox
99% Visible

Chapter 13

It was a minimum day at school, and Riff and I snuck out to eat lunch at PJ's. We were actually supposed to be at an assembly, something to do with school elections, but neither of us cared much about school government, much less the "beautiful people" who always got elected. Nothing ever changed—it was middle school, after all. Beth, still in fifth grade, wouldn't be out of school for a couple of hours, so Riff and I decided to skip out early and grab a bite.

When we got there, we didn't even bother to look at the menu. We always ordered the same thing—he had a double-decker cheeseburger and chili-cheese fries, and I couldn't get enough of PJ's pastrami. She served it on a fresh-baked onion roll piled high with lean meat and tons of pickles. Slathered in mustard, it was the best meal in town. That and an icy-cold Coke hit the spot.

One of the best things about Diane, the server, was that, as soon as she saw us, she put in our order. We didn't even have to say anything. As she gave our orders to PJ, I studied the other diners. Mr. Anderson sat in the next booth facing Mr. Ingstrom, who sat next to Ms. Glass. She inherited The Quiet Riot bar from her father a few years back. At the counter, Mr. Winkler, who owned

The First Edition Bookstore, made a big dent in his greasy Reuben sandwich while Thousand Island dressing dripped off his chin.

Deputy Riggs walked in and motioned first at Diane then over at an empty table. Leave it to Riggs to actually want to sit at a table instead of a booth, like most people. He always had to be noticed. Diane nodded back. He swaggered over, pulled out a chair, put two fingers to the brim of his hat in a kind of military salute, and sneered at me. "Jaime."

"Deputy." When I was Beth's age, I got into a little bit of trouble and Riggs never let me forget it. I turned away and picked at my napkin, hoping he'd leave me alone for once.

"Sheriff Brazelton and that idiot deputy of his couldn't find their butts with a brand-new GPS system," Ms. Glass stated loudly. Even though she was looking at Mr. Anderson, she was actually talking to Riggs.

The deputy took the toothpick out of his mouth and pointed it at her. "Seems to me," he said quietly, "someone's still a little pissed off about having her liquor license pulled awhile back. Something about selling to a minor?"

She nearly pushed poor Mr. Ingstrom off the end of the booth. "Get out of my way."

Ms. Glass only stood about five foot two, dripping wet as my dad always said, but she was meaner than a pro football player on steroids. When she marched over to Riggs's table, I tried not to snicker even as I silently rooted for her to beat the crap out of him.

"Well, seems to me there's a skinny little fart who should learn how to keep his big mouth shut."

Riggs jumped up and towered over her, getting right in her face, but she didn't budge. The air in the diner went still, while everyone held their breath. Even me.

"Oh, hell," Riggs muttered then sat at the counter. "Coffee, Diane. Please."

"Yeah, that's what I thought." Ms. Glass triumphantly returned to stand in front of her booth, then turned and addressed everyone in the diner. "We pay our city taxes so the police force will keep our town safe, but Stan Brazelton isn't doing a thing about those murders."

"Seems to me just last month I read in the town report that you were in arrears in your taxes, Donna," Mr. Ingstrom drawled with ill-concealed humor. "Guess you're all paid up now?"

Everyone laughed. Ms. Glass poked him in the shoulder. "What're you, some kind of smart ass, Gus? I don't know about you, but I want someone who can do the job and make this a safe place again."

PJ came out from the kitchen so quietly no one noticed until she took hold of Ms. Glass's arm. "Cool it, Donna," she growled. "Or I'll have to ask you to leave."

"Wow," Riff whispered. "Do you think there'll be a cat fight? Nothing cooler than two chicks fighting."

"Don't know," I replied. "Maybe."

"Fine." Ms. Glass glared at PJ. "I'll catch you later. Penelope Jane."

PJ winced. She hated her real name. Dad told me once that she went by her initials since before she was my age. I could totally empathize.

"Okay." She rubbed her hands together. "Who's up for pie?"

☽

Later on, we were hanging out on the sidewalk in front of the diner while we waited for Beth to meet us after school. Riff and I played *The Legend of Zelda* on our Game Boys. He loved the puzzles in *Oracle of Ages*, but I preferred the action of *Oracle of Seasons*. We picked the consoles and games up on e-Bay for less than thirty dollars. Sure, they were old news, considering everyone had iPhones, iPads and iPods, but we didn't much care. They were new to us, and that was all that mattered.

Beth snuck up and pushed me from behind. "Boo!" she shouted.

Lindy giggled.

I jumped about a foot. "Hey, knock it off. Can't you see I'm busy?"

"You and your stupid video games. When are you going to grow up and stop messing around with those things?"

"Ha," I retorted. "How about you and those dumb water globes you collect?"

She started to say something, but shut her mouth so hard I could hear her teeth click. She pulled on Lindy's sleeve. "Come on, let's go. Who needs these morons, anyway?"

They headed home. We jammed our GBAs into our backpacks and started after them. We found them sitting under a jacaranda tree. Its messy lavender flowers littered the ground beneath them.

Beth got up and wiped the dirt off her butt. "'Bout time."

"Dude, give me a break, will you?" She was starting to get on my nerves. I wished she'd find more friends to hang out with besides Lindy. Especially since Lindy's dad kept her practically chained to the house when she wasn't in school. Maybe then she'd stop hanging around me all the time.

"Fine," she huffed, and stomped off.

We followed along after them. I pulled my GBA out and returned to *Zelda*, trailing after Riff, who was downing yet another Dew.

He crouched on the grass and peered into the hedge lining the sidewalk. "Oh, wow."

"What?" I was engrossed in battle, trying to defeat TwinRova's fire and ice witches.

"Look."

Seriously? I was so close to saving Zelda. "What?" Couldn't he shut up and leave me alone? When I didn't look up, he shoved something in my face.

I grabbed his wrist and pushed it away until I could focus on what was in his hands. "Gopher snake. Cool. Let me see."

I uncoiled the black and brown snake from his arm and watched as it twisted itself around mine. I was surprised it didn't hiss at me. Guess it realized I wouldn't hurt it.

"I have an idea." Riff had an evil grin. "Give me the snake. This is going to be awesome." He looked up the path at the girls.

"Oh, you wouldn't." I really hoped he would.

Riff reached out, unwound the snake from my arm, and held it behind the head and on the tail until it was stretched to its full length. It was about four feet long, not yet full grown.

Second thoughts flooded my brain. It might get me into trouble. In fact, it probably would, but I just couldn't help it. The look on her face would be hilarious. Besides, she might even laugh afterward. "Okay. Go ahead, but take it easy. Beth's still a little shaky."

"Whatever." He started up the hill. I followed. The girls were walking close together, like girls did. Beth held something out to Lindy, but I couldn't see clearly. We snuck up behind them.

"Hey, Beth," Riff said.

"What?" She turned, and he tossed the snake at her. It hit her in the face. She stumbled backward, screaming louder than I would have thought possible. Then she tripped and went down, hard. Riff and I watched as the snake slithered away. She started to cry.

"Aw, come on, you big baby. It's just an itty bitty gopher snake. It won't bite. Much." Riff was laughing so hard at his joke he was snorting.

"I. Hate. You!" Her face was contorted with rage. "You, you booger!" She started to push herself up, but stopped and cried out. She scrambled onto her knees, hunching over something on the ground. I noticed a puddle spreading across the sidewalk, and my stomach flip-flopped so quickly I was afraid I might puke.

"Beth, your language. I'm shocked and appalled." Riff was still laughing. He never knew when to stop.

"Shut up, Riff." I started to help her up, but Lindy pushed me out of the way.

"Leave her alone, you creep," Lindy yelled. "Why are you guys always so mean to her?" She knelt and put her hand between Beth's thin shoulders. "Are you okay?"

"No. Look at what he did." She cradled something in her hands. She lifted her head and glowered at me with such hatred, it caught me off-guard. "Look what you did."

I went over and winced as I saw what she held. When Riff threw the snake at her, she was showing Lindy the water ball Uncle Fred gave her for her birthday, right before he died. It was his last present to her, and we had broken it. I reached out to help her up. "Gee, I'm sorry."

She jerked away. "Yeah, sure." She picked up the shattered glass and placed each piece gingerly on top of the plastic stand.

"I didn't mean to—"

She looked at me, tears running down her cheeks, her breath coming in great big hitches. "You never mean to."

After picking up all the pieces, she folded them inside her hoodie and carefully put the bundle in her back-pack before wrapping her arms around it.

I tried again to apologize.

"Beth," I started.

"I hate you." The words were so quiet I almost didn't hear her.

"I hope you guys are happy." Lindy slung her arm around Beth's shoulders. "Come on, Beth. Let's go home."

Riff chuckled as they walked away. "Dude, we got her good that time, didn't we?" He shook his head and ran his hand underneath his nose.

"Riff, will you shut up for once? You're warped. Seriously."

"Dude, chill."

"Whatever." I took off after the girls, catching Riff's puzzled look as I left. It made me want to punch him in the face. Sometimes I wondered how we ever became friends in the first place.

☽

Beth couldn't understand what was up with Jaime these days. He was always so nice to her, even when she was little. But now it was like he was tired of her. Was he mad that he had to give up his room? It would be an easy problem to fix. She'd just give it back to him, and sleep on the couch.

But part of her knew it wasn't the couch. Ever since she told him what happened that night, outside her window, he'd been different. Which was exactly why she hadn't wanted to tell him about it in the first place.

"Beth, angel, dinner's ready," Aunt Annette called. It was hard getting used to eating dinner every night at exactly six o'clock. Things were always the same here. Dinner at six, breakfast at seven fifteen, chores before homework. Never homework, then chores. But since her stomach had rumbled for the past half hour, she must be getting used to having a strict schedule. She got off the porch and headed in to dinner.

Everyone was already at the table. Jaime usually sat next to her, but tonight he chose a spot directly across from her. As she pulled out the chair to sit down, he stared at her. It made her uncomfortable.

"Stop staring at me," she demanded.

"What?" All innocent. "I'm not doing anything."

"Jaime," Uncle Robbie warned.

"Dude, I said I wasn't doing anything."

"Watch it, young man," Uncle Robbie scolded. "And don't call me 'dude.'"

"I didn't do anything," Jaime muttered into his mashed potatoes.

It was too much for her.

"Yeah, and you didn't do anything on the way home from school, either."

Aunt Annette stopped eating, her fork in mid-air. "Sweetie, what happened on the way home from school?"

Beth glanced first at Aunt Annette then at Jaime. His head was bent over his plate, but she could see the scowl on his face clearly enough. She also saw him shake his head ever so slightly. "Nothing."

"Well, something must have happened or you wouldn't have said that. Come on, tell Auntie what happened."

Beth put down her fork and leaned her head in her hands. She wished she'd never said anything. Now she'd catch it from Jaime for sure.

"Spit it out, honey," Uncle Robbie coaxed.

She looked up at them, unable to hide the welling

tears. She couldn't hold it back any longer. "He and Riff threw a big snake at me," she blurted out. "And made me break my water globe. The one Daddy gave me."

"James Robert Mannaro, you apologize to your cousin this minute."

Uh, oh. She'd gone and done it now. Aunt Annette only used complete names when she was pissed. *Is he going to give me the silent treatment because I tattled on him?* Beth didn't know if she could handle that on top of everything else.

"But—"

"Now."

"Sorry."

"Say it like you mean it, young man."

Jaime cleared his throat and glared at her. "I'm sorry we broke your water globe."

"That's better. Now, I want you two to bury the hatchet."

She just couldn't help herself. Silent treatment or not, she wanted him to pay for what he'd done. "But did you hear what he did? He broke my water globe."

"That's quite enough, young lady." Her mother had to throw in her two cents' worth. Naturally.

Ignoring her mom, Beth focused on an adult who cared. "Uncle Robbie, he broke it on purpose."

"I'm sure he didn't mean any harm. And he did say he was sorry."

"You know how Riff is." Jaime shrugged. "Once he gets his mind set, no one can stop him."

"That's right," her mother agreed. "You know as well as anyone here, he couldn't have stopped Riff."

"You never take my side."

"Look, he's apologized. Now drop it."

"But—

Beth's mom stood up with such force that she

knocked over her chair. She loomed over her daughter, her face turning an ugly shade of red. Then she stuck her finger in Beth's face and yelled, "Knock it off, missy, or I'm going to smack you."

Uncle Robbie tried to pull her mother away. "Calm down, Judy. Everyone just calm down. It's okay. Everything's going to be okay."

He picked up the fallen chair and eased her mom into it. Then he reached over and, with a wink and a smile, gently tugged on one of Beth's braids. She knew she was expected to smile back, but she was just too angry.

"We didn't mean for it to break." Jaime's voice broke a little. He tapped his chest with his palm and looked Beth in the eye. "And I tried to stop him, honest to God, but he wouldn't listen. You know how he is."

The rest of the meal was eaten in silence. Having lost her appetite, Beth mostly chased her food around her plate. Finally, she pushed herself away from the table. "I'm done."

"You didn't eat very much," her aunt remarked.

"Guess I'm not very hungry."

"Okay, you're excused."

"But first, you clear your plate."

There her mother went again, voicing her unneeded opinion. Why couldn't she just stay out of it for once? Beth picked up her dishes and carried them out to the kitchen.

"Make sure you rinse them off," her mother called after her.

"'Make sure you rinse them off,'" Beth muttered sourly.

When she had cleaned off her dishes and stuck them in the dishwasher, Uncle Robbie came into the kitchen. He opened the fridge and examined the insides. After he pulled out a small bottle of orange juice, he peered over the top of the refrigerator door. "Don't sweat the small stuff, honey."

She didn't bother to respond. Who were they to decide what was big and what was "small stuff"? Jaime had broken the very last thing her father had given her. It was not small stuff, no matter what anyone said. They just didn't understand. No one did.

First, Jaime made fun of her when she told him the killer was a werewolf, then he was mean to her. And today he had that stupid Riff throw the snake at her to scare her. He knew she hated snakes. So that wasn't small stuff, either. Maybe she should run away. Pretend she'd been eaten by the monster. Then they'd see.

Then they'd take her seriously.

☽

I couldn't believe what happened to Beth's water thing. How was I supposed to know she had it with her? She shouldn't have taken it to school. But when her mom jumped down her throat at dinner, it somehow made what she'd said about the werewolf a little bit more believable. I wanted to make it up to her, wanted her to know how sorry I was. For everything.

I played couch potato while watching the muted television flicker. There was some dumb horror movie on. Some ancient black and white thing with someone in a really bad rubber monster suit running around killing everyone. It was pretty stupid, and my mind started wandering. I wrestled back and forth. Did I want to give Beth something of mine to make up for the broken water thingy? Would she even accept something? After all, she was pretty pissed off. Finally, right before the end of the last commercial break, I made my decision. Reaching into my backpack, I pulled it out and held it for a few seconds. I think I even kissed it goodbye.

I got up off the couch and crept into the bedroom. I watched for a few seconds from right inside the door to see if she was asleep yet. "Beth?" I whispered. "You awake?"

There was a sharp intake of breath, but otherwise, nothing. Taking a few steps into the room, I called to her again. When she still didn't say anything, I walked over to the nightstand next to the bed and laid my prized possession on top of the clock radio. Her eyelids flickered rapidly, and I knew she only pretended to be asleep. Typical little girl move. I shook my head, leaned over, brushed her bangs off her forehead, and gave her a little peck.

As I turned to go, she switched on the light. She saw what I'd put on top of the radio and picked it up. "What's this for?"

"To make up for breaking your water thingy."

Her smile was small as she corrected me. "Globe. Water globe."

"Yeah, that's what I said. Anyway, I'm sorry about what happened. Cross my heart and hope to die. It was all Riff's idea."

"Stick a needle in your eye?"

"Yeah, yeah. Stick a needle anywhere you say."

"Dude, you don't have to give *Zelda* to me. It's okay." She tried to hand the Game Boy back, but I pushed it toward her.

"No, I want you to have it."

"Really?"

"Really."

"Well, okay. Thanks."

"Still love me?" I teased.

"Yeah, I guess so."

I stood up and danced around the room. It made me feel stupid, but it would make her laugh. I was right; she tried to hide a giggle behind one tiny hand as her eyes twinkled. That was good enough for me. It meant everything was all right again.

I spun around like a ballerina. "Still think I'm cute?"

"Hey," she teased me right back. "I wouldn't go that far."

"Thanks a lot," I retorted, then turned out the light. "Night."

"Night, Jaime. I mean, James." She pulled the covers over her shoulder and closed her eyes. Things were getting back to normal.

Or as normal as they could be, what with how crowded it was. That, and the whole werewolf thing.

Saturday, September 28, 2013

WANING CRESCENT

Old moon
Growing smaller
37% Visible

Chapter 14

On Saturday nights, there wasn't a whole lot of things to do in town. Adults either went to the Quiet Riot to get drunk, or to PJ's to eat. Kids either went to the bowling alley or the movies then on to the diner for burgers and shakes afterward. Beth and I were excited about going to see an old horror movie called *Bubba Ho-Tep* at the three-dollar theater. It was about Elvis, who hadn't died but actually lived in a rest home in East Texas with an identity he took from an Elvis impersonator. Beth loved Elvis—and horror movies— so Mom gave me money for us to go, in hopes it would cheer Beth up and take her mind off things. Afterward, we were going to PJ's, where Riff was supposed to meet us for Cokes.

On our way out the door, Dad stopped us. "Kids," he called from the kitchen table. "Come here a sec."

"Aw, Dad." I made a point to stare at my wrist even though I never wore a watch. Then I elbowed Beth, who'd taken forever to get ready. "If we don't leave now we're going to be late."

She elbowed me back.

"You've got plenty of time, Jaime. I want to talk to you about something."

I looked at Beth and rolled my eyes. She stifled a giggle, and we went into the kitchen.

"You kids need to be extremely careful." He sounded worried, and that scared me. Dad was the kind of guy who hardly ever got upset about anything. Things seemed to roll off his back, and he never, ever got scared. Except now. "Something strange is going on in this town, and I think it would be best if you were home by six-thirty."

"Aw, geez, Dad, that's so early." It was bad enough Mom made us go to a matinee in the first place. "It's Saturday night for Christ's sake."

"Watch your mouth, boy, or you can just forget the whole thing and stay home altogether."

"Sorry."

"Six-thirty gives you almost an hour and a half to eat and hang out with your friends."

"But," Beth interjected. "There's nothing to do when we get back."

"Sorry, puppy. It's for your own good."

She gave him those big green eyes of hers, batting her eyelashes so hard it was all I could do to keep from laughing.

"Tell you what," he said. "Sunset's a little before seven. You can have an extra twenty minutes. How's that?"

"How 'bout nine?" I pushed.

"Ten to seven," he said firmly.

"Eight?" She smiled her big goofy grin again, but this time it didn't work.

"Six-fifty, guys."

"Fine."

We got up and pushed our chairs under the table. When we got to the front door, we grabbed our hoodies off the hook on the wall and headed outside.

"Don't be late, you two," he called after us. "I mean it, now."

I scowled over my shoulder. "All right, all right all ready. Ten minutes to seven. We got it." Then I slammed the door behind me.

☽

"So, what'd you think?" I asked.

The movie had ended but we always stayed to watch the credits.

Beth took one last sip of her Coke. "That had to be the dumbest movie I've ever seen."

"So, I take it you didn't like it?"

"Are you kidding me? I loved it!"

"Yeah, me too." I chuckled. "Let's bounce and get some fries."

"'Kay."

She pulled on her hoodie and headed for the exit. I followed her out the door. PJ's was across the street and down about a block. As soon as we stepped off the curb, someone came barreling around the corner, tires screeching madly. The car was only inches away when I yanked her back onto the sidewalk.

She gave the guy the finger. "Jerk."

"Come on." I patted her on the shoulder. I had to smile though, since she was beginning to act more like herself again.

We carefully looked both ways then crossed the street. As we approached the diner, angry voices filled the cool fall air.

"God, let's go already." It sounded like Mr. Winkler, but he seemed edgy. Weird since he was almost never impatient.

"Okay, you all know which group you're in, so let's review the hunt one last time." I couldn't tell whose voice that was, even if it was familiar.

"Fine, but hurry up, will you?"

We peeked in the door and couldn't believe it. There had to be thirty people all crowded around one of the tables. Mr. Anderson had a map spread out. We inched closer and peered over Mr. Anderson's shoulder. The map was marked with several red X's.

"Groups one, two and three," Mr. Anderson instructed, "you take Heritage Park. Make sure you search in the woods surrounding it. Don't miss anything."

Everyone picked up their weapons: guns, shovels, baseball bats, golf clubs. Even an axe or two. Beth stood there with her mouth hanging open. Neither one of us could believe it. What was going on? I'd read about lynch mobs in Social Studies class, but this was the first time I'd ever seen one in real life. What was the town turning into?

"Groups four and five," Mr. Anderson continued, "you guys search along the tracks all the way over to the town limits."

"Yeah," people said. "Will do."

Mr. Anderson snapped the lid onto his Sharpie with an audible click, then sneered. "I promise you, if that thing comes out tonight for a little midnight stroll, we'll nail the son-of-a-bitch."

"Hey, wait a minute."

Mr. Anderson turned and glared at me.

I swallowed audibly and scratched behind my ear. "You can't just go out and hunt it down."

"It?" Mr. Anderson gawped at me like I was nuts, but I could say the same thing about him.

His eyes were bloodshot, bugging out so far they might actually pop out of his head at any second.

He scared me.

"Well…um…you know." I tried to cover up my mistake. "The killer. You can't just go out and hunt the killer down."

"Yeah? And who's going to stop us?" Mr. Anderson smirked. "You? Don't make me laugh."

"Maybe the boy can't stop you." The sheriff's voice was saturated with controlled anger. "But I sure as hell can." He stood there, filling the whole doorway, one hand on his baton and the other on top of his service revolver. Riggs was right behind him. "Unless I'm mistaken, people—" Sheriff Brazelton eyed Mr. Anderson. "—I haven't deputized a single one of you." He regarded the others. "I want everyone to go home and let us handle this."

"That's right, Sheriff," Mr. Anderson practically spat. "So far, it's only been you and that skinny little dung heap you call a deputy running around, acting like you know what you're doing. But there's still a maniac out there killing people."

"You sanctimonious wind bag," Riggs challenged.

The sheriff put out a hand to restrain him. "Whoever it is, Larry," he said calmly, "we'll catch him."

"You couldn't catch the clap from a two-dollar whore."

Beth and I giggled since we never heard Mr. Anderson, or any adult, talk like that.

The sheriff sighed heavily and walked across the diner. He seemed to be memorizing everyone who was there. When he reached the far end of the room, he turned. "Do you folks know what you're planning? It's called vigilantism. Is that what you all want? To be vigilantes? To form a lynch mob?"

People shuffled, looked at their feet, the walls, anywhere but at the sheriff.

"And what if you do find the killer? What then? Are you going to bring him to justice? Or maybe you'd rather shoot him yourselves?"

Mr. Anderson gazed around and licked his lips. "Come on, he's just trying to scare us. What's he done to catch the killer, anyway? Nothing. Doesn't even have so much as a fingerprint. Or any other evidence."

Sheriff Brazelton got right up in his face. "And what if you find him, Larry? Will you kill him? Pull the trigger yourself? What if later on someone else is killed and you realize you murdered the wrong person? Hmm, Larry? What then?"

Mr. Anderson's face was as red as a raw hamburger. "That's not going to happen."

"How do you know for sure?"

People put down their weapons. The sheriff eyeballed everyone. "Henry? Steve? Are you all willing to take that chance?" More shuffling and murmurings.

"Don't listen to him. He's—"

"Shut up, Larry," Mr. Winkler barked. "I, for one, would never be able to forgive myself if that happened. Could you?"

Deputy Riggs took the opportunity to strut his stuff among the townspeople. "All right, everyone. You heard the sheriff. Let's move along. Go on home, now. Come on."

He ushered everyone out the door. They all brushed past us like we were invisible. We pushed up against the wall and waited for everyone to leave. In less than two minutes the place was deserted, except for us and the two cops. Beth and I quietly headed for a booth in the back.

"Boy, that was close." Riggs ran his hand through his hair. "For a minute there, I didn't think we were going to be able to stop them."

"I'll say," the sheriff agreed. "I've never seen Larry

Anderson so worked up before, not since Donna Glass threw him over for Martin Petrelli back in high school."

Beth raised her eyebrows. Mr. Anderson and Ms. Glass? Quiet Mr. Anderson had once been in love with the obnoxious and loud Ms. Glass? It was all we could do to keep from laughing out loud. I had to look away or else I would have.

"Yeah, and even then he never talked about hunting the guy down."

"Well, just goes to show you never can tell," the sheriff mused.

They pulled out their chairs and sat down. Riggs glanced up and saw us pretending to read the menus. "Hey, what're you two punks still doing here?"

Sheriff Brazelton glanced over at us. "Leave them alone, Riggs. They're not hurting anything."

Riggs pushed back from the table and started to get up. "Punk's probably waiting for another opportunity to steal something, Sheriff."

The sheriff didn't even look at him. "I said, leave them alone. Now, sit down."

With ears as red as a blood orange, Riggs begrudgingly sat, but he glared at us the entire time, me in particular. The sheriff, on the other hand, never seemed to hold my past against me, and didn't pay any more attention to us. He motioned to Diane, who had retreated to the safety of the kitchen as soon as the fireworks started. When she saw him wave, she picked up her order pad and sashayed over to their table.

"So, Sheriff," she said. "What are you going to do about finding the murderer?"

"I'm going to do my job, Diane." He scratched the end of his nose. "So, how's PJ's world-famous pie tonight?"

"Good as ever. Apple, cherry, and banana crème."

"I'll take apple. Riggs?"

"Cherry. Heated. A lá mode."

"Got it." She went to retrieve their order.

"And two coffees," the sheriff called after her.

"Right." She turned to us. "Be with you in a sec."

"No problem," I assured her. We only had about an hour until we had to leave, and we still hadn't heard what the sheriff planned to do. In fact, they didn't talk about the murders any more while we were there.

Friday, October 18, 2013

BLOOD MOON

First full moon after Harvest Moon
100% Visible

Chapter 15

Dinner time. Alone. Again. Lately, if Lindy wanted company during a meal, she had to sit in the living room and eat off a rickety old TV tray.

Her father seemed to be glued to the tube these days. He thought cable sports were the best thing ever invented and loved being able to watch Mike Napoli plow one over the fence. Personally, Lindy didn't give a shit about baseball or any other sport, but it was the only way to connect with her father anymore, so she studied the sports section and watched as many games with him as she could stand.

"Okay, boys," Homer yelled at the television. "We're going to kick some butt tonight."

Lindy sighed and pushed her green beans around. Hopefully her father's team would win this one, because if they didn't, he would take it out on her. He had no issue with waking her and shaking her like a can of spray paint. She half expected her brain to make the same sound as the little ball in the paint can did when you shook it. Here it was, two days later, and she still had a bad headache from the last time. Even her eyeballs felt like they were going to crack like eggs that had been cooked too long.

By the second inning, Lindy was bored stiff. She glanced at her father, who dozed in his chair. There were several beer bottles decorating the floor around him. She got up and cleared the trays, careful to move her father's without banging it into him and waking him. After she put them away, she tossed out the trash and headed to bed.

As she switched off the kitchen lights, her father shouted and she froze. "Hey, batter batter. Swing, batter. Yeah, that's my boy. Throw him another one, just like the other one. C'mon, you pussy. Strike him out!"

Good. He was so involved in the game, she was sure he'd leave her alone. Maybe she could actually get a decent night's sleep for a change. As long as the Red Sox won. That was the main thing.

She'd just started to doze off when a crash jarred her awake.

"Lindy," her father yelled and threw open her bedroom door with so much force that the doorknob gouged a big hole in the wall. "Girl, get up. Come see."

He grabbed her by the wrist and dragged her out of bed. Her legs got tangled in the blankets and she stumbled into her father's belly. He smelled of stale beer and sweat, and she wondered when her father last took a shower. She was afraid he would yell at her for bumping into him, but instead, he put his arm out to steady her.

"You okay?" He put his arm around her shoulders and pulled her close. She was so surprised all she could do was nod. "Good." He shoved her across the room. "Come on, you gotta see this."

They walked down the hall and into the living room. Lindy had no idea what he wanted to show her, and she regarded him questioningly. "What is it, Daddy?"

"Sit down. Watch with me. We're actually winning."

Relieved, she let out a tiny sigh and dropped into her chair. "Thank you, God," she mouthed.

He only wanted her to keep him company. And his team was winning. She settled back in her chair and waited for her father to start a conversation. If he wanted to. If not, she'd just sit here and try to relax without falling asleep. Maybe try to enjoy the fact he actually wanted her around. And not as a punching bag. At least for now.

"C'mon, you bums. Hit the ball." Homer took a long swallow from the bottle, then belched. "Hey, baby," he slurred. "How's about another brew for your old dad?"

"Sure." She jumped up and took the empty bottle he waved at her. She tossed it into the recycle bin and grabbed a fresh one out of the refrigerator.

"Oh, foul ball," the commentator remarked. "Too bad."

"Too bad, my eye," Homer mumbled. "Just kill the stupid thing, will you?"

"It's going, going, it's gone."

"Atta boy, Napoli!" Homer pumped his fist. "That's what I'm talking about. Calls for a celebration. Gherkin, another round." He chuckled at his own joke.

Lindy didn't get it, but she wasn't about to say so. Instead, she tittered and hoped it sounded real. "Good one, Daddy."

"Huh?" He didn't seem to recognize her at first. She watched his eyes as he tried to focus, then guided the bottle into his hand when he reached out for it. "Oh. Sit."

She'd rather go to bed, but did what she was told. With any luck, he'd pass out soon and she could go back to sleep. Living with her dad exhausted her. She couldn't take much more. Leaning her elbow on the arm of the chair, she rested her head on her hand. Her eyes quickly grew heavy and, before she realized it, she fell asleep.

☽

He awoke with a start, disoriented and a little scared. Lindy was sleeping in her chair. The TV blared a few feet away. The floor was showing through the carpet in spots—he could see the bare cement where his feet wore it out directly in front of the chair. Under his left arm was a big stain and a Coors bottle balanced precariously next to his right hand. So as not to waste a drop, he grabbed the bottle and took a long draw. "Lizzie? Lizzie Bear, you there?"

It hit him then, as if a train slammed into his gut. Lizzie, his beautiful Lizzie, was dead. Almost a year now. He collapsed back into the overstuffed chair, his head in his hands. How could he have forgotten? Eyes closed, he put the still-cool bottle to his forehead and rolled it back and forth. He'd been so angry when she'd died. Still was.

He hoisted himself up out of the depths of his Laz-E-Boy and headed for another Coors. He thought he heard something, but wasn't sure. He stopped and listened. Nothing. He shrugged and took another step. The noise came again, louder this time. It almost sounded like a growl. But how could that be? They didn't have a dog. He shook his head to clear it and continued toward the kitchen and another brew.

As he stood in front of the refrigerator, he tried to focus, but couldn't get anything to come in clearer than double. He aimed his hand in the general direction of the handle. It took several tries before he finally latched onto it and opened the door. The bright white light filled his vision and made his eyes throb.

A quick look inside told him he was down to his last sixer, and he cursed his rotten luck. There were still five and a half innings left in the game and six beers wasn't enough.

"Oh well." He sighed heavily. "Have to pace myself, I guess." He pulled out a bottle and used the door handle to pop the top. Just as the glass touched his lips, he heard it again. Louder still. Definitely a growl. "What is that?" He took a long sip and slammed the bottle on the counter, spraying suds everywhere. "Going to have to do something about that."

He lurched back into the living room, tripped, and stumbled into the back of Lindy's chair. He caught himself in time, but his beer bottle crashed to the floor.

"Crap."

Beer splashed all over his pants, the chair, the floor, pretty much everywhere. What a mess.

"Daddy, what is it?" Lindy jumped up from her chair. "What's wrong?"

He reached out and slapped her across the face. At least, that's what he meant to do. Maybe he'd hit her too hard, because she stumbled backward and nearly knocked over the television. Or maybe, she knew what that noise out back was, and was trying to pull a fast one.

☽

Lindy sat on the floor—after her father's fist flew out of nowhere and slammed into her—and rubbed the side of her face. He hadn't hit as hard as usual, but it was enough to knock her down. She didn't even bother to cry. It was a big waste of energy.

"You keeping secrets from me, girl?" He grabbed her by the arm and yanked her to her feet.

"What? No!" What was he talking about?

"You got some kind of dog hidden out in the shed? You and them rotten friends of yours?"

"No, Daddy, there's no dog out there." Had he heard the growls, too?

"Sit down and shut up." He practically threw her into the chair. Lindy tucked a loose strand of hair behind her ear and watched her father leave the room. There was a loud crash, and he cursed. *Must've tripped over the rug again.* The thought was accompanied by a near-hysterical giggle. She tried to catch it with her hand before it escaped. If her dad realized she was laughing at him, she'd be in big trouble.

From the noises she could tell he was rummaging around looking for something, but she couldn't imagine what it was. But then it came to her on a sudden wave of nausea, causing her dinner to jump into her throat. The gun? Did he want the gun? Oh, God, was he going to try to kill the monster? If he did, there would be a death, all right, but she seriously doubted it would be the monster. If her father tried to shoot it, the monster would kill him for sure. She was going to be left all alone and there was nothing she could do about it.

Her father was going to die.

☽

Homer intended to show his daughter and those cretins she hung around with not to mess with him. If they were hiding a dog out there, they'd regret it. Thought they could put one over on him, did they? He'd show them.

He walked down the narrow hallway, tripped on the rug directly in front of the linen closet and crashed into the door. "Damn rug."

He kicked it out of his way. After fumbling with the latch on the closet, he tugged it open and rummaged around the top shelf until his hand closed on his gun. Pulling it down, he clicked off the safety before heading back into the living room.

"Don't just sit there." His lazy daughter had the audacity to stare at him as if she was totally clueless. "Get over here. You're going to watch me kill your dog. Maybe it'll actually teach you something."

"But, Daddy—"

"Don't 'but Daddy' me." She made him grab her by the arm and yank her to her feet. "Just get your skinny little butt outside."

They went out the door, into the back yard, and over to the far corner where the once pristine shed sat. Seeing how much it had fallen apart pissed him off.

"Your dog do this?"

"Daddy," Lindy whined. He hated it when she did that. "There's no dog. Remember all those winds we had? That's what ruined your shed."

"How stupid do you think I am?" A part of him knew she was telling the truth, even as they heard the growls again. Still, she needed to be taught a lesson. "You hear that? Don't tell me there's no dog."

He reached for the doorknob and Lindy grabbed his arm, trying to pull him away. "No, Daddy. Don't!"

Sure now that she was hiding something, he shoved her out of the way and turned the handle. "Gonna open me up a can of whup-ass. Stupid dog. Bust up my shed, will you? We'll just see about that."

The growls got louder. The shed started to shake. The windows rattled.

"Daddy, please."

Tools fell off the pegs nailed into the walls and clattered to the floor. "What the—"

A sick feeling grabbed hold of Homer's stomach and he took a step backward. The building stilled, and the noises stopped.

Homer snorted. *Stop being such a pussy and open the fricking door.*

Filling his lungs with air, he burst through the door and nearly decapitated himself on the rusty bicycle frame hanging from the roof.

☽

Lindy didn't like the way her father kept smirking at her. It was almost evil. Where he got the idea she was keeping a dog in the shed was something she didn't understand. Daddy hated pets. Everybody knew that. She'd no sooner try to hide a dog in his shed, than she'd tell him to get his own beer for a change.

"Still insist there's no mutt?"

What would he do when he went into the shed and realized there was no dog? Still, it didn't explain where the growls came from, or what made them.

She was scared, really scared. And not scared like when Dad was on the warpath. This time, she was more frightened than ever.

"Come on, Daddy," she pleaded. "There's nothing there. Let's go, okay? How about I pour you a beer? A nice cold one?"

His response was to shove her back. She tripped and fell. When the growls got louder, she scrambled up off the grass and threw herself into the nearby bushes.

☽

"Come out, come out, wherever you are," Homer

called as Lindy disappeared into the hedge. When there was no response, he rubbed his hands together in anticipation of the lesson he'd teach his daughter when this was all over. "You still gonna tell me there's no mutt in here?" He turned his attention back to the inside of the shed. "Wassa matter, little doggy? 'Fraid to show yourself?"

In response, there was a deep, guttural growl. Homer froze. It was hard to see in the gloom. Dust motes rained down from the ceiling, highlighted by the moonlight shining through the windows. He grabbed a flashlight off the workbench, switched it on, and aimed it at the bushes, spotlighting Lindy's pale face.

"Daddy?" She blinked and held her hand up to shade her eyes from the harsh light. "Let's go back inside, Daddy. Please."

Something rustled. He aimed the flashlight into the nearest corner of the shed, peering into the darkness. "Did you hear something?" He slowly approached the spot where the noise came from. As soon as he got there, the growls came again, this time, from directly behind him. "Girl, if you're screwing with me, you'll be sorry."

No answer. He turned. At first, he couldn't see her. Then he caught sight of her foot as she disappeared back into the bushes. He'd deal with her later.

The growls swelled until they came from all around him. His heart beat rapidly and it was getting hard to breathe. Sweat poured down his forehead and stung his eyes. "Good dog?" He tried to sound authoritative, but, even in his drunken state, he recognized the warble of fear in his voice. Trying to see what was right beyond the range of his flashlight, he wiped his face in an attempt to clear his vision again. Tentatively, he took a step forward. Something wrapped itself around his head. He fought it off. Threw it onto the floor. Raised his gun. Shot four bullets into it. Took a deep breath. *You got it.* He inhaled deeply. *Everything's okay now. You're safe.*

He bent down to inspect the stringy pile. A tiny chuckle started at the back of his throat, turned into a giggle, then became a chortle, before finally escalating to near hysterics. *Cobweb, you just shot a frigging cobweb!*

The growls returned. Harsher. More intense. He spun around, feeling as if he was being watched. His skin crawled as he backed out of the shed, the light bouncing rapidly from side to side as he checked for the all clear.

Suddenly, from out of nowhere, a large shadow appeared. The thing was behind him. He whirled and emptied the gun, too scared to aim.

What he saw was so hideous, so unbelievably repulsive that he lost control of his bladder. As a large puddle formed at his feet, he watched with fascinated terror as huge serrated teeth, putrid and decayed, rose to fill his vision. The stench of rotten meat hung in the air, and he vomited all over his Wolverines. When he was done, the face of the monster loomed before him. Just before it tore into him, Homer could have sworn it was laughing at him.

$$\mathrm{D}$$

Her father's screams made Lindy's skin crawl. She whimpered and wormed herself deeper into the bushes. She didn't care her face and legs were bloody and raw from the prickles. Her hands flew to her ears as she began to sing tunelessly. "La, la, la. Laddy da da. La. La." Anything to drown out the sounds of flesh being torn. But that wasn't the worst of it.

The worst was the screaming.

Saturday, October 19, 2013

FULL MOON

Second day of lunar cycle
100% Visible

Chapter 16

It was a few minutes after nine o'clock Saturday morning, and Beth and I stood outside Lindy's front door. There was no answer to our repeated knocking. "I don't like this," Beth whimpered. "I don't like it at all."

"Yeah, me neither," I agreed.

"Try the knob."

"You try the knob."

"James, come on. This is serious."

"Sorry." I took a deep breath. "Here goes."

Taking hold of the doorknob, I glanced at Beth. She was chewing on the string of her hoodie, just as nervous as me. Lindy was supposed to come by the house about eight for some of my famous blueberry waffles and thick maple bacon. No one would mistake me for a gourmet chef, but I wasn't bad with breakfast foods. Maybe because breakfast was my favorite meal. But when eight o'clock came and went and our waffles got soggy, we started to worry. And when no one answered the phone, even though Beth let it ring over a dozen times, we got scared. Dad said she'd probably just overslept, but he hadn't seen the fear in Lindy's eyes when she'd told us about the growling. Something told me it was more than

Lindy sleeping in. More, even, than her father deciding he wouldn't let her out of the house. Especially since he usually slept off his nighttime activities until early after-noon.

I twisted the knob, but the door was locked. I gave Beth a raised eyebrow. Wolf Creek wasn't a town that locked its doors at night. At least, not until people started getting murdered.

Beth chewed on her lower lip and frowned. I started to tell her that we should try the back door but before I could she sprinted around the side of the house. Once again, I found myself trotting after her.

As I rounded the corner, I pulled up short but still nearly ran her over. "What'd you stop for?"

Her only response was to point. I followed the line of her finger and saw the back door standing wide open. Something was wrong. Really wrong.

All the color drained from her face and she moaned way down deep in her throat. Putting my hands on her shoulders, I gently shook her. "Beth? It's going to be okay. Stay put." I took a few steps then turned and point-ed at her. "Don't move. Hear me?"

She nodded. I took a deep breath and headed toward the open door.

☽

"Jaime, take your cousin outside."

I'd called my dad as soon as I found Lindy, huddled in the corner of her bedroom with her comforter thrown over her as if to protect her from something. I had no clue what had scared her so badly, but she was staring into space and sucking her thumb.

"But, Dad—" I started to protest.

He had hunkered down on his haunches directly in front of her and gently lifted her comforter, slowly unwinding it from around her. His large, hairy hands captured her tiny brown ones.

"Just do it." His eyes flicked toward Beth before returning to search Lindy's face. "She doesn't need to see this."

He was right. She stood in the middle of the doorway, crying silent tears. I went over to her and leaned down, blocking her view. We still didn't know what had happened, or where Mr. St. George was.

"Come on. Let's go sit outside."

She didn't answer, but allowed me to steer her down the hall and out the door. I had her sit on the back steps then settled in next to her. She kept crying, as if on mute. It freaked me out, so I tried to get her mind off what was going on so she'd stop.

"Hey, how 'bout you and I go over to PJ's later for one of Diane's famous root beer floats?"

No response.

I tried again. "Okay, if you don't want to do that, little girlie, how's about we go down to the Rite Aid and get an ice cream? See if they have any of those water thingies I can get you."

Still nothing. I'd expected her to act pissed at me for calling her "little girlie," even though I knew she secretly loved when I called her that. But instead, she just sat there, not moving at all. Frustrated and not knowing what to do, I scanned the back yard and tried to figure out how to get her to talk to me. Man, the tool shed was a mess. Even so, something seemed a little off. It took me a few minutes to realize what it was. The door hung by a single hinge and stood partially open. Something was sticking out of it, but I couldn't tell what it was from where we sat. I knocked shoulders with her.

"Be right back."

I waited for an answer that didn't come. Sighing, I headed down the steps and across the backyard. Approaching the shed, I slowed way down, not sure what I would find or if I wanted to find anything. The door was splintered all the way through and looked chewed on the bottom.

When I saw a beat up Wolverine steel-toed work boot sticking out of one of the holes in the side, my breath caught. Not many people in Wolf Creek wore Wolverine boots, but Mr. St. George did.

"Dad?" I croaked even as all the spit in my mouth dried up. I cleared my throat and tried again. "Dad!" When there was no answer, I yelled. "Dad! Dad, come quick!"

I couldn't seem to take my eyes off the boot. Every time I tried, my eyes immediately returned. I licked my lips and took a step forward. Afraid I was right about the boot, I'd taken several more steps and knelt for a closer look when I heard footsteps behind me.

"Jaime? You okay?" Then Dad saw what I was looking at. "Oh, my God, don't touch anything."

I yanked back my hand and frowned at him. "Dad?"

He gently took my arm and pulled me up. He said something, but I think I was in shock, because nothing made sense until something was jammed into my hand. When I looked down, I was surprised to see I was holding Dad's cell phone.

"Son, go into the front yard and call the sheriff."

"Oh, yeah, right. Okay. I will. What about Beth?"

"She's fine where she's at. Now go."

Edging my way past the demolished shed and shredded fence, I did what Dad asked, my mind spinning. Had it been a month since Lindy first showed us the wrecked shed and claimed the damage was because of a monster?

As I dialed nine-one-one, I wondered what the sheriff would say.

$$\newmoon$$

While we were waiting for the sheriff, I went to bring Beth out into the front yard, but when I got to the steps, she was gone.

"Beth?" I called. When there was no answer, I entered the house and went from room to room. "Beth, where did you go?

"Here we are." She led Lindy by the hand, and they both seemed to be a little bit steadier. At least neither one of them looked whiter than snow anymore.

I nodded at her. "Hey, Lindy."

"Hey." Her voice shook a little.

"You okay?"

"No, not really."

"Come on. Let's go wait outside."

Beth's eyes were wide and she pulled Lindy closer. "What for?"

"I called the sheriff. He'll be here any minute."

Lindy sniffed and dug a knuckle into the corner of her eye. "Where's my dad?"

"C'mon, let's go out front." I stalled, because even though I suspected she knew her father was dead, I didn't want to be the one to confirm it.

"I want to know where my father is." Her voice was stronger, a little closer to normal.

"Just come outside."

"Where is my dad?" she demanded.

"Lind—" Beth started, but Lindy balked and backed away.

"No. No, you tell me. Tell me right now. What happened to my daddy?"

Her voice was eerily calm.

I tried to think of something to say, but nothing came to mind. I took hold of her wrists and decided to level with her. "Here." I motioned to the couch. "Sit down."

"He's dead, isn't he?" She plopped down into one of the saggy living room chairs and crossed her arms as if to ward off an unseen evil. She seemed so tiny, wadded into the chair like that. Something came over her face, a kind of resignation, maybe. She rubbed her eyes with the heel of her palm and wiped her nose on the back of her hand, snuffing all the snot back into her head.

"Yes. I'm sorry."

Beth picked up Lindy's hand and held it in both of hers. "Oh, Lindy."

"The monster got him, didn't it?"

There was so much sadness in her eyes I almost started to cry myself. "I think so."

☽

Stan Brazelton couldn't believe everything that was going on in Wolf Creek these days. He'd lived there all his life, except for that time in the mid-eighties when he'd moved to Moreno Valley and joined the Riverside County Sheriff's Department. The things the warring gangs did to each other were too much to bear, and, after a year there, he'd fled back to his peaceful hometown.

He'd been unprepared for the events of the past couple of months. After they'd scraped up what remained of Homer St. George, he went back to his office, a place where he felt safe. Now, he sat at his desk and tried to figure out what to do. Never having investigated a murder before, much less three, he was in over his head. There was no getting around it, he'd have to swallow his pride and take his chances next year when it came time for re-election. This was far more important. Human lives were at stake.

It was time to call for reinforcements. He picked up the phone and dialed.

Deputy Riggs walked in toward the end of the conversation, and the sheriff motioned for him to sit down. While he waited, Riggs picked his teeth with the edge of a matchbook. This really irritated the sheriff, but he couldn't seem to break him of the habit.

Brazelton covered the phone's mouthpiece. "Riggs, for God's sake, not now, okay?"

Riggs appeared puzzled. Brazelton pointed to the matchbook and gave Riggs an exaggerated frown.

"What, this?" Riggs indicated the somewhat frayed and soggy matchbook cover.

The sheriff held up a finger to silence the deputy. "Well," he uttered into the phone. "Whoppee. We got some dead bodies here. You think you'll send a team out sometime this week?"

"Sure, we can do that," the officer on the other end of the line said.

"Good. When?"

"We'll be there sometime in the next day or so." The line went dead.

"Oh, bite me." Brazelton slammed down the phone.

Riggs went back to picking his teeth. "That the Highway Patrol?"

"Yep. Still can't get over the fact that they're the ones to call to conduct a criminal investigation. Seems like we should have a State Police force, like other states do."

"What'd they say?"

"They're sending someone out. Should be here within twenty-four hours."

"Good." Riggs hesitated, giving the sheriff a strange look.

Brazelton leaned back in his chair and laced his fingers behind his head. "What?"

"Do you think it was a good idea to tell that Chippie to bite you?"

The sheriff snorted and shook his head at his deputy's gullibility. "Riggs, I waited until he hung up, you goofball."

Riggs blushed a deep scarlet.

The sheriff ran his fingers through his hair. "Jesus, we're in real trouble here. What a mess."

He wasn't sure, but he had a strange feeling it was only the beginning.

☾

October 19, 2013. That was the day the town changed. If I thought people were jumpy over the summer as the Santa Ana's blasted through town like an Angry Bird on speed, I must not have known the meaning of the word jumpy. Wolf Creek used to be a sleepy little town where nothing ever happened, but after Mr. St. George was eaten by whatever monster stalked the town, mothers no longer let their toddlers play outside. Fathers glanced nervously over their shoulders while guarding their sons as they practiced Little League. The Gun Rack, the local hunting supply store, had a run on guns like never before. Mr. Connor ran completely out of ammo by the end of the day, and every single gun in his inventory was gone by the end of the week.

You could feel the change in the air. It practically

pushed in against you, sucking the soul from the town. People no longer stopped to chat with each other. Instead, they hurried about their chores, racing inside the Circle K or the Rite Aid to get whatever they needed and then rushing back out to their cars to hustle home again before dark. Home was the only place people seemed to feel safe anymore. And even then, everybody started locking their doors and windows.

The day after Mr. St. George's murder, the mayor activated the town's phone tree and called a town meeting for one o'clock at the Community Center. The topic of conversation was how to make the town safe again. All suggestions were welcome, including any reasonably intelligent theories as to what was happening.

Beth and I figured no would listen to us—because, frankly, no one ever listened to kids—but we decided to go down to the sheriff's office anyway and feel him out about our werewolf theory. Even though Dad let us out of the house during the day, our curfew was four every afternoon. Guess the parental units figured that, since all the murders had taken place after dark, there was no point in confining us while the sun was out.

Still, we snuck out of the house that morning while Dad was engrossed in the newspaper, Aunt Judy was soaking in the tub, and Mom was doing whatever it was moms did on Saturday mornings. We left the TV on, a little loud but not blaring, to cover our tracks. We figured we had forty-five minutes until someone discovered we were gone, and we hoped to be back before then.

"Come on," I whispered during a particularly obnoxious commercial where the guy screamed at us to buy his oxygen-based cleaning products. "Let's go."

We got up, walked quickly past Dad, with his nose buried in newsprint, quietly opened the front door, and left. We walked down the sidewalk into the heart of town and to the sheriff's office near the corner of Remus Street and Wolf Creek Road. It took less than ten minutes to get there.

"Hope the sheriff's the only one there." I still wasn't a hundred percent sold on Beth's werewolf theory. It was all so incredible. Maybe it was some kind of psycho serial killer or something. Michael Meyers or Jason, someone like that. Because if it did turn out to be some escaped lunatic instead of her monster, everyone in town would find out about the werewolf thing and laugh at us. "Let's keep walking right on past the window," I suggested when we were about three stores away. "That way, we can look and see who all's inside before we go in."

"Good idea." We slowed to a crawl as we walked by the office and tried to glance in the window without being seen. Once we got past it, she turned to me. "I couldn't see anything, could you?"

"Nah, the window's all dark."

"Should we try it again from this side?"

"Yeah, okay," I agreed. "Maybe the sun was shining on it weird or something."

We walked past the window a lot quicker this time. Hopefully whoever was inside wouldn't notice we'd just walked past ten seconds ago.

Beth, walking on the other side of me, leaned back and squinted in an attempt to see inside as we walked past. "See anyone?"

"Nah, the window's all backlit, so whoever's in there can probably see us, but we can't see them."

"Shoot." She snapped her fingers. "Well, should we just go in?"

"Don't know." I shrugged. "What do you think?"

Before she could answer, the door opened and Sheriff Brazelton poked his head outside. "Well, are you two coming in, or what?" He held the door open for us and we scooted in. "James." He nodded a greeting. "Beth, how you doing?"

Beth gave him one of her all-star smiles. "Pretty good, Sheriff. You?"

He chuckled and shut the door. "Fine and dandy." Then he eyeballed me. "What can I do you for?"

I licked my suddenly dry lips and glanced at Beth. She busily chewed a hangnail on her thumb and wouldn't meet my eyes. It was up to me to start the conversation. I took in what my mother called a cleansing breath, and let it out slowly. "Sheriff, we know who the murderer is." He simply sat there and stared as I shared our suspicions. "You know how each murder's happened on the night of the full moon?"

The words fell fast, as I was afraid he would laugh like I did when Beth first told me about the werewolf. Especially when the corners of his mouth started to turn up. The best thing to do was to plow forward and hope for the best.

"Oh, let me guess," came a voice from behind us. We turned in our chairs to see who had spoken.

"Oh, God." I rubbed my forehead so hard it felt like the skin was peeling off. Riggs leaned against the door-jamb, a paring knife in one hand and a half-eaten Granny Smith in the other.

"The murderer is..." he said dramatically. "Drum roll, please." He played air drums and punctuated them with a strike to the cymbal. What a doofus. "A werewolf. Sheriff, we'd better run and grab all the silver bullets we can."

"Riggs, cool it." Sheriff Brazelton hid a flash of a smile behind his hand. "Okay, kids, that's a very funny joke, but I have work to do."

I felt like a fool, but couldn't give up. "But, Sheriff, this isn't a joke. There really is a werewolf on the loose."

Before he could say anything, someone grabbed the back of my collar and jerked me out of my chair. I caught sight of a wiry arm with a ton of fine brown hair and knew that hair went all the way down to the first knuckle. Somehow, my feet got all tangled up and I stumbled into Riggs's stomach.

"Oof!" he cried out.

Beth didn't bother to hide her giggle.

"Riggs, let go of him." The sheriff was halfway around his desk, but Beth beat him to the punch.

"Come on, let's get out of here. Riggs couldn't find his way out of a wet paper bag with a flashlight and a compass." She grabbed my hand and stared defiantly at the deputy. "Gonna move so we can get by, or what?"

She flared her nostrils and gave him the typical Beth stance. I raised an eyebrow, but kept my mouth shut.

Riggs raised his hand in a backhand. "Why, you little—"

"Riggs," the sheriff warned, still standing beside the desk, but looking like he was more than ready to deck Riggs himself.

Riggs sighed and let his hand fall to his side. He took a loud bite out of the apple, chewed with deliberate care, and moved aside just enough for us to get by. When we got to the door, I held it open for Beth, who hesitated in the doorway, then turned back to the cops.

"Beth," I whispered. "What are you doing?"

"I'm going to give them a piece of my mind," she answered loudly. "They sure could use some extra." She marched over to Riggs, stood on her tiptoes and got right up into his face. "You'll be sorry you didn't believe us next month when the werewolf strikes again." She shook her index finger at him. "And we'll tell everyone that you could have done something to keep someone from being murdered, but decided to sit on your skinny butt and do nothing instead." Then she turned and stomped out of the office. I was amazed at her gall, but it sure made me laugh. Which I did, loudly, and directly, at Riggs. Then I followed her out the door.

☽

The sheriff shook his head in disbelief. James Manarro had always seemed to be a pretty levelheaded kid, with the singular exception of that one incident three or four years ago. He was fairly certain James had been put up to it by that delinquent-in-training friend of his, Riff…what's-his-name. But there was that "honor among thieves thing," and James had refused to incriminate the little punk. Instead he'd ended up with a hundred and seven community service hours, served while wearing a greasy orange jumpsuit as he painted picnic tables in the park and picked up litter. The kid never complained once, though. Brazelton had to admit that he had more respect for the kid than he did for many of the adults in town.

He sighed. A werewolf? Really? It had to be a joke, a stupid kid's hoax, maybe even an initiation of some sort. Still, it didn't seem like something James would do. And that little Beth. What a spitfire. The way she'd marched right up to Riggs and given him what for. It cracked Brazelton up. Not many kids her age would dare speak to an adult, much less a cop, that way, even one as smug and sanctimonious as his pencil-necked geek of a deputy.

But Riggs wasn't all bad. He was a whiz at organization, and kept the departmental files in order. In spite of the things Larry Anderson said last month at PJ's, most of the town respected Riggs, or at least pretended to.

Riggs snorted and took another bite of fruit. "Can you believe that little snot?"

Brazelton thought he looked like a roasted pig with an apple in its mouth. "Oh, the kid's not so bad."

"Not so bad?" Riggs snorted again. "You got to be kidding me, Sheriff. Do you honestly believe there's a werewolf running around killing people?"

"Of course not. But they believe it. I think maybe I'll talk to them about it some more. They might know more than they're telling."

"Well." Riggs shrugged. "It's your time you're wasting." He sniffed and hitched up his utility belt. "Think I'll go on patrol, maybe see what's up at the Community Center. Make sure everything's ready for this afternoon."

"You do that." The sheriff glanced at his Timex. If he hurried, he might be able to catch the kids before the town meeting. If not, he could search for them afterward.

Something seriously nagged at him, though. His stomach was acidy, his palms were sweaty, and his blood pressure was up again. All were symptoms that spelled trouble, and over the years he'd learned to listen to the signs. That old drunk, Homer St. George, was nothing more than shredded beef when they found him. The county coroner hadn't ruled on the cause of death yet, but the sheriff was willing to bet it wasn't a bad case of the flu.

Maybe the kids really did know something about the murders.

Could there actually be a werewolf out there, ready at any time to prey on the town?

☽

Thirty minutes before the town meeting, we piled into Mom's Corolla. The Community Center was only five minutes away from our house, but Dad wanted to get a good seat up front. When we got there hardly any seats were left, and we were forced to sit about three rows from the back, wedged in between the Gonzalez family, with their bazillion kids, and the Connors.

Mr. and Mrs. Connor had two sons, but one had been killed in a drunk driving accident five years back. The remaining son weighed at least three hundred pounds, and his butt hung way over the tiny metal folding chair. I could hardly breathe because I was way too smooshed. I sat there a few minutes and tried to concentrate on the buzz of conversation around me. So many people were talking that it was hard to think.

Beth leaned over and stage-whispered in my ear. "Let's get out of here."

"Not yet." I stuck my finger in my ear to clear out the sound. "I want to hear what's going on."

"Okay, but can we at least get closer to the door? All these people are giving me the willies."

"Sure." I tried to un-wedge myself from the chunky monkey next to me. It soon became obvious that it wasn't going to be easy or even possible unless he moved over. I tapped him politely on the shoulder. "'Scuze me."

The guy just glanced at me out of the corner of his eye while he continued to munch on one of the mini-donuts from the back table, powdered sugar decorating the front of his black Rolling Stones T-shirt. In his plump hand he clutched a half dozen more.

When I realized he wasn't going to move on his own, I rammed my elbow into his side and wondered if he would even feel it. But he must've been ticklish, because he cackled so hard that he spit soggy crumbs all over the back of the girl who sat quietly in the chair in front of him. She touched the back of her neck and discovered a mushy mess.

She shot him a disgusted look. "Ew. Gross."

Her mother leaned over, whispered something, and

patted her on the thigh. The girl gave the guy one last dirty look, then turned back around and used the tissue her mother fished out of her purse to clean up.

"Let's get out of here before we get sucked into the black hole of death." I jerked my thumb back over my shoulder at the guy.

Beth tittered and worked her way down the row. There wasn't much legroom between the rows, and, as I followed, I tried not to step on anyone's toes.

As we headed down the side of the room toward the door, I noticed Riggs and the sheriff leaning against the wall. Their arms were folded across their chests, their eyes searching the crowd. But the resemblance ended there. Where the sheriff was fair and impartial, commanding—and getting—the respect of the town, the deputy was ill tempered, judgmental, and just plain nasty most of the time.

The mayor stood in the doorway, apparently looking for someone. As soon as she spotted the cops, she walked directly over to them. The trio huddled together, each one occasionally glancing around the room before quickly returning to the huddle.

Beth flicked her head toward them. "Look."

"Yeah." I gave her a little push to urge her to walk faster. "Hurry up, I want to see what the sheriff plans on saying."

"You mean about the werewolf? Think Riggs'll let us get that close?"

"Probably not, but it's worth a try. Move it."

We wove our way in and out of the crowd. There were so many people. I'd never seen so much of the town in one spot, outside the Labor Day Festival every year, and maybe when the town lit the Christmas tree every December first. But we weren't crammed inside like we were now. It took us several minutes, but we finally made it close enough to the mayor and the two cops to hear what they were saying.

"So." The mayor searched Sheriff Brazelton's face. "Until the Highway Patrol arrives, what leads will you be following up on?"

Riggs chuckled roughly. "I know which one we won't be following."

"Riggs," the sheriff cautioned. He turned back to the mayor. "We had a couple of citizens come in to the office this morning to report their suspicions."

"Which citizens?"

Riggs snorted loudly. Sheriff Brazelton scowled at him then seemed to notice Beth and me.

"Us." Beth pushed her way through the rest of the crowd. "We're the ones."

I wanted to melt right into the floor. "Beth, shut up."

"What could a couple of kids know about three murders?" Mayor Willoughby grunted her disbelief. "You two run along now. The grown-ups are talking."

Beth and I grimaced at each other. What, did the mayor think we were five?

"She told you the truth, Mayor." It was going to be an uphill battle, I could tell. "We really do know who killed those people."

The mayor completely ignored us. "Sheriff, as you know, I am not only the mayor but head of the City Council. As such, I am your direct boss, and I demand that you discuss with me every lead you have."

"And as *you* know, Mayor," the sheriff retorted, "the sheriff of Wolf Creek County is an elected position, and as an elected officer, the citizenry are the people I'm ultimately responsible to. So if you don't mind, I think I'll keep the information to myself a while longer."

I almost laughed at the look on the mayor's face. Guess she wasn't used to anyone talking to her like that, because her cheeks turned bright red, sweat started to bead on her forehead, and her mouth moved but nothing came out.

"Riggs," the sheriff continued. "Time to get started."

They made their way up to the podium. We headed back to our seats, and, as we did so, it occurred to me that maybe Sheriff Brazelton believed us after all. Or at least, he didn't entirely *disbelieve* us.

Only time would tell if he was taking us seriously. I hoped someone else wouldn't have to die before that happened.

☽

From where we sat near the back of the meeting hall, we could see the whole room. Riggs followed the sheriff with his usual swagger, and Mayor Willoughby brought up the rear. The way she trotted along behind them reminded me of a toddler trying to keep up with an impatient mother who was late for her mani-pedi.

Giggling, Beth elbowed me and pointed. "Hey, the mayor's short little legs make her run like a munchkin."

"Yeah, if we're lucky, maybe she'll burst into song." We grinned at each other and sang in high, nasally voices. "We represent the Lollipop kids, the Lollipop kids, the Lolli—"

"Pipe down, you two," the man behind us demanded.

We tried, but every time we caught each other's eyes, we cracked up. Aunt Judy leaned across Mom and glared at both of us, but mostly at Beth. She caught her mother's scowl and slumped back in her chair, viciously kicking the legs of the chair in front of her.

"Beth, stop it right now," Aunt Judy insisted.

Beth gave it one last kick, then crossed her arms defiantly and mumbled something under her breath.

I was about to whisper that Riggs was acting like a strutting peacock when Sheriff Brazelton banged on the lectern. People quickly quieted down, and the meeting was called to order.

"Okay." The sheriff's voice needed no microphone. "We all know why we're here."

"Damn straight," someone in the back shouted.

Others murmured in agreement.

"All right, all right. Settle down, people." The sheriff came out from behind the lectern. Riggs stood off to one side watching the crowd, one hand on the top of his baton, the other on his gun. He'd unsnapped the strap securing it in the holster and I wondered if he actually thought he might need to use it here. "Deputy Riggs and I are doing everything we can to track down the person or persons responsible for the recent deaths. In the meantime, I don't want anyone taking this matter into their own hands. No lynch mobs, no private retribution."

He gazed around the room, stopping at each face from the diner that day when the Rotary Club had been all riled up and wanted blood. "I promise you, we will find the killer or killers and justice will be served."

"You and that fish-faced barracuda you call a deputy couldn't find an X-ray machine with a Geiger counter," someone shouted from the middle of the room.

Riggs stepped to the edge of the podium. "Who said that?"

"I did."

People looked all around, trying to figure out who had spoken.

"Identify yourself."

Riggs spread his legs apart and took up what my dad once called his "official" stance, which made him appear even more like a douche than usual. The sheriff put out a hand to restrain him, and I wondered if he ever got tired of always having to rein the tool in.

"You couldn't find your way out of a phone booth with a pith helmet and a pick axe."

I finally placed the voice at the same time its owner stood up. Mr. Anderson, the guy who'd tried to get everyone worked up enough to hunt for a killer they had no chance of capturing. "Why don't you just get in your little squad car and drive your little selves right out of the county, so we can get someone in here who actually knows what they're doing?"

"Shut up, Larry."

Everyone turned around and gawked as Mr. and Mrs. Fitzpatrick stood right inside the doorway, clinging to each other.

"Don't tell me to shut up."

"I said, shut up." Mrs. Fitzpatrick's voice was so calm it was eerie.

"You have no right," Mr. Anderson blustered, even as he began to visibly sweat and the vein in his forehead throbbed prominently.

"I have every right," Mrs. Fitzpatrick retorted. "You didn't see what our baby girl looked like. They had to pick up what was left of her with tweezers and a baggie."

Sheriff Brazelton stepped off the podium and headed down the aisle toward them, weaving quickly in between the townsfolk who'd crowded into the walkway to watch the spectacle with the Fitzpatricks. "Evan, Margaret. I'm truly sorry for your loss." He motioned with his arm to indicate everyone in the room. "We all are."

"Our loss?" Mr. Fitzpatrick shouted, in direct contrast to his wife's quietness. "Our loss?"

The sheriff reached out and put his hands on the Fitzpatricks' shoulders as he tried to calm them down and usher them out the door at the same time.

"Evan, I know how upset you must be."

Mr. Fitzpatrick pushed the sheriff's arm away. "How dare you?"

As soon as he did so, the sheriff yanked his other hand away from Mrs. Fitzpatrick as if burned.

"How dare you condescend to know how we feel? Our Mary was ripped to shreds. Ripped to shreds! You saw her. Or what was left of her." At this, Mr. Fitzpatrick began to sob.

"Our daughter is dead." Mrs. Fitzpatrick rubbed her husband's back and continued. "You come in here with your platitudes and your smugness, and you talk to these people about retribution? Why don't you go to the cemetery, Sheriff? Go down there and talk to our Mary. Explain it to her, all about private retribution and justice for all. You'll be able to find her easily enough. Just find the tombstone with all the fresh flowers around it. We take flowers out to Mary's grave every day. So you go out there and explain it to her, Sheriff."

There was a moment of stunned silence, then Mr. Anderson started up again.

"Woo hoo," he hooted, nearly knocking over the poor lady sitting next to him in his rush to get out of his chair. "You heard him. We're going on the hunt. Come on, everyone, let's go!"

He ran down the aisle, nearly knocking the Fitzpatricks over in his rush to get hunting, and practically flew out the door. It didn't take long before about a hundred people stampeded after him.

"People!" The sheriff raised his voice, but it was no use.

There was no stopping those who wanted to go. Riggs actually drew his weapon and pointed it toward the ceiling, but then lowered it again without firing. You could hear car doors being slammed and the screech of tires as people couldn't leave for the hunt fast enough. Mayor Willoughby looked like she was about to lose her lunch, and, for once, Riggs clearly didn't know what to do.

We quietly watched it all. No way would they find the monster tonight. After all, she was there, sitting right next to Beth, calmly watching everything that was going on.

Biding her time until the next full moon. Until she could kill again.

☽

Larry Anderson was glad to see so many of his buddies had the guts to do something about what was happening to the town. A good-sized crowd had gathered in the lighted basketball court of the park. Larry nodded at Gus Ingstrom and Irv Winkler, then smiled at Donna. It amazed him that such a tiny little thing had bigger *cajones* than that skinny geek Riggs, or even the sheriff.

"Okay, guys, gather round." He never claimed to be a natural take-charge guy. If he was, maybe he and Donna would have stayed together back in high school. But she chose that football creep Martin Petrelli over him. Something he never quite got over. But now, he had a chance to show her she made the wrong choice, and he was eager to get started. "Everyone remember what group they're in?"

People nodded and murmured quietly. Men and women, including some barely old enough to vote, cast elongated shadows on the cement.

The air was crisp and cool, a typical Southern California October night. The woods bordering the far side of the park were full of live oaks whose leaves were now red and umber and lined the forest floor with a thick layer of mulch.

The chaparral thrived during the long drought periods typical of the area, and the scrub brush had dried nearly to the point of breaking loose in the heavy winds and tumbling through town.

"What group am I in, Larry?" Gus Ingstrom called.

"For the third time, Gus," Larry replied. "You're in Group Three."

"And where do we search?"

"For God's sake, are you retarded or what? Search the woods behind the park. Think you can remember that for the next five minutes? Can you do that?"

"I don't know." Gus wiped the spittle from the corner of his mouth and glanced at the other hunters. "Do you really think we should be doing this?"

"Well, who else is going to hunt the killer down?" Larry regarded the hunters grouped around him. "Do you see the sheriff or that moron Riggs anywhere?"

"No, but—"

"But nothing. If we don't do this, the killer may never be found. Is that what you want?"

Gus shook his head and stared at the ground.

"Okay, then." Larry clapped his hands together. "Everyone ready?"

"Well, it's about time," Irv Winkler grumbled. "Let's get going."

The crowd eagerly dispersed, shovels, baseball bats, and guns in hand. About half headed for the woods, while the rest fanned out to search the nooks and crannies of the town.

☽

Thirsty. Need water. Soon.

Even though the first night of the normal three-day lunar cycle was last night, the werewolf managed its transformation tonight with great difficulty. Since it had gotten sick, its need to hunt had outweighed the common sense of its human side. In fact, most of its humanity was already lost. Before long, it wouldn't be able to change at all.

It would forever be a hunter. Predator.

And humans would be its only prey.

☽

Although he would never admit it, not even to himself, Larry Anderson was severely creeped out. He'd never outgrown his childhood fear of the dark. A mockingbird cried out, its annoyingly persistent search for a mate piercing the silent night. Another scary thing about nighttime. All those damn birds and crickets and things.

He hated fall and winter. He supposed his so-called friends would snicker and call him a pussy, but the way the trees looked without their leaves, as they threw dark and spooky shadows, reminded him of the boogeyman of his childhood. He hid it well, though. Didn't think anyone knew or even suspected. Still, it was basically the reason he'd positioned himself in the exact center of the search line. If that crazy lunatic grabbed someone, he'd likely start on one of the ends, which would leave Larry plenty of time to get away.

He pulled the collar up on his Levi jacket and wished he had worn his thick hunting coat. The wind was aggressive, and he was cold.

"Come on, you pussies," he called to the searchers nearest him. "Step it up. Let's find this scumbag so we can beat the crap out of him and go grab a beer."

"We've been out here for an hour," Gus Ingstrom whined.

"Yeah, I'm cold," some other pussy moaned. "Let's go home."

Larry stopped and broke formation to turn and scrutinize the searchers. "Look. Those of you who want to go home, go. Be a big, useless wuss. We don't need to be slowed down by cowards. But those of us who stay will know we've done everything we can to keep this town safe." He studied each of the hunters on either side of him. "We're going to catch the murdering scumbag, and when we do, those of you who leave now will all be sorry you left with your tails between your legs. Now, who's with me?"

"Oh, for God's sake, Larry," Donna snapped with her usual impatience. "Just shut up and get back in line. Who elected you king of the mountain?"

He stepped so close to her they were nose-to-nose. "Listen, you cow."

Several people broke ranks to circle the warring pair. It reminded Larry of the playground fights he used to get into in the third grade. The ones he always lost.

"Shut up, both of you," Irv Winkler said.

They turned toward him.

"Who you telling to shut up, old man?" Donna demanded.

"Shut up, you damn fools," he repeated. "Can't you hear that?"

Larry and Donna glared at each other even as they stood still for a few moments. And so did everyone else. Before long, people shuffled back and forth. Someone coughed. The tension was a heavy weight holding them in place.

"I don't hear—" Larry started, then he understood.

The birds weren't singing. No chirps from the crickets. Even the wind had died down.

Gus Ingstrom backed up and spun around wildly. "I don't like this. I don't like this at all."

"Yeah," Irv Winkler agreed. "For once, Gus, I got to agree with you."

All thirteen hunters tightened their grips on their weapons. A loud pop came from deep within the trees, followed by a low rumble.

"Oh, my God," Donna whispered. "What was that?"

"Don't know." Larry no longer cared what people thought. "But I, for one, ain't gonna stick around to find out." With that, he pushed several people aside and ran back toward the lights in the park and the safety of his car.

"Wait up, Larry," Irv called after him. "We need to watch each other's back."

Yeah, I'll watch my own back, thank you very much. Larry didn't intend to find out where the sound came from. Or what made it.

☽

It lifted its nose and sniffed. The werewolf skulked in the shadows downwind from the humans and relished the musky odors vaguely reminding it of something, although it couldn't remember what.

It watched, amused, as the humans searched. They would never find it. Not before it killed again. It growled low in its throat and licked its lips. Bubbles foamed along its muzzle.

So hungry. Unquenchable thirst. Only blood would ease its pain. Human blood.

☽

Larry paused to catch his breath. Somewhere behind him, a branch snapped, and he whirled around. No one was there. Where was everyone? He could hear muffled voices, but couldn't make out where they came from.

His hackles rose. Someone—or something—watched him. He could feel it. His blood coursed heavily through his veins. His heart beat erratically, thumping against his chest until he felt it throbbing in his temples, his neck, even in his abdomen. He couldn't move, couldn't even breathe.

The bushes stirred slightly. Whatever it was stalking the town was close. Too close.

It was going to get him.

☽

It could smell the man's fear. Hear his blood as it pumped through his veins. The werewolf watched as the man stopped to catch his breath. Rattled the bushes, enjoyed the deepening of the human's fear.

It would have to strike soon, though, before the hunger weakened it much further. Before it lost its ability to hunt. While it could still kill.

☽

"Oh, crap." Larry licked his lips and backed slowly away from the rustling brush. Whatever was in the woods was right behind him. "Oh, God in heaven. Help me!" His high-pitched scream echoed through the trees and came back to him in an eerie imitation of his voice.

"Geez, Larry, get off me, will you?"

He was shoved from behind, and stumbled over a tree root. He whirled around and stood face to face with

Irv Winkler, who grinned like a dribbling idiot.

"Holy cow, Irv. You scared the crap out of me."

Irv patted him on the shoulder. "Come on, you big wuss. Let's go."

The bushes rustled again, followed by the same deep rumble. It sounded like a cross between the purr of a big wildcat and the roar of an old leaf blower.

Donna climbed through the bushes and stood next to Irv. "What was that?"

The rest of the hunters followed suit, huddling a little closer to one another and tightening their grips on their weapons.

"Don't know," Irv said. Everyone glanced nervously around. Several whipped around in tight circles as they tried to cover their backs and protect their flanks at the same time. Irv pointed over Larry's shoulder. "But it came from over there."

"No," someone else shouted and pointed in the opposite direction. "It's over there."

"All right," Donna chimed in. "Everyone calm down. Won't do no good to panic."

"She's right," Irv said. "Let's stick close together. Everybody, arm's length from your neighbor. No more."

Larry stretched his arms and shifted so that he was the proper distance from his neighbors. "Sucker tries to get by us, we'll kill the crazy mother."

Donna cackled. "Big talk for someone who nearly pissed his pants a minute ago."

"Drop dead."

The rumble came again, louder this time. Clearer. It was definitely some kind of animal. Something really, really big was out there, and Larry didn't want to wait around to find out what it was. He stepped away from the group.

"Wait." Donna grabbed his arm. He shrugged it off. "Larry, wait, I think it's behind us."

Everyone whirled around to see if they could see whatever was making the noise. There were more growls, deeper, angrier than before.

"Oh, no," Gus whined again. "Can't you guys feel it? It's right here with us."

"I'm outta here." Larry broke away and ran in the direction he thought the park and safety was in.

When he disappeared behind a tree, Gus called after him.

"Larry, come back." Then, quieter, "Coward."

They were all nuts if they thought he would stay out here and be a sitting duck. What with the cloud cover that hid the moon and the trees and brush, the woods were scary enough. But add in those strange sounds and the feeling of being watched he couldn't shake—there was no way. He wasn't about to become a midnight snack for whatever was out there.

☽

Larry stopped to rest against one of the less ominous trees. He studied the path behind him and tried to slow his breathing. Faint voices floated through the air. He squinted and peered into the gloom. Other than a spare word here and there, he couldn't hear what was being said, but he could tell from the few words he could make out that that loudmouth Donna Glass was listing her little and loud complaints about him. Again. Boy, if he could only get his hands on her, he'd give her something to complain about.

As he pushed away from the tree trunk, he heard signs of the group as they moved toward him and figured they'd finished griping and were heading home. He scanned the darkened sky and wished the cloud cover would break. His MagLite flickered, and he banged it against his palm. When was the last time he changed the batteries? He couldn't remember, but he wasn't waiting around to see if they would fail before he got back to the car, so he broke into a trot and wished again for the clouds to break so the woods would be flooded with moonlight.

A scream, high and full of terror, pierced the night. Larry froze. People crashed through the bushes. Growls and snarls were followed by more screams. This was no crazed lunatic stalking the town. This was some kind of monster. It not only killed people, but it sounded to Larry as if it were *eating* them.

"Oh, God," someone screamed from directly behind him. He turned around and saw Gus. Half of his face was gone, and he looked like he'd been scalped. His clothes were shredded, and there was an enormous hole where his left hip should be. His remaining eye bounced up and down on his cheek as he lurched toward Larry.

"Help me—" he began.

Then an enormous paw, almost as black as the shadows it seemed to catapult out of, sliced through the air. Larry watched as Gus's head spun toward him in a perfect spiral. It landed a few feet in front of him and bounced across the tops of his boots.

For a moment, Larry stared at it, unable to comprehend what just happened. Then he looked to where Gus had been and saw an enormous beast. It sat hunched over Gus's body, guarding it like a gargoyle atop an ancient church. The thing was covered in gore, its fangs dripping red foam. Blood spurted from what was left of Gus's neck and darkened the ground beneath it. The monster plunged its paws into Gus's innards and gnawed hungrily on them.

Larry's right eye twitched. He whimpered. The creature ceased chewing and seemed to listen. Then it whipped its head around and glared directly at Larry. Its eyes glowed as red as the Blood Moon. Then it roared, an earsplitting clap of thunder that nearly knocked Larry down.

Instead, he fainted.

Sunday, October 20, 2013

WANING GIBBOUS

Old moon
Growing smaller
98% Visible

Chapter 17

Riff and I got up early Sunday morning to shoot hoops at the park. I worked on my hook shot while Riff mostly dicked around. He even managed to bounce the ball off the backboard once in a while.

As I was about to push the ball into the air, he spoke. "Dude, how much longer is your cousin gonna be in your crib?"

"Hey, you mind?" I managed to catch the ball before I released it. "I'm trying to shoot, here."

"Sorry."

I lined up the shot, bounced the ball my usual four times, then lined it up again. Holding my breath, I closed my right eye and pushed the ball up and away, watching it fly through the air. It hit the rim, circled once, twice, three times. Then in. Rim shot.

I pumped the air with my fist. "Yeah." Then I turned back to Riff. "So, what's up?"

Before he could respond, I caught a flash out of my line of sight. I turned and walked a few feet toward the edge of the court, in the direction of the woods and away from Riff.

"Hey, where you going?"

"Did you see that?" I was afraid to look away from

the spot in the woods for fear I'd lose it.

Riff walked over and stood beside me. He glanced at the trees, then looked back at me. "See what?"

I pointed to the approximate spot. "There."

Riff squinted at where I pointed, then shook his head. "Am I supposed to be seeing something? 'Cause, dude, all I see is trees."

The flash didn't return, but the bushes surrounding the spot rustled crazily. Then a scary-looking Mr. Anderson stumbled out of the woods. The knees of his Wranglers were torn, one of the sleeves of his Levi jacket was missing, and his flannel shirt was untucked on the right side. His face was splattered with dark, gooey spots. He kept compulsively peering over his shoulder like something was chasing him.

"Whoa." Riff took a step back. "Freaky."

I ran toward him. "My God, Mr. Anderson. What happened? Are you okay?"

He stared at me with haunted eyes, but didn't seem to recognize me. Then he started babbling incoherently as he pointed back into the woods, over and over again, but I couldn't figure out what he meant.

"Thing—eat—kill—" he sobbed hysterically and collapsed so quickly I didn't have time to catch him. As soon as he hit the ground, he curled up like a baby.

"Dude's in serious need of a straitjacket." Riff came up beside me and poked at him with his foot. "What's up with that?"

I knelt next to the panic-stricken man. "Do you have your phone on you?" I asked Riff.

"What?"

"Your phone, dude. Do you have it with you?"

"Oh, yeah."

"Call nine-one-one. Have them send an ambulance." I tried to calm Mr. Anderson down, but Riff just stood there with his nose wrinkled in disgust. "Riff," I commanded. "Call. Now."

He grabbed his phone out of his pocket, walked a few feet away, and put the phone to his ear, plugging his other with his finger so he could hear. Meanwhile, I turned my attention back to Mr. Anderson, who whimpered like scared puppy.

"Mr. Anderson." I shook him gently by the shoulder. "Mr. Anderson, it's James. James Manarro."

There was no response. I looked around for something, anything, to help me figure out what to do, but all I saw was an empty park and Riff's back as he talked on the phone. I tried again.

"It's okay. Everything's going to be okay. Nothing's going to hurt you."

He continued to snivel, but calmed a bit. He pulled his head out from under his Levi jacket collar, his eyes glazed.

"It's okay," I told him. "You're safe now."

"The dispatcher said she'd send the sheriff and Riggs as soon as she got a hold of them, right after she called the ambulance." Riff gestured at Mr. Anderson with his head. "How's he doing?"

"He doesn't seem to be hurt anywhere." I fingered Mr. Anderson's head and legs and tried to see under his jacket, but his arms were crossed too tightly and it was impossible to pry them apart. "I think he's just scared."

"What happened to him?"

I scrutinized the woods. As a kid, I'd played in those woods a thousand times, but now they somehow seemed sinister.

"Don't know." I wasn't lying. *Not exactly, anyway.*

Barely three minutes later, the early morning stillness exploded into chaos. The ambulance pulled into the parking lot, siren blaring and lights flashing, and Riff trotted over to direct them to us. Next to me, Mr. Anderson still whimpered quietly. The ambulance was followed almost immediately by two patrol cars that hopped the curb and skidded to a stop just short of the blacktop's edge where I was still trying to comfort Mr. Anderson.

The attendants pulled the gurney and their medical junk out of the back of the ambulance and raced over. Riff pulled one of his nasty Mountain Dew's seemingly out of thin air and guzzled it.

I watched Riggs climb out of the first cruiser and sighed heavily. He was such a douche, and I dreaded the third degree coming my way. My only hope was that Sheriff Brazelton wouldn't let Riggs get too over-zealous before he muzzled the guy. But when Riggs headed directly over to the second cruiser, I wondered if the sheriff had already done me a big favor and told him to back off.

My thoughts were interrupted when both the driver and passenger doors opened on the second cop car. It was a small county with a limited number of cops and the sheriff, Riggs, and one part-time deputy were all that were assigned to Wolf Creek County. I wondered who could possibly be riding shotgun. Whoever it was, wore a khaki-colored uniform. The county cops wore that ugly green color.

The unknown cop also wore a huge Pharell William's hat and Ray Bans. The cop slammed the door shut and stood next to the cruiser. The sheriff climbed out of the driver's side and they both walked over, with Riggs following behind like an obedient child.

"James." Sheriff Brazelton addressed me with a nod. He indicated the other cop. "This is Sergeant McNeil of the Highway Patrol."

I gave a half-hearted wave. "Hello."

"Morning."

Oh, my God, it was a girl. I couldn't believe it. I

never figured a Chippie could be a girl. My surprise must've shown because the sheriff chuckled.

"Sergeant Mindy McNeil," he added. "Now, can you tell us what happened?"

"Not really. We were shooting some hoops..."

Sergeant McNeil pulled her sunglasses down her nose and peered at me over the top of them. "We?"

I pointed to Riff, who was watching the medics work on Mr. Anderson. "Riff and I."

Sergeant McNeil pushed her glasses back up her nose.

"Go on," the sheriff prodded.

"Anyway, we were shooting hoops when there was a flash, and then Mr. Anderson came stumbling out of the woods, all bloody and crying and shi—uh, stuff."

The Chippie adjusted her Ray Bans again. "Exactly where did he come out?"

I pointed. "Over there."

"Show me, son."

I bristled. Why did adults who didn't know you think it was all right to call you "son"? I sighed and walked the few yards to where Mr. Anderson had escaped whatever he thought was chasing him. I was pretty sure I knew what it was, but I didn't plan on saying anything to Smokey the Bear. Or anyone else. If Sheriff Brazelton wanted to know what I thought happened, he'd have to come right out and ask me.

The Chippie walked beside me, the sheriff a step or two behind her. Riggs went to where the paramedics were working.

I had no idea why the Highway Patrol was involved, but it was obvious from the way she acted that she thought she was in charge. I wondered what the sheriff would say about that.

When we got to the spot at the edge of the woods, I

contemplated her shiny sunglasses and wondered what was going on behind them. "Here."

"Thank you." She turned away deliberately and scanned the trees. "Would you mind waiting over there."

It wasn't a question. I was dismissed like I was some rubbernecker who wanted to see a bunch of blood and guts and wasn't the one who took care of the guy.

"Whatever," I muttered, hoping to piss her off.

Jamming my hands in my pockets, I headed toward Riff. He met me under the basketball hoop.

"How's Mr. Anderson?" I asked.

"Still blubbering, but they can't find any cuts or holes in him or anything. Just a bunch of scratches." He motioned toward the cops with his head. "What's going on over there? Who's the new cop?"

"Some Chippie Sergeant."

"Chippie, huh? Sheriff must be scared."

"Yeah, but why call the Highway Patrol? Don't they just hand out tickets and pick up road kill and stuff?"

"No, dude," Riff explained. "My sister's boyfriend is one. He told me once that they get called in when local yokels get voted off the short bus and can't figure out what to do when someone gets murdered or something."

"Hmm," I grunted. Who'd've thought Riff would know something like that? Just goes to show you never can tell about people.

We watched as the gurney was loaded into the ambulance.

One attendant jumped in the back with Mr. Anderson, while the other ran to the front, then they peeled out, red light flashing and siren screaming.

I needed to get home and tell Beth what happened, so we could talk about what to do next. I figured we had until the next full moon before someone else was murdered.

☽

They were all exhausted from everything that had been going on around town, so they hadn't gone to church, even though they should have. Beth got up before the adults and was surprised to find James already gone. It was so boring here without him. She tried to stay out of her mother's way, so that usually meant hiding in her room. What happened to the fun she used to have here before Daddy died? She loved playing Monopoly with her aunt and uncle, being chased around the living room by Uncle Robbie the Tickle Monster, and baking ginger snaps with Auntie Annette.

Her mother never seemed to do anything anymore but drink tea. Last night, Beth hid in her room, pretending to be asleep, listening to the adults laughing and having a good time without her. They never once thought about her, all alone in her room.

Fortunately, her mother was still snoring away in the alcove off the kitchen and hadn't heard Beth get up. This meant she could set up camp on the living room couch, surrounded by the sleeping bag James used when the couch was his bed; the rest of the crumb doughnuts, now stale, left over from yesterday's breakfast; and his Game Boy. It was cool that he'd given it to her to make up for Daddy's broken water globe, but she wasn't in to video games. If she was, she'd rather play something with zombies or vampires. Anything but werewolves.

There was nothing else to do while she waited for James to come home, so she switched on the video game and gave it a try. She was deep into saving the dumb chick from the witches when he burst through the front door. Startled, she dropped the game on the edge of the coffee table and cracked the cover. Scowling, she was afraid he would think she did it on purpose. "I'm sorry, I'm so sorry. I didn't mean to."

"Where're the parental units?"

"What?" How come he wasn't having a cow about his precious Game Boy?

"Mom. Dad. Aunt Judy. Are they still asleep?"

"Yeah, why?"

He snatched the remote off the couch and turned off the TV. He quickly folded the sleeping bag, tossed his pillow on top of it, grabbed Beth's wrist and pulled her up.

"Come on," he whispered. "I've got to tell you something. But not here."

She'd never seen him so freaked. "What's going on?"

"Let's go for a walk."

"Fine." She pressed her lips together in a tight frown. "This better be good."

"Better than you could ever imagine."

She got her sweatshirt while he tapped his foot impatiently on the front porch.

"Come on," he insisted.

They hopped off the porch and headed for town. He walked so fast, she had a hard time keeping up. *At this rate, we'll start flying any minute.*

She stopped short, already winded. "Slow down, James," she complained. "What's your boggle, anyway?"

He glanced furtively over each shoulder, then back at her. "Okay, here goes. Riff and I were shooting hoops this morning over at the park, when what do you think happens?" He didn't wait for her answer. "You know Mr. Anderson, the guy who owns the hardware store? He came stumbling out of the woods, right there in front of where we were playing. And he was covered in blood and dirt."

She felt her eyes grow wide, even as her stomach cramped. Had her mother struck again? Had she killed someone else? "What happened?"

"Well, he was crying so hard, I couldn't understand him at first. He ran over to me and then collapsed. I told Riff to call for an ambulance, and I checked Mr. Anderson over to see if he was hurt."

"Was he?"

"That's the weird thing. He had some minor scratches and stuff, like he fought with some of the bushes in the woods, but he wasn't really hurt. The blood was from somewhere else." An old truck rattled down the street. James watched it disappear. "Come on. We'd better get moving before someone wonders why we're just standing here."

As they continued toward town, the truck appeared again and passed them slowly enough for them to see the driver. It was Ms. Glass, and she looked as mean as ever. Why was she glaring at them? They weren't doing anything wrong.

Then she did something totally out of character. She stopped and called them over to the truck. "Hi, kids. Got a minute?"

James and Beth exchanged a look. James shrugged. "Um, okay." They walked across the street to the vehicle. "Weren't you part of the hunting party last night?" he asked.

"Yeah, but I was one of the lucky ones. I got out alive." She gestured at him with her head. "You were the one who found Larry Anderson this morning, weren't you?"

Beth frowned. Word sure got around fast in a small town.

"Yeah, we were shooting hoops, and—"

"Catch you later." Ms. Glass sped off down the

street, turning at the first corner she came to and disappearing. They gaped at each other.

Then Beth spotted another car and pointed.

"Oh, great."

It was a squad car, driven by none other than Deputy Riggs.

"Come on, let's get out of here." James didn't wait for her to respond, just hustled over to the sidewalk and headed back the way they'd come.

She was confused because he was headed away from town, but she could tell by the look on his face that now wasn't the time to question him. She followed along in silence.

It didn't take long for Riggs to catch up to them. At first, he paced them. It made her nervous. But when she looked at James, sweat was trickling down the side of his face, and his upper lip had tiny beads of moisture on it.

The deputy must have noticed it, too, because he started to harass James. "Hey, punk," he jeered. "What're you so nervous about?"

James didn't answer, but kept his pace steady and stared straight ahead. His jaw clenched and unclenched, and she could hear his teeth grinding together.

"Hey," Riggs practically shouted. "I'm talking to you, boy."

James still didn't say anything. The squad car lurched forward and turned into the driveway ahead of them, blocking their path. Riggs threw open his door so hard it bounced back on him and he was forced to shove it open again so he could get out. He darted around the front of the car and stopped directly in front of them. With two fingers and a nasty grin, he poked James in the shoulder. Trouble was about to go down, and she was worried.

Riggs was so mean to James. She couldn't figure out

why he hated him so much. Just because he'd broken those car windows that one summer, but it wasn't like he hurt anyone.

He'd also stolen the car stereo, but feeling guilty, he'd given it back.

The sheriff made him pick up trash and repair the picnic tables in both parks and all the benches around town until school started, so he'd paid for it already. The sheriff didn't seem to have a problem with him, so why was it such a big deal to Deputy Riggs?

"What's the matter?" Riggs poked him again. "Cat got your tongue?"

"Leave him alone." Beth took a step toward them, warily looking from James to Riggs and back again. What would happen if he took a punch at Riggs? He'd get thrown in jail for sure, and maybe worse.

James flashed her a warning look. "Shut up, Beth."

"Yeah," Riggs mocked. "Shut up, Beth." He poked James again, this time hard enough to make him take a step backwards. "Let the pussy fight his own battles."

"Leave her alone." She peered around him, not wanting to miss anything.

Spittle flew from Riggs's mouth into James's face as the deputy poked him over and over. "Yeah? What're you going to do about it?"

Before James could answer, the car radio crackled.

Sheriff Brazelton's voice came through loudly, but not very clearly. "Riggs. You find those kids yet? Come back."

Riggs hesitated, looked from the car to James and back again.

"Riggs? You there? Come back."

Riggs looked James right in the eye. "This isn't over yet," he said quietly. He opened the passenger door, sat on the seat, and reached for the mike. He brought it to his mouth and pushed the talk button. "Yeah, Sheriff, just found them. Over."

"Bring them to the park. I'll be sitting on the bleachers. Come back."

"Roger that," Riggs replied. "Out." He replaced the mike and got out of the car. He slammed the driver's door shut and opened the back door. She saw his nasty smile. It was the one that rarely spoke to his eyes. Fear burned a hole in her stomach, like a worm through a rotten apple. "You heard the sheriff. Get in."

Unsure if she should get in or not, she looked to her cousin to see what he was going to do. He crossed his arms tightly and appeared calm, although she could almost feel his jaw as it worked. That sick feeling was back, and she idly scratched the side of her neck.

"Make me."

She couldn't believe James was challenging Riggs. That couldn't be good. The leer returned to Riggs's face. He clearly enjoyed James's reaction. Another step closer put them nose to nose. Riggs's hand rested on top of his gun. She noticed that at some point he had unstrapped the holster.

"Oh, I would love to."

"Then do it."

"Why, you little..." Riggs was interrupted by static from the mike. It was loud enough to make her jump, and she glanced at the car and then back at the guys.

"Riggs. Where are you? Come back."

Riggs squinted at the car and frowned.

"Riggs, you there?"

"Just you wait, you little thief." He shoved James away, walked back to the car, reached inside, and grabbed the mike. One foot rested on the bottom of the doorframe. "Here, Sheriff."

"Where the hell are you?"

"About three blocks away, on Remus Street."

"What's taking so long? Get over here. Now."

"Right." Riggs replaced the mike, glaring at James the whole time. "Get in."

They climbed inside the back seat. Riggs released the brake, hung a U-turn, and sped off toward Heritage Park and the mystery of what happened to Mr. Anderson. At least, it was a mystery to her. James never finished telling her exactly what happened, and she was dying of curiosity. Curiosity killed the cat, her mother was fond of saying, but her dad had told her that curiosity built a strong mind, and to never lose that quality. She sure did miss him.

She glanced at Riggs to make sure he wasn't watching them in the rear view mirror and nudged James's leg. When he looked at her, she raised her eyebrows. He frowned and shook his head slightly, then glanced over at Riggs. The deputy hummed something that passed for music.

"Tell you later," James mouthed. He moved his eyes slowly and deliberately toward Riggs, then back to her. She nodded. They turned away from each other and gazed out the windows until they got to the park.

Riggs got out of the car and headed over to the bleachers. The sheriff puffed on a cigarette as he waited. There were no handles on the inside of the back doors, and they found themselves stuck in the car until someone let them out. She figured now would be a good time to get the gory details.

"So," she demanded. "Tell me what's going on. Why're we here? What do the cops want to talk to us for? What'd you do, anyway?"

"Wait." He glanced out the window to see where the cops were. Riggs stood in front of the sheriff, who gestured with both hands and seemed like he was yelling at his deputy. She noticed that James smiled slightly when he saw that. "I'm not sure," he finally told her. "But from what Mr. Anderson said before the paramedics took him away, a lot of people were out in the woods last night."

"Hunting for the monster?"

"Yeah, I guess. Anyway, something started chasing them, and he didn't think many people got away. Said the thing almost got him, but it went for Mr. Ingstrom instead. Sliced off his head and ate his insides."

"Oh, my God," she moaned as her nausea rose to a painful level. She swallowed a few times and willed the nasty stuff in her mouth back to her stomach. She didn't want to throw up, especially not in the cop car.

He bumped her with his elbow. "You okay?"

"Yeah. We've got to do something."

"Shhh." He thrust his head forward and back again. "Riggs's coming."

The door on James's side flew open. Riggs reached in, grabbed him by the back of the shirt, and yanked him out of the car. James tripped and fell to his knees. Riggs started to say something, but stopped when the sheriff came over.

"What do you think you're doing?" He pulled James away. "Knock it off."

"This punk—" Riggs started.

"Never mind him. Go find Sergeant McNeil and see if she needs help."

"Aw, Sheriff," Riggs complained.

Beth wondered if he would throw a tantrum because he didn't get his way.

"Don't give me attitude right now. I'm not in the mood. Just go."

Riggs stomped off like a spoiled child who'd been told he can't have a cookie before dinner. The image made her snicker. Sheriff Brazelton looked at her, and she stopped. Then he grinned slowly, and she knew they were okay.

"Why don't we step into my office?" He headed over to the bleachers and they followed. When he got there, he climbed all the way to the top before sitting down. "Okay, kiddo." He flashed his eyes to the bleacher seat and back to James. They sat down. "I want you to tell me again everything that happened this morning, from the time you and Riff got to the park. Don't leave anything out, no matter how trivial you think it might be." He turned to Beth. "And when he's done, I want you to tell me about your werewolf theory."

She listened to James as he spilled it all out in a rush, not minding a bit that she had to wait to tell what she knew. At least someone was finally listening to them. And maybe, just maybe, no one else would have to die.

☽

Sheriff Brazelton listened attentively to the kid who'd helped poor, stupid Larry Anderson. From what James told him, Anderson had been scared to death, babbling repeatedly about the monster he swore was chasing him.

"Okay, wait," the sheriff interrupted. "Are you saying that this thing, this monster or whatever, *ate* Gus Ingstrom?"

"That's what Mr. Anderson said." James swiped his hair out of his eyes. "I even made him repeat it, because I wasn't sure at first what he was saying. Then I made him tell me again, just to make sure I heard it right. He saw the monster cut Mr. Ingstrom's head off with its claws. Then it started eating his insides, and Mr. Anderson passed out. The next thing he knew, it was morning, so he ran back to the park and found us. How's he doing, by the way?"

"Don't really know yet. They sedated him, so we won't be able to talk to him until tomorrow."

The little girl looked like she was about to toss her cookies. Maybe this was too much for her. Should he have talked to the boy alone? But she was the one who seemed the surest about there being a werewolf preying on the townsfolk.

This wasn't the first time he'd heard rumors to that effect. After all, they did live in a town called Wolf Creek. He remembered a similar incident from when he was just a kid about the girl's age. Only then, it was just a few horses and dogs being slaughtered, and the word "wolf" written in blood on the side of the barn where the horses were stabled. Werewolf, indeed.

"Okay." He turned to Beth. "Now your turn. Tell me why you think there's a werewolf running amok."

He waited while she gathered her thoughts, looking at James. Only when she got his slight nod did she begin.

☽

Beth told him everything she knew about what happened to her father. She began with the constant bickering between her folks and ended with the glowing pair of eyes peering in her window that time.

"There was a full moon that night, too," she told the sheriff. "Just like last night."

"That's a pretty hard story to swallow," he commented.

"That's what I thought at first," James said. "But when you think about it, it makes sense." He counted off on his fingers. "One. Beth sees the werewolf outside her house. Two. Her father dies in a mysterious car crash on the way home from work."

"He was the best driver in the world," she added. "He never would have driven so fast in the rain. There weren't even any skid marks."

"Yeah, that's true." James turned back to the sheriff. "Three. This place has been Boredom Central all my life. Nothing ever happens. Then all of a sudden, we have several murders in a little over a month? And four, all the murders happened on the nights there was a full moon."

"Look it up if you don't believe us," she told the sheriff, sure that he didn't.

"Oh," he responded. "I believe you believe it."

"And don't forget about what happened last night. All those people Mr. Anderson said he saw the werewolf slaughter."

"Well, right now all that's hearsay." The sheriff sighed and rubbed the back of his neck. "We only have your word that's what he actually said. And so far, no one's been reported missing. Except for Gus Ingstrom, of course."

She crossed her arms and stood. Why did adults have to be so stupid all the time? All those people were bound to turn up missing. Did he think they sprouted wings and flew away? "I knew you wouldn't believe us. Come on, James, we're just wasting our time here. Let's go."

"Now, just hold on there." The sheriff grabbed her arm. "I never said I didn't believe you. But until Larry wakes up, I can't verify that what he told James is what actually happened."

"Yeah, Beth," James agreed. "He's just doing his job. At least he's not blowing us off."

She sat back down. "Whatever."

"Now, what do the two of you know about werewolves in general?"

James shrugged. "Just the usual stuff." He looked at Beth. "Right?"

"Uh huh. They're usually people who've been bitten by a werewolf. Every full moon, they change and roam the land, killing anything and anyone they come across. If they bite someone and that person dies, then that's it, but if they live, they turn into a werewolf."

"And the only way to kill them is by shooting them with a silver bullet?" Sheriff Brazelton looked serious, but she still wasn't sure he actually believed them.

With every full moon, she was more and more scared that her mother would come after her. Maybe she wouldn't kill her, since Beth was her daughter. Maybe she wanted them to be some sort of mother-daughter werewolf team. Who knew? Stranger things had happened.

She mentally shook her head. Stranger than that? No way.

"As far as we know," James answered.

They sat in silence for a few minutes and watched the woods, waiting for some sign that Larry Anderson really had seen what he said he'd seen.

Finally, Sheriff Brazelton took his sunglasses off the top of his head and chewed on the end of the temple. "Okay, here's what we're going to do. You." He pointed at Beth. "I want you to find out everything you can about werewolves. Where they came from, how the first one came to be. See if you can find out how many of them there supposedly are in California. Most of all, find out all the ways to kill them. Got all that?"

She nodded. Then he turned to James. "And you. Two things. First, make sure that friend of yours, Riff what's-his-name, make sure he keeps his mouth shut about what happened. And two, I want you down at the hospital first thing in the morning. I want you there when

I question Larry, make sure he tells me the same story he told you. Can you do that for me?"

"Sure."

"We can do that, easy." She was excited. She loved to Google things and already had several searches in mind.

"Okay, you guys get going. I'd better go make sure Riggs hasn't fallen into a big hole or anything." He winked at her, and she smiled. Then he went down the bleachers, across the basketball court, and disappeared into the woods. She and James sat there a minute and watched until they couldn't see him anymore. She didn't know about James, but she finally felt they might actually be getting somewhere.

$$\mathbb{D}$$

We sat on the bleachers until our butts fell asleep, waiting to see if they found anything. After about half an hour of nothing happening, we decided to go for donuts and were about halfway across the basketball court when Sergeant McNeil stumbled out of the woods, holding her stomach.

Except for the deep red circles high on her cheeks, her face was stark white. Beth and I frowned at each other then looked back at the woods as Sheriff Brazelton lurched from the tree line like Mr. St. George used to after too many beers.

We ran over to him, but before we could ask what happened, he put one hand on a tree, leaned over, and threw up on his shoes.

"Sheriff, what's wrong?" I put a hand on his shoulder but yanked it back when he stared up at me, wild-eyed.

Sweat ran down his face while his eyes bugged out

so far I was sure they would fall and bounce across the asphalt. "Don't," he started, then he stopped to draw in three huge breaths. He wiped his mouth with his sleeve. "Don't go in there. You don't need to see it. No one needs to see it."

"Sheriff, you all right?" Sergeant McNeil didn't look much better than he did.

"No," he replied. "Jesus, Mary, and Joseph. I never saw anything so…so…so…gruesome. Those people were torn to pieces." He shook his head and ran a trembling hand across one eye. "How're you supposed to get used to something like that?"

"You don't." McNeil took a big breath and let it out slowly. "You find somewhere private to toss your cookies then get on with it as best you can. Do you have any crime scene tape? We need to cordon off the area as soon as possible. Too many people have tromped through here already."

Riggs appeared out of nowhere. "Tape's in the trunk."

"Get it, will you?" Sheriff Brazelton asked him. "And bring a couple bottles of water."

Riggs nodded and headed toward the cruiser. But not before he bumped me with his shoulder hard enough to make me take a step back. Buttwipe.

"God," Beth commented. "He never lets up, does he?"

"Nope."

"Why does he have such a hard on against you?"

"Beats me."

"You two." The sheriff pointed a shaky finger at us. "You go on home like I told you, and stay there. Do what you need to do." His weak smile did nothing to reassure me. "And James? I'll see you in the morning. Eight o'clock. Sharp."

"Right. Come on, Beth, we'd better get home. Mom and Dad'll freak if we're not there in time for Sunday brunch."

"Okay." She shoved her hands into the pockets of her hoodie. "But I'm not going to eat any of my mom's pancakes, no matter how much she yells at me. Damn things taste like sawdust."

I chuckled. "They're so heavy, you could knock somebody out with them."

"The way she never fails to burn them you could use them to start a barbecue."

As we walked home, we found new and funny ways to degrade Aunt Judy's cooking. It was a good way to keep Beth's mind occupied. I was worried about what happened and how the cops planned on figuring out who—or what—had done it. If those people were ripped to shreds, I was sorry more people had to die, but now the sheriff would be forced to believe us. He had to realize that he needed to hunt for a werewolf, not a human being.

Because if he didn't, we would figure out a way to do it ourselves.

☽

Beth spent the rest of the day researching werewolves. Most of the things she found were pretty much what they showed in the movies. If you were bitten by a werewolf, you became one. A werewolf was human most of the time, and only when the moon was full did they turn. And only a silver bullet could kill them.

Her stomach growled wildly, complaining about missing dinner. She told everyone she wasn't feeling good so she wouldn't have to stop her research. Maybe it was time for a break so she could get something to eat.

Then she found a blurb on the 'Net.

After reading it, she was so excited she decided to find James and share it with him. It might be the key to the whole thing. She poked her head outside her door. The light from the television flickered, but otherwise the living room was dark. Uncle Robbie snored quietly in the big chair. Aunt Annette and James sat on the couch watching some sappy Lifetime movie. Her mother was nowhere to be seen.

There was a box of tissues in Aunt Annette's lap, just like every time she watched Lifetime movies. James's back was against the arm of the couch, his chin resting on his knees. He looked like a big dumb dog. Getting his attention without being seen by anyone would be tricky.

She went back to her bedroom, closed the door, and leaned against it, gazing around the room for something she could use to make him notice her. The only thing she could think of was to shoot tiny spitballs at him. But what could she use to shoot them with? Then she remembered the giant Pixy Stixs she'd hidden under her mattress and reached underneath it to search for them. At first, she panicked because she couldn't find them, but then her hand brushed against one. Pulling them out, she put them on the bed. She ran to the desk and yanked a piece of paper out of her One Direction notebook. Ripping open one of the striped straws, she dumped the candy out onto the paper, wet her finger and stuck it into the mound of powder. As she sucked the sweet treat off her finger, she opened the other end of the straw and blew into it. She nodded. It just might work.

Tearing a second piece of paper out of her notebook, she ripped it into thin strips. Then she rolled one of the strips into a ball, put it in her mouth, and used her tongue to get it good and wet. Ammunition prepared, she aimed the straw at her stuffed Elmo, took in a huge breath and blew as hard as she could into the straw. At first the spitball stuck, but then it launched itself all the way across the room. A direct hit, right in the eye. It should work.

After taking another quick finger full of sugar, she opened the door a crack. James had moved onto the arm of the couch. Good. He made a better target that way. She launched a wet one at her cousin, and snickered quietly when it hit him on the cheek. He was startled so badly that he almost fell off the couch.

"What the—"

He touched his cheek, then scanned the room. When he saw Beth, she put her fingers to her lips in warning. Then she gestured for him to come over. He glanced at his mother, saw that she was engrossed in the show, and climbed off the couch.

"What do you want?" he whispered.

"Get in here." She pulled him into the room and shut the door behind him. "I found out how we can kill the werewolf."

"Really? How? Silver bullet?"

She shook her head. "Not just that. They can be killed by any wound that destroys the heart or the brain, as long as we use something made of silver."

"So, if we shot it in the head or heart with, say, Mr. Anderson's shotgun, that would kill it?"

"As long as we used silver bullets. Or if we stabbed it or cracked open its head with one of your mom's silver candlesticks or something." There were lots of ways to kill the monster, and now that they'd figured it out, she couldn't wait to get started. "We got to do it, James. Before it kills again."

"Hold on," he said. "We don't even know who it is yet."

She swallowed hard. "Yeah, we do."

"We do?"

"Uh huh."

"Well, are you going to tell me, or what?"

She licked her lips and tried to swallow the huge lump in her throat. She guessed that now was as good a time as any, so she plunged in headfirst. "It's my mom."

"What?" He gawked at her, his face scrunched up like he was smelling something bad. He shook his head and snorted. "You've got to be kidding me. I know you guys don't get along any more, but Aunt Judy a werewolf? No way."

She'd just have to convince him, that's all. "Way. I can prove it, too." She went over to her backpack, pulled out a small piece of cloth, and held it out for him to see. "Do you recognize this?"

He shook his head. "What is it?"

"It's a piece of Mom's favorite dress. The blue one with green swirls all over it. Remember? She used to wear it all the time."

"Yeah, I remember it. But that doesn't prove any-thing. Lots of ladies have blue and green dresses."

"True. But what about this?" Opening the folded bit of cloth, she revealed a knot of coarse brown hair. "I found this outside my windowsill that day after I first saw the werewolf. And the next day Mom had a bare spot on the side of her head. Said she'd pulled it out in her sleep."

He screwed up his face and shook his head. "But that still doesn't prove anything. Maybe she really did pull it out in her sleep."

"Yeah." Frustration rose and tears began to burn in back of her eyes. "Right. Do you have any idea what it's like for me, knowing what my mom is? Knowing that she's really a monster? Think that's easy for me to be-lieve? Well, it isn't."

"Okay, okay." He waved his hands in a "stop" mo-tion. "I believe you. Just don't cry."

She sniffed and wiped her eyes. "I couldn't believe it at first, you know? But the more things happened, the more I realized that there was no other explanation. Like Katniss Everdeen always said, 'if you eliminate the impossible, whatever's left, no matter how improbable, is the truth.' Or something like that."

"That was Sherlock Holmes."

"What?"

"Sherlock Holmes said that, not Katniss."

"What. Ever. Anyway, I know it's my mom."

A minute ticked by as James studied her. She tried not to fidget, but he either believed her or he didn't. Finally, he seemed to make his decision. "All right," he said. "Guess we should make our plans, decide what we're going to do, and figure out a way to kill it, no matter who it turns out to be. Let's just hope you're wrong and it's someone else. Okay?"

"Fine." At least he'd agreed to help her and that was all that mattered. That was the main thing, even if he didn't believe who it was. Killing the thing would be hard, maybe the hardest thing she'd ever have to do, but it had to be done.

He squinted at the clock on his dresser. "Right now, though, I need to go to bed. It's late, and I have to get up early to meet Sheriff Brazelton at the hospital before school."

"Are you going to tell him what I found out about how to kill it?"

"Yeah, I'll tell him. But just about how to kill one, not about who you think it is."

"Whatever." She folded the scrap of cloth around the tuft of hair and shoved it back into the secret pouch hidden inside her backpack.

After zipping it securely, she turned to tell him to be sure to ask the sheriff what he could find out about who the werewolf was, even if he didn't let on who Beth suspected.

But he'd already left the room. At least he'd be able to get things started. People liked him and usually listened to him. Maybe the sheriff could come up with some ideas about how to stop the murders. But even if he didn't, it seemed like he was going to help them. Hopefully.

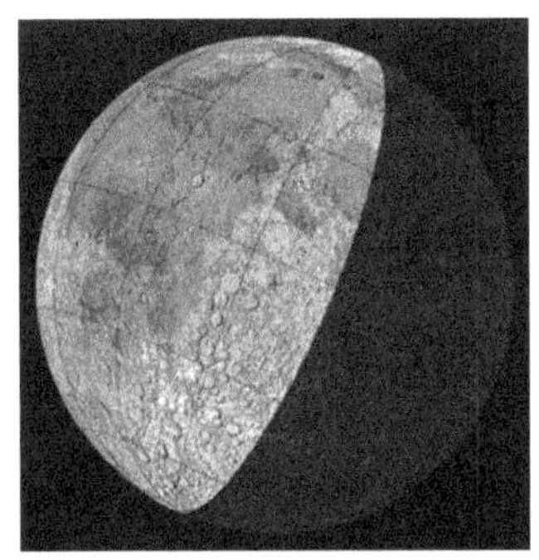

Thursday, October 24, 2013

WANING GIBBOUS

Old moon
Growing smaller
73% Visible

Chapter 18

The meeting with the sheriff went well. Mr. Anderson repeated everything he said to me as he stumbled out of the woods. His story of death and a mysterious creature was incredible. When he was done, Sheriff Brazelton listened to me share Beth's research, but I left out who she thought the werewolf was. When I was done, he told me to go home, that school was cancelled again, and he had some things to think over. He did promise to look into it and get back to us.

That was two days ago, and I was beginning to think he'd forgotten. Or chickened out. Or, even worse, hadn't believed us in the first place. Beth and I were sitting in church during the service for the hunters. I was trying really hard to concentrate on Father Michael's sermon, something about all those souls going to heaven to be with Jesus, and for some reason we couldn't know, God had called them home. All well and good, but I'll bet even He didn't expect them to be killed by a werewolf.

The fact that she was so positive it was Aunt Judy didn't make it any more believable. Actually, it made it harder. How could someone I loved, someone Beth loved, be a monster? And if she was, how come no one knew about it until now? And how long had she been a werewolf? Had she started killing right after being turned into a monster, or had she been a werewolf for a long time, and only now started killing people? Confused to the point that my brain hurt, I didn't know what to think.

Maybe I should worry about all of that after the service. All those people, almost everyone who'd hunted the werewolf that night, had died. Only Mr. Anderson and Ms. Glass had gotten away. After what she'd said to us the other day, I was dying to talk to Ms. Glass, but I hadn't had the chance ever since she drove off that day.

"The Bible teaches us that in death, there is life, as long as we believe in Jesus Christ." Father Michael contemplated his parishioners. When his gaze seemed to settle on me a bit longer than I was comfortable with, it freaked me out, and I couldn't help but squirm on the pew.

Mom reached over and grabbed my leg.

"Sit still," she demanded. "What's the matter with you? You're acting like a seven-year-old."

"Sorry." I kept myself still by sitting on my hands. Beth fidgeted with the hem of her skirt, probably as antsy as I was.

"We must hold the families who lost their dear ones close to our hearts in this, their time of greatest need." Father Michael bowed his head. "Let us pray."

Everyone closed their eyes. Father Michael led the prayer, advising us not to be sad because our friends and loved ones were in heaven. Right. Let someone in the father's family be torn to pieces, and we'd see how easy it was for him not to be sad. This was all such bullshit.

Getting that squirmy feeling again, I fought to sit still. Didn't want to get Mom pissed or she'd have Dad ground me for sure. I cracked open an eye and looked around. Dad was dozing. Mom's eyes were closed but her lips were moving. I shut both eyes and tried to offer up my own prayer, but that feeling you get when someone's watching you, the one that makes the hair on the back of your neck stand up, made it hard to concentrate. It creeped me out, so I opened my other eye to check the rest of the church. At first, all I saw were bowed heads, but then someone moved and I realized that Ms. Glass was watching me.

I nudged Beth. She frowned. "Shh," she mouthed without opening her eyes.

So I pinched her leg, hard, and her eyes flew open. She wore that Angry Bird expression, but before she could say anything I nodded over at Ms. Glass. Beth followed the direction of my nod then looked back at me with a question on her face. When I looked over at where Ms. Glass sat, I couldn't find her. Had she left the church without being seen? How could that be? I'd only looked away for a split second. Twisting in my seat, I checked to see if she had walked down the aisle. The heavy oak doors were swooshing silently closed. I started to go after her, but my mom pulled me back. Great, I was stuck waiting until the service was over. Thank God, Father was finally finishing.

"Amen." Father Michael smiled at his parishioners. "Peace be with you."

"And also with you." Everyone responded as we were taught. I didn't think many people even listened to the sermons. They just knew all the right answers and said what they were supposed to say at the right times. It bugged me, made me feel like a tool, but there wasn't a thing I could do about it now. As soon as the first person stood up to shake hands with her neighbor and wish them peace, I was out of there. Beth was right behind me.

A lot of other people made it to the doors ahead of us, so by the time we got outside, Ms. Glass had vanished. "Shit."

Beth punched my arm. "What's up?"

"I think Donna Glass wants to tell me something."

"What makes you think that?"

"Because she was staring at me in church just now, that's what. Plus, she stopped to talk to us that time, remember?"

The parental units came out of the church and walked up behind us. "Come on, kids." Dad put a hand on our shoulders. "Time to go to the cemetery."

"The graveside service shouldn't be too long." Mom straightened my tie and smoothed the shoulders of my coat. "I expect you to mind your manners a little better than you did in the church. You hear?"

"Sure, Mom." I grimaced as she fidgeted with my clothes. "Sorry."

"That's okay. Afterward, we'll go get something to eat. How about some waffles? How's that sound?"

"Great." She could suggest we go get some lizard guts and bat wings and I would've agreed to it. I just wanted to find Ms. Glass and see what she wanted.

"We're going to pass." Aunt Judy grabbed Beth's arm roughly. Beth winced. "Come on, Beth. We're going back to the house."

"Ow, Mom, you're hurting me."

"Nonsense. Now come on."

"But I want to go to the funeral." Beth tried to pull away, but Aunt Judy's grip tightened. Beth's lower lip trembled and she kept blinking unnaturally fast.

I couldn't let her be alone with her mother the werewolf, so I blurted out the first thing I could think of.

"Let go of her."

The adults all scowled at me like I'd just announced that I'd crapped my pants. "I mean, can't she go with us? Seeing as how she loves waffles and all."

"Since when?" Aunt Judy's nostrils flared as big as a

horse's, and she got right in my face. I thought for a minute that she was going to bite me. "And no, she can't go with you. I want her with me. Where I can keep an eye on her."

All of Beth's suspicions roared to life in my brain at her mom's unusual behavior. What did she have planned for Beth? Was Aunt Judy a monster, a real live werewolf who became a vicious killer once a month, like clockwork? I took a step back and looked at my dad.

"Are you sure?" He put his hand on Aunt Judy's arm and pulled her gently back a step. "We'd love to have you two join us."

"I said—" Aunt Judy's voice grew louder—and meaner. "No. Thank. You. We'll be fine."

Poor Beth. Lately, she'd served as Aunt Judy's verbal punching bag. I suppose if Aunt Judy was a werewolf, it could explain her behavior. Couldn't it?

☽

At the graveside, Father Michael droned on about souls being called home and something about the Father, Son, and the Holy Ghost, but I wasn't listening. From where I stood next to my parents, I could barely see Ms. Glass. She stood apart from everyone, underneath an oak tree. Why wasn't she down here with the rest of us?

When everyone filed past the caskets, paying their last respects by placing white roses on them, Ms. Glass motioned to me. She pointed toward the mausoleum where the rich people were buried, then walked away quickly, disappearing around the corner. I was about two-thirds of the way back in line, so I figured I had about twenty or twenty-five minutes before I would be missed. It was all I could do not to bolt, but I managed to look cool and slink far enough away so no one would see me trot over to where Ms. Glass waited. As I rounded the mausoleum, she reached out and yanked me forward so hard I almost came out of my shoes.

"Hey," I yelped like a puppy. I'm not afraid to admit I was scared. What did she want? For all I knew, she could be the werewolf.

"Shh, not so loud," she instructed. "Want someone to hear us?"

Before I could answer, she disappeared inside the crypt. Talk about scared. I sure didn't want to go inside some creepy tomb, but I needed to find out what she wanted. After all, we weren't exactly friends or anything. If she wanted to talk to me, it had to be something important.

☽

In its human form, it watched the parade as everyone piled out of their cars and filed over to the graves. From its place high on the hill overlooking not just the cemetery, but the entire town, it snickered. No one knew who it was, or that it grew stronger every day.

Soon it would be unstoppable.

☽

Ms. Glass and I stood inside the dank crypt for a few minutes and waited for each other to start. Unable to stand it anymore, I said the first thing that came to mind. "Nice day for a mass funeral." Dumb, I know, but it was out before I could stop it.

"Cut the small talk," she said. "I know why you're here."

"What do you mean?"

"Don't be coy with me, boy. You know more about the killings than you let on, don't you?"

"W—well—" I sputtered. "Um, I was there when Mr. Anderson came staggering out of the forest. Is that what you mean?"

"What I mean—" She emphasized each word. "—is that you know what the killer is."

My mouth went dry and the corner of my right eye twitched. Could I trust her? She was always mean to everyone. Was this some kind of sick joke? "What do you mean, *what* the killer is?"

She poked her head out of the crypt's door, maybe to make sure no one was around. Then she looked me directly in the eye. "You know that the killer isn't human, don't you?"

I scratched the side of my face. Did I want to risk saying it first? No, I wanted her to, so I nodded. Slowly.

"It's not a bear, like some people in town are saying. Or a mountain lion. You know that, right?"

Again, I nodded.

"Or a wolf."

All of a sudden, the air inside the crypt felt heavy, pressing in all around me, and it smelled funny. Musty, dirty. Like death. I was having trouble breathing. My heart raced and my throat was dry. Would she really say it? Did she actually believe in the unbelievable?

"Not a normal one, anyway," she continued with a funny expression and reached out toward me. Instinctively I took a step back and tripped over a broken piece of marble. She grabbed me so I wouldn't fall. "Hey, kid, you okay?"

"Um, yeah, I'm okay."

"You're going to make me come right out and say it, aren't you?"

"Say what?"

"Oh, for God's sake, cut the crap. Werewolf, kid. The killer's a werewolf."

I tried to keep my cool, but the crypt's walls started to close in on me. The stale air sucked what little breath I still had out of my lungs. I wiped my mouth with the back of my hand. "How do you know that for sure?"

"Never mind how I know." She whirled around. "What was that?"

She crept to the door, pressing her back against the wall, to sneak another peek outside. I scratched my cheek again and wondered what she'd heard, since I hadn't heard a thing.

"Can't talk anymore," she whispered. "They might hear. They're everywhere. Whatever you do, do not contact me. We have to wait until it's safe."

She waved at me. "Good luck, kid. I'll be in touch."

Then she vanished out the door and down the hill, leaving me to wonder who she was afraid would hear her, and what they might do to her if they did.

☽

Beth paced nervously back and forth in her room, the back of the chair jammed under the doorknob for safety. She wished they would hurry up and get back from the service. She needed to talk to James. They'd barely gotten home before her mother had mumbled some excuse about going to the market and practically ran out the door. Why was she in such a rush to get home, if she just wanted to go right out again? It didn't make any sense. Could she be preparing to kill someone else? How could that be? The full moon was four or five nights ago.

A car door slammed, and Beth ran to the window.

James and his parents were walking up the driveway. Finally. She grabbed the chair and tossed it behind her, then ran to the front door. Just as she was about to open it, behind her someone cleared their throat. She turned. Her mother stood in the kitchen doorway. Where had she been? And more importantly, how had she come in without making any noise?

"As far as anyone's concerned…" Her mother straightened her collar and then smoothed her skirt. "I've been here the whole time. Got that?"

"But you weren't here."

"Listen," her mother spat. "I've had just about enough of your crappy attitude. You are not to tell anyone I was gone. Do you hear me?"

Beth nodded.

"What? I can't hear you."

Beth gulped. "I got it."

"Good. Make sure you do." Then her mother did something really strange. She went into the kitchen, stuck her hands under the running faucet, and then picked up a dishtowel to dry them off when Aunt Annette and Uncle Robbie walked in the door.

"There." Her mother hung the damp kitchen towel over the oven door handle and went into the living room. "That does it. Kitchen's clean."

Puzzled, Beth frowned. Her mother had insisted Beth clean the kitchen when they first got home. Now Beth was really confused. And scared.

Her mother smiled at Aunt Annette and Uncle Robbie like she hadn't known they'd come home. "Oh, hi. How was the service?"

"Fine, as far as these things go," Uncle Robbie commented.

Aunt Annette put her arm around Beth's mom and squeezed her shoulders. "How about a nice cup of tea?"

"I'll make it for us," Beth's mom offered.

Aunt Annette followed her back into the kitchen.

Uncle Robbie loosened his tie and unbuttoned his collar. "I really hate these things," he told Beth. "Feels like a damn dog collar around my neck. I'm going to get changed." He turned to James. "Why don't you guys take advantage of this nice weather and go down to the park? Maybe shoot some hoops. Just be back by three."

"Sounds great." James turned to Beth. "Want to?"

Judging by the smile that didn't reach his eyes, something was up. He moved his gaze rapidly back and forth between her and the front door. She didn't really want to shoot hoops, but was eager to go along to see what he wanted. Maybe something happened at the funeral. Who knew?

☽

After I told her about how Ms. Glass pulled me into the crypt and what she'd said to me, Beth's eyes were huge.

"So, what do you think?" I asked, and bounced the basketball I'd brought along.

"She really said she knew it was a werewolf?"

"Yep."

"Then—" she said slowly, as if measuring her words, "—then I think we should ask her to help us. Kill it, I mean."

"Yeah, me too. But you want to know the really weird thing about it?"

"Being yanked into a tomb and told that werewolves are real isn't weird enough?"

"Ha, ha, very funny. No, seriously. She acted like there were lots of others around."

"Other what? Werewolves?"

I nodded. "Either she knows more than we do about what's really going on, or she's ready for a room with rubber walls."

"I can't believe we're talking about this. That this whole thing isn't some awful nightmare that I can't wake up from." Her eyes filled with tears and she sniffed. I couldn't blame her, what with finding out her mother was a monster that she was going to have to kill. "So what do we do now?"

"Beats me." I tossed the basketball at the hoop. It slammed against the backboard. "Maybe we should talk to the sheriff again."

She watched the ball as it bounced past her. "But didn't Ms. Glass tell you not to talk to anyone?"

When I realized she wasn't going to shag the ball for me, I jogged after it. "I can't just sit on my hands and do nothing. What if someone else gets killed in the meantime?"

"Look, there's still some time until the next full moon. Maybe Mom won't turn any more. Maybe it was just one of those things. You know, something that happens once or twice and then stops all on its own. Can't we just wait and see?"

"Fine. But I still think we should at least come up with a plan, some way we can lure it out into the open so we can kill it."

"Hey, that's my mom you're talking about."

"I know. I'm sorry. But we still need a plan, just in case. Don't you think?"

She sighed heavily. "Okay."

If the time came, would Beth be able to kill her? I wasn't even sure I could, and Aunt Judy was only my aunt, not my mom.

Beth scooped the ball out of my hands, threw it at the

hoop, and turned her back to it. "She shoots." Her voice was monotone. "She scores." Amazingly, the ball went in the hoop, catching nothing but net.

"Show off," I teased, hoping she'd laugh, but knowing she wouldn't. I wasn't sure she would ever laugh again.

☽

After that, we left the park and got a root beer at the Circle K. We were sitting on one of the benches lining Wolf Creek Road when Beth told me something weird.

"You know," she began. "I'm not supposed to tell you this. Not supposed to tell anyone."

"Tell me what?"

"As soon as Mom and me got home from the service, she left. That little act she put on for your folks, the one about just washing the dishes? She made me do them while she was gone."

"So? Maybe she just went for a walk."

"Oh, yeah? Then how come she told me not to tell anyone that she'd been gone?"

"She actually told you that?"

"Uh huh."

"Where do you think she went?"

"Don't know. Maybe stalking her next victim."

I hadn't thought of that, but when she said it, a chill came over me, and I rubbed my forearms to get rid of the goosebumps. There had been someone way up on Impasse Hill, hidden behind a tree, watching the funerals. As soon as she talked about the werewolf stalking its next victim, it made me think she might be right.

Maybe Aunt Judy really was a werewolf.

Thursday, October 31, 2013

WANING CRESCENT

Old moon
Growing smaller
11% Visible

Chapter 19

After the funerals, things went pretty much back to normal. We kept a close eye on Aunt Judy, but for the most part, all she ever did was talk on the phone to her friends, drink tea, and watch talk shows. She especially liked Jerry Springer.

Riggs was his usual mean self. The sheriff went about his business, and never got back to us. Maybe Riggs convinced him we were playing some sort of elaborate joke. I don't know and I never got the chance to ask.

One thing the sheriff did was set a curfew. In October it got dark around six o'clock, so everyone had to be inside for the night by five-thirty. Which was fine with me after Beth's Internet research discovered that werewolves didn't necessarily need a full moon to change, that they could do it any time they wanted to. Talk about creepy.

At least before, we'd been confident that we were a little safer in between full moons. Now, I didn't even want to leave the house to go to school, but I couldn't stay home when Aunt Judy was there.

Too scary.

Then came Halloween night, and Beth and I were

playing with the Game Boy. I was glad it still worked even after she cracked the screen.

"Hey, no fair," I exclaimed. "You just killed one of my men."

"Tough shit," she replied. "Deal with it."

"Nice talk, gutter mouth."

"You're just jealous because I'm better than you, and I don't even like this stupid game."

The parental units sat at the kitchen table in their usual adult huddle and drank yet more tea as they argued about something, which they were doing more and more of lately. The result of too many people in too small a space. I was tired of the couch. A few weeks had turned into over three months, and my back had a permanent kink from the couch spring that dug into me every time I tried to get comfortable.

I cocked my head to try and hear what they were saying. All I caught was something about someone needing to know something. What were they talking about? Who needed to know what? Were they talking about something to do with what was going on in town? I couldn't tell, so I leaned forward and whispered for Beth to mute it.

"Why? Can't stand the sounds of me winning?"

"Shut up. I'm trying to hear what they're saying in there."

She hit the mute button and looked at me questioningly. We listened, but couldn't hear what they said. We were concentrating so hard we didn't hear my dad until he suddenly appeared in the doorway.

"What's the matter? We not speaking loud enough for you?"

Busted.

Beth tried to cover for us. "No, Uncle Robbie. Spoil sport here—" She thrust the Game Boy at me. "—can't stand that I'm winning, so he made me turn it down so he wouldn't have to hear all his men dying."

"That true?" he practically growled.

I swallowed noisily. "Brat's blowing me out of the water."

"Um hum." He didn't sound convinced. "Remember, if any trick-or-treaters come to the door, you just ignore them."

"I know, I know." I crossed my eyes at Beth and she giggled.

Then in perfect harmony, we both mimicked his earlier words. "It's just not safe. You never know who's out there these days."

He smiled like he thought it was funny. Only his smile didn't reach his eyes. "There might even be monsters out there. Witches. Vampires. The Boogeyman." He smirked. "Or werewolves."

We just stared at him. What made him say that? And why was he acting so strange? What was going on?

He started back into the kitchen, then turned to Beth. "Whip him good, puppy. Kid needs to learn a lesson."

Her face was so white her freckles had all but disappeared, and there was sweat on her forehead. She belched, and I was afraid she would puke. "Um, okay." When he disappeared back into the kitchen, she wiped her forehead. "What was that all about?"

"I'm not sure."

"Your dad's really starting to freak me out."

"Yeah. Me, too."

"Do you think he said that, about monsters and werewolves, because he suspects something?"

I thought about that for a second. Truth was, I didn't know. "He's pretty smart. He might." I didn't add that I was beginning to wonder if Dad could be the werewolf. But that was crazy, wasn't it?

"What should we do?"

"Just act like everything's cool. Tomorrow we'll go to The Quiet Riot and see if Ms. Glass will talk to us again."

And talk she did. Just not right away.

Sunday, November 18, 2013

TOTAL LUNAR ECLIPSE

The moon passes directly behind the Earth
into its umbra, or darkest part of its shadow.
This only occurs when the sun, Earth, and moon
are aligned exactly, with the Earth in the middle.

Chapter 20

Nearly three weeks later, there was another full moon. We still hadn't been able to connect with Ms. Glass, and I was worried that someone else might be murdered. But since we didn't have a plan yet, I told Beth to spend the night with Lindy, who was living with her grandmother now, just to be safe. Especially since there was also supposed to be a lunar eclipse, too. I was glad Beth was gone, because she was so convinced the werewolf was her mother, she was starting to scare me. What if we lured it into a trap, killed it, and it really was Aunt Judy? What if Beth went to kill the werewolf, couldn't do it because she was positive it was her mother, and it killed her instead? Or what if it wasn't Aunt Judy? What if it was someone else? Would Aunt Judy ever forgive Beth for thinking she was a monster? Would Beth ever be able to trust her mom again? It was too much to deal with, and I didn't want to think about it anymore. At least not for a while, anyway.

I gave Riff a call. If anyone could take my mind off things, he could. Usually on Saturday afternoons, he and I would hop on our bikes and ride out to this place in the woods that was perfect for jumping and racing and just having fun. But last summer, I crashed my bike and bent the frame. Mom wouldn't let me get it fixed until I'd "learned how to be responsible." Besides, the woods were now a scary place, and pretty much everyone avoided them these days. So now the only things we could do was shoot hoops or toss the ball around at the park. He was only allowed to use his cell for emergencies, so I had to call his house phone.

"Hello?" His mother never did like me.

"Hi, Mrs. Wozniak. It's James Mannaro."

"Yes?" Frostbite warning.

"Is Riff there?"

"Yes."

She banged the receiver down and I could hear her footsteps as she walked out of the room. I sat on the floor and leaned against the wall, scratched my side and tried to think about anything but monsters. You never could tell how long it would take her to tell Riff I was on the phone.

"Dude," Riff yelled into the phone, practically breaking my eardrum. "Save me. I'm dying of boredom here."

"Same here." I forced out a laugh. "You up for a game of hoops?"

"Nah, how's about we get rid of a few beautiful people instead?"

"You got it!"

Riff was a freak for anything dark and futuristic and was dying to get his hands on a copy of *The Purge* DVD ever since it came out last month. "My grandmother sent it to me."

I laughed. His grandmother on his father's side absolutely hated Mrs. Wozniak and would do anything she could to piss her off, like buy her fourteen-year-old grandson an R-rated movie.

"So get your skinny ass over here and let's watch it," I told him.

My parents didn't care what I watched, as long as it wasn't sex.

"On my way. Have to ditch Ma, but I'm there."

The phone clicked on the other end as it was replaced in the handset. Riff was all right, despite what a lot of people thought. He could be obnoxious, and he sometimes drove me nuts, but most of the time, he was a pretty good guy. His mouth was his way of making sure no one hurt him. Constantly bullied in school when we were kids, he didn't want anyone to see how much those experiences had hurt his feelings. Not even me.

We became friends in the first grade when we were at PE choosing teams for kickball. I was a captain, and the other captain was a mean girl named Becky. Riff was the last one to be picked, as usual. It was Becky's turn, and when the teacher turned her back, Becky walked over to Riff and pushed him down.

"No one wants you on their team. You stink."

You could tell he wanted to cry, but even then his pride wouldn't let him. I helped him up. "You can be on our team," I told him. We've been friends ever since.

"What're you doing on the floor?" my dad asked. "Everything okay?"

I hadn't even heard him walk down the hall. I stood up and smoothed out my pants. "Yeah, I'm fine. Riff's coming over."

"Okay, I think we might have a couple of those green things he drinks way back in the corner of the fridge."

"Great, thanks."

My dad liked Riff.

"Well, you guys have fun."

"We will. He's got a new movie. No sex," I promised.

Dad nodded. "Just make sure he leaves in plenty of time to get home before curfew."

"'Kay."

"In fact, it probably wouldn't be a bad idea if he went home before the eclipse."

"What time is that again?"

"I think about quarter to five, maybe ten till. Not sure. To be safe, have him leave by four-thirty."

"All right," I agreed.

The last thing I wanted was for Riff to be out after dark. Going into the kitchen, I went to hunt up some snacks to munch on. After rummaging in the pantry, I found some Fritos, bean dip, and cheesie poofs. I pulled them all out, then on impulse snagged the last bag of dried fruit. The apples were my favorites. I was dumping the chips into a bowl when the back door flew open and in popped Riff, seemingly propelled by the wind. Lots of dead leaves followed his entrance, and a few were stuck in his hair.

"Hey, close the door," I told him. "You look like hell."

"Love you too," he replied. "Out of my way, douche bag."

He pushed past me into the living room and plopped down on the couch. Grabbing the snacks, I followed. Riff pulled his backpack off his shoulder and dug around inside. Out came the DVD.

"Awesome." I ripped open the case and shoved the movie into the DVD player. We settled into the couch as the FBI warning flashed on the screen.

Normally, we made cracks all through the movie, but this time, my mind wandered back to the full moon and everything that went along with it, and I kept missing what he was saying.

After about half an hour in, Riff paused the movie. "Dude, what's up with you?"

"What?"

"You're just not into it. I thought you'd be all-intense and stuff. What's up?"

"Nothing. Really."

"Don't lie to me, dude. I've known you forever, re-member?"

Checking over my shoulder to make sure no one was around, I made a decision. I didn't want to say anything to Riff, but I couldn't pretend anymore. He knew something was up. I took a big breath and let it out slowly.

"I know who killed Mrs. Sommes and those other people. Or rather, what."

"Huh? What do you mean, what?"

"I mean…" I took a big breath and let it out slowly. "A werewolf killed those people."

Riff gawked like I'd just told him I was a Martian. Then he burst out laughing.

"Dude, stop," I told him. He grabbed his sides and started rolling around on the floor. "I'm serious."

But he didn't stop, not for a really long time. When he finally sat up, he'd laughed so hard tears were actually streaming down his face. He wiped them away and chuckled.

"Had me going there for a minute."

I didn't respond. I expected him to laugh at first, but I honestly thought he'd believe me.

"You can't be serious." He cocked his head. "Can you?"

I nodded.

"But that's impossible. There's no such thing as werewolves. Or vampires. Or Frankenstein. That's all baby shit."

"I don't know about vampires or Frankenstein, but I do know that werewolves are real."

"Since when?"

"I don't know." I shrugged. "Since now, I guess."

"Right." Riff snorted. "And Wolf Creek is such an exciting place that one decided it had to come here and start eating people. Dude, give me a break."

"Whatever. Don't say I didn't warn you."

"Yeah, okay. I'll thank you when I'm being chased by one." He picked up the remote. "Now, we gonna finish the movie, or what?"

He turned the movie back on. I finally stopped thinking about monsters and actually enjoyed it. But just when it got to the good part, there was a tap on my shoulder.

"Time's up, guys," Dad told us. "Eclipse will be here in a few minutes. You really need to go now, Riff."

"Just a few more minutes till it's over, Mr. Mannaro." Riff grinned at me. "We gotta see who makes it through the night alive."

"Riff, go home." He put his hand on Riff's shoulder. "Now."

Riff squinted and you could tell he was wondering how far to push. "All right, I'm leaving."

"I mean it, guys," Dad told me. "Pack it up. Now."

"Fine."

We pretended to shut off the movie, but as soon as he left the room, we turned back to it and time got away from us. By the time it was over, the eclipse had already started.

"Shit, Riff, it's way late. Look." I pointed out the window. The sky was dark red. It was freaky, and when Riff saw it, he paled.

"Oh, crap." He stood up. "I got to go."

"Let me get my dad." I gestured toward the hallway, where he'd gone. "He'll run you home."

"Nah, I'm cool." After shaking the can to see how much Dew was left, Riff took a long draw and tugged on his jacket. "Later, dude."

I walked with him to the front door. The sky was so

weird. There were lots of clouds, but you could still see the sun set at the same time the moon rose. The way the moon looked like a shiny new penny on one side and a puddle of blood on the other was freaky. I'd never seen anything like it, and probably never would again.

We stood there and watched the sky. Then we heard voices in the kitchen and I nudged Riff. "I'm going to get my dad to drive you home."

"Don't be such a pussy. It's only a few blocks." He pulled his iPod Shuffle out of his back pocket and jammed the buds into his ears. "Later."

"Later." I watched my best friend head home and a strange feeling came over me. "Riff?" I called after him.

He turned and took one of the ear buds out.

"Yeah?"

"Sure you don't want a ride?"

He shook his head. "I ain't afraid of no boogeyman. Or anything else."

☽

Riff chuckled as he finished the soda he bummed from James's fridge. Werewolves? Seriously? He had to be kidding. Riff laughed and shook his head. Werewolves.

As he tromped up the hill toward the easement, he watched the sky. The eclipse made it look so cool. Too bad there were so many clouds up there, but at least you could see how weird the moon looked. Or was that fog? Nah, couldn't be.

Something rattled in front of him and a momentary flash of fear zipped through him, only to vanish when he saw a candy wrapper bounce rapidly across the path. He snorted and realized he was glad cooler weather was on the way. Even though it always brought the Santa Ana winds, which made everyone a little jumpy, at least things were finally cooling off.

He turned the volume up on his iPod, then stuck his hands back in his jacket pockets and leaned into the wind. Even as a little kid, he always loved the feel of air pressing against his face. He would roll down the window of their beat up Honda and stick his whole head out. Hot or cold, it didn't matter. He loved how it made his face tingle.

Quickening his pace, enough so he was breathing harder than normal, he walked up the hill. He needed to get home soon since he was already way late. His mom was going to kill him. He should've left James's when Mr. Mannaro first said so. If he was lucky, he might be able to sneak in without his mom hearing and then he could say he'd gotten home on time.

He tossed his empty can into the bushes and sang tunelessly along with Gwen Stefani about being "Just a Girl." *And what a girl.* That chick was smokin'. He bobbed his head in time to the music. While he may never admit it, he loved No Doubt and wished he'd been able to see them in concert. His hands jabbed and poked the air from inside his pockets, punctuating the lyrics.

Underneath the music, he could have sworn someone was behind him. He tugged the ear bud out of his right ear and listened. He frowned, but didn't hear anything else. The artificially dusty red night made things hard to see. Everything appeared distorted and weird. He tripped on a plastic Dr. Pepper bottle and stumbled several feet back down the hill. His elbows flailed wildly but he couldn't yank his hands free from his pockets. Then, just as he finally managed to right himself, he lost his balance and sat down hard, uttering a loud "humph" when he hit the dirt.

"Shit." He stood up and wiped off the seat of his jeans. "Idiots got nothing better to do than toss their crap on the ground for people to trip over."

His thumb hooked into the hole he tore under his back pocket, and he hitched up his right hip and bent backward for a look. "Oh, great. Just what I need. Very cool. Damn."

Jamming the ear bud back into his ear, he turned up the volume to drown everything but the music out, then trudged back up the hill. The trees and bushes lining the path were bare, their gold and red leaves littered across the narrow path up the easement. It made him long for the East Coast where it actually rained in the fall. Not the dry and drier crap here in So Cal. If it weren't for his best bud, he'd have gone cray cray a long time ago.

Maybe that's what was happening now. Maybe he was losing his marbles and going crazy, thinking someone was following him. Maybe he was so far gone he'd never be able to find his way back. Climb the clock tower and shoot everyone in sight. And maybe the monster running around killing everyone just happened to be behind him. *Yeah, right.* Still, he walked a little faster. Just in case.

James will have a good laugh when I tell him about my walk home. After only three steps, he stopped and strained to see into the murkiness. Of course, no one—or nothing—was there.

"Oooh, better watch it, dumb ass." He tried to chuckle, but it got caught in his throat, so he shook his head sadly. "You're freaking yourself out. Just chill. There's nothing following you."

☽

It loved the feel of the wind as it ruffled its fur and

cooled its hot skin. The transformation was quick, but the aftereffects left a burning under the skin and a blood lust that grew more and more vicious if not immediately relieved.

It loped along the deserted streets and easily avoided streetlights, preferring the shadows. The humans built a wall around the railroad tracks bordering the southernmost side of town. They tried to beautify the wall by planting lots of flowers and trees around it, but that created more places to hide

The moon was full behind the clouds, and the air held a strange heaviness. As long as it ran on all fours, it would be safe along the tracks, hidden from view by the fence. This part of town had trees and areas untouched by humans with their buildings, so crowded together, where they sold the cars that filled its nose with horrid exhaust and cooked their cow meat, which smelled almost as bad.

On its way to the tracks, it picked up the scent of a lone human. It stopped, stuck its nose into the wind, and inhaled the pleasant aroma. The werewolf wrinkled its muzzle with delight. It ran its tongue over the end of its nose and bared its teeth as its stomach rumbled loudly.

Human! It ran toward the smell.

☽

Riff couldn't believe his friend. How could James believe the rumors about some monster or other roaming the streets during the full moon? That was so lame. Like a monster had nothing better to do than come to this crappy little town and eat people. It was all bullshit. Riff didn't believe what that old fart Anderson claimed happened in the woods. Probably some sicko Jeffrey Dahmer wannabe. But whatever it was, one thing was for sure, there was no werewolf preying on the people of Wolf Creek.

There it came again, the sneaky sounds of someone as they tiptoed along behind him. Which was really lame—who would want to follow him? *There's no one there, douche bag.* Still the impulse to glance over his shoulder was strong enough to give in to. When he did, he laughed because, of course, there was no one there.

"Stop being such a pussy," he told himself, and helped Gwen finish her song before he heard what sounded like a branch being snapped in half.

He glanced over his shoulder again and hurried on. *Why you so mental?* It had to be the weird red semi-darkness that made him think someone was there when no one was. Right? His parents always said he had an over-active imagination that would get him into trouble someday.

"But not today," he muttered under his breath, and then chuckled. No one was behind him. *Gotta stop watching those slasher movies.* He vowed to lay off the scary movies—for a week or two, at least.

Several candy wrappers and a bright red and blue Doritos bag blew across the path in front of him. The bag caught briefly on a gnarled tree root before sailing on its way. He watched it rise quickly in the tiny twister sur-rounding him before it disappeared from sight.

Time to make like the twister and blow before he got into big trouble.

☽

The fragrant odor of human filled its nostrils. The hunger grew as it closed in on its prey. It must feed again.

The smell came from a small, wooded hill with heavy scrub brush and trees to hide in. On all fours, it charged up the dirt trail where the scent of Man was the strongest.

It must be quiet, but it was so hard. It was starving, and its head was fuzzy. Its ears rang. Before long, it would weaken and have trouble hunting. It followed the human aroma that made its stomach rumble painfully. Bushes provided adequate cover, and it slowed to a trot.

Then it pulled up short and sniffed the air again. Focusing, it spotted its prey. It licked each side of its muzzle with deliberate care then watched the boy and waited for the moment to attack.

☽

Riff glanced back down the path a final time and shook his head at being such a loser. As he started down the other side of the hill, the footsteps grew louder and more insistent. This time, he didn't bother to look. Someone was behind him, all right. *Oh, God, it's the maniac!* He took off down the hill in a haphazard fashion, zigzagging from one side of the path to the other. Breath ragged and harsh joined the painful stitch in his left side under his ribcage.

Without warning, he was pushed from behind and careened down the hill so fast, his arms pin-wheeled wildly and he struggled to stay upright. One foot hooked around the other, and he screamed as he went down. His face hit the trunk of a tree with a loud crunch.

"Uh nuh," he screamed.

It was a struggle to sit up. First, he had to roll onto his back. That tired him, so he leaned back against the tree trunk and closed his eyes. *What just happened?* He brought his hand to his face and touched something thick and wet. When he pulled his hand away and tried to focus on it, it remained fuzzy and undefined. He moved his hand a little closer to his face and narrowed his eyes until his vision cleared. When it did, and he was able to see what was in his hand, he wished he couldn't.

Blood dripped down his wrist and onto the sleeve of his jacket, staining it a bright crimson. His eyes grew wide and his breath came in great, lurching sobs as he realized he was holding almost two bloody inches of his tongue.

He moaned and kicked his feet blindly. Not knowing what to do with his tongue, he stuck it in his right jacket pocket and tried to push himself off the ground. As he did so, something flickered in his peripheral vision. Before he could see what it was, a white-hot slice raked down his cheek, under his jaw and across his throat.

Warm blood spurted from the side of his face and patterned the trunk of the tree in a design resembling the whirly-paint pictures he made at school carnivals when he was a kid.

His mind refused to believe what was happening, even though he wondered where all the blood came from. God, there was so much of it. His knees went weak, and he fell into a bunch of poison oak.

Oh, great, I'll be itching like crazy in the morning. The thought was distant and unreal as he tried to roll out of it. *Sure hope Mom has a big bottle of that pink stuff to rub on it.*

Something grabbed him around the calves even as he struggled to get away. Teeth bit deep into his ankle, shredded the gristle, and ripped the tendons from the bone.

Riff's flayed skin burned and he tried to scream, but with all the blood in his mouth, the best he could do was gurgle.

As he was dragged deeper into the dense undergrowth, he wished he could take back everything he said to James. His friend was right, after all.

There really was a werewolf stalking the town.

Tuesday, November 19, 2013

FULL MOON

100% Visible

Chapter 21

The day after the eclipse, breakfast was interrupted by the phone. Dad growled and I wondered who was calling so early in the morning.

"I swear." Dad pushed his chair back. "If it's one of those damn telemarketers—"

"Settle down, Robbie." Mom put her hand on his forearm as he walked by her. "They don't call this early. Besides, if it is a salesman, just hang up."

"I will, but not before I say a few choice words."

After he went into the living room to answer the phone, I went back to my eggs. Or at least tried to. I managed to swallow a bite or two, but couldn't seem to get any more than that down. Strangely, Aunt Judy had insisted on making them for us, along with bacon, sausage and whole-wheat toast. It was weird considering she hadn't cooked anything for a long time, and I was afraid she was trying to poison me.

I was pushing my eggs around with my toast when Dad appeared in the doorway. "Jaime?"

He caught my eye, and I could tell something was wrong. "Yeah, Dad." I put down my fork, almost knocking over my orange juice in the process. "What's wrong?"

"It's Mrs. Wozniak. She wants to talk to you."

"Me?" I squeaked, then cleared my throat and tried again. "What for?"

"I don't want you to get upset, but—"

Mom twisted her wedding ring around and around. "Robbie?"

He was scaring me. "What is it?" I could hear my voice shake. "What's wrong?"

"Riff's missing. He never made it home last night."

Bolting from the table, I charged past him. When I picked up the phone, I held it to my chest and closed my eyes. "Please, God," I prayed. "Please let him be okay." Then I took a deep breath, put the phone to my ear, and spoke.

"Mrs. Wozniak? It's James."

"James?" I could tell right away that she'd been crying. "Do you know where Harold is?"

"No. He left here a little late yesterday, what with the new—" I stopped, not wanting to get Riff in trouble. I'd almost forgotten he didn't want his mother to know about the DVD his grandmother had sent him.

"The new what?"

I didn't know if I should tell her or not, so I hesitated.

"James, please. If you know anything about where my son is, tell me." She started to cry.

If Riff was missing, it wouldn't hurt if his mom found out about the movie. "We were having so much fun watching the movie his grandma sent that we lost track of the time. He meant to leave before the eclipse, but we got involved in the movie and by the time he left, it had already started. I wanted my dad to drive him home, but he said he'd walk."

From behind me, Mom said, "Oh, Jaime."

Everyone was listening to my side of the conversation. I couldn't look them in the eye, especially not my dad.

"It's okay." Mrs. Wozniak blew her nose into the phone. I grimaced and pulled the receiver away from my ear. "It's not your fault."

There was a loud knock on the front door, and Aunt Judy went to answer it.

"Was he going anywhere else after he left your house?"

I glanced up as she opened the door and let Sheriff Brazelton in then turned my attention back to Riff's mom. "He told me he was going straight home. He didn't want to be late and make you mad."

"Okay. Well, if you do hear from him, you'll have him call me, won't you?"

"Yes, ma'am." I turned to the sheriff as I hung up the phone. "That was Riff's mom. Are you here because he's missing?"

Sheriff Brazelton nodded. Sitting down heavily on the couch, I put my head in my hands. "Why, Riff?" I whispered. "Why didn't you let me have Dad drive you home? I should have made you leave when you were supposed to."

Mom sat next to me and rubbed my back. "Everything'll turn out okay, you'll see."

"Okay? Okay?" I bolted from the couch and charged across the room. "Everything's not okay, Mom." I crossed my arms and turned back to face them. It wasn't her fault Riff was gone, but how could she possibly think things would ever be okay again? "My best friend has been eaten by a werewolf. Nothing will ever be okay again."

"Honey, calm down. You're just upset." She walked over and guided me back to the couch, gently urging me to sit. "Let's talk with the sheriff and see how we can help." She patted my leg and looked at the sheriff expectantly.

"Are you okay?" Sheriff Brazelton seemed genuinely concerned.

"I'm fine."

"Good. Then I need to ask you a few questions." He pushed aside the magazines strewn on top of the coffee table, sat directly in front of me, and pulled out a small spiral notepad and pen. "You say Riff was here last night?"

I nodded.

"What time did he leave?"

"About quarter to five."

The sheriff made a note in his pad.

"Is anyone trying to find him? Maybe we should go out and see if we can find him." I started to stand, but the sheriff pushed me back down.

"There's a search party out looking for him. Did you see which way he went when he left?"

I nodded. "Same way he always went. We stood at the door a few minutes and watched the sky. You know, how weird it was because of the eclipse. Then he took off down the street, toward the easement."

Sheriff Brazelton's head whipped up from his notes. "The electrical easement?"

"Yeah." I stood up again. "I have to go find him."

The sheriff stood and adjusted his duty belt over his spare tire before gently pushing me back onto the couch. "I have people out looking for him as we speak. I'll radio in and have Riggs take part of the search party over to the easement. The best thing you can do is to stay here in case Riff calls or comes back. In the meantime, I'll be speaking to all his other friends."

"Besides me, Riff doesn't have any friends." I was suddenly very tired.

I should have made him stay over. Or insisted on Dad driving him home. Something. Anything. *Just please, please, please, please let him be all right,* I prayed.

"Okay." The sheriff put his hand on my shoulder and tried to look me in the eye, but I was too worn-out to look up. "You let me know if you hear from him, right, James?"

I didn't answer him. I was too busy making a deal with God that I would go to church every single Sunday for the rest of my life and even listen to all the sermons, if He would just let Riff be alive.

Dad let the sheriff out. They whispered back and forth to each other before the sheriff said, "Will do." Then he was gone.

When I heard the door close, I looked up to find my parents watching me with their sad puppy faces. I couldn't stand it. I had to leave. Now.

"I'm out of here."

Dad blocked the front door. "Just where do you think you're going, young man?"

"Out of my way, Dad."

"Jaime, you've got to calm down. Getting hysterical won't help find Riff."

Turning the other way, I walked the length of the couch. Mom stood beside the coffee table blocking my way.

"Neither will just sitting here, twiddling my thumbs." I grabbed her by the shoulders, only meaning to move her out of my way, but she tripped over the table leg and fell.

When she landed on the floor with a thud, Dad raced over to help her up.

"Annette, are you hurt?"

She put her hand to her forehead and frowned. "No, I'm okay."

As he bent over her, I hurried to the door and paused to consider those I loved more than anyone else on the planet. "Sorry, Mom. I didn't mean to knock you down."

"Honey, wait."

But I had to do something. I couldn't just sit around and make nice-nice with the grown-ups when I didn't know if my best friend was hurt or dead.

Or worse.

☽

Bolting out of the house, I headed for the easement. If something happened to Riff, it happened there. Everywhere else was wide-open spaces. The woods were where it had probably gotten him. Much more cover. And other animals lived there, so it would feel safe. Invincible.

If he wasn't there, he might have made it to the grade school's kickball field on the other side of the easement. Maybe he'd gotten so scared he hid somewhere. After all, there were lots of trees and bushes to hide under between his house and mine. Maybe that was what had happened. If so, I could kick his ass for scaring everybody. But the fire in my belly told me he wasn't hiding.

It only took about three minutes at a dead run for me to reach the woods. As soon as I got there, I knew something was wrong. There were several Highway Patrol cars parked all over the place, along with both Wolf Creek squad cars. People milled around, not really talking to each other, just walking back and forth on the dirt path. An officer wrapped yellow crime scene tape around the trunk of a big oak tree and then walked across the path. He stopped and did the same thing to another tree on the opposite side.

"Oh, shit," I groaned.

The fire in my belly had become an erupting volcano

spewing molten lava. I caught sight of Sheriff Brazelton and Sergeant McNeil as they came out of the trees, stepped underneath the tape, and walked slowly toward their cruisers.

I waved my arms above my head, trying to get their attention. "Sheriff," I called. They both looked up. When I got to where they stood, I couldn't catch my breath, and McNeil was once again condescending.

"Take it easy, son." She patted me between the shoulder blades. Ordinarily, it would have irritated me, but while I heard her say it, it didn't really register until Sheriff Brazelton put his arm around my shoulders and walked me a step or two away, just far enough so that the sergeant couldn't pound on my back any more.

"James," he said. "Slow down. Take a deep breath before you hyperventilate."

I bent over and put my hands on my knees. "Is it Riff? Is he dead?" I only had to see his face to know for sure. Just like some part of me had realized, when Riff left my house last night, when I got that weird feeling, that I'd never see him again.

"Oh, God, no. No, please, no, no, no."

The sheriff's hands tightened on my shoulders. "I'm sorry, he's gone."

I tried to shake off his hold, but he must have expected it because his fingers squeezed into my flesh hard enough to leave marks. "All right, settle down."

"It's best if you don't see what's left of the body." McNeil was probably trying to help, but all I got from it was that Riff was now in pieces.

"Let me go." I struggled, but it was no use. Once I realized it, I slumped against the sheriff.

"That's better." He loosened his grip. "Now, you go on home. I'll stop by later, after I break it to the Wozniaks." He turned to the sergeant and relaxed his hold on me a little more. "God, how do I break something like this to a child's parents? What can I say to them?"

Seeing my chance, I wriggled free and ran toward the easement, ducking under the tape and charging up the hill. It was easy to figure out where Riff's body was because a small crowd of cops gathered there, poking the underbrush with sticks. They talked quietly among themselves. I plowed through them and into the bushes before anyone could stop me.

Running about a hundred feet through the undergrowth, I stopped in front of a manzanita tree. The dirt underneath it was dark and muddy, and there were deep furrows through it, as if someone had been dragged through the puddle. I crept through the brush and had lifted the low branches of the scrub oak up when I saw Riff. Or rather, a piece of him. I think it was a shoulder and part of his back, but I looked away so quickly I wasn't sure.

The next thing I knew, I was in the back of a cop car with a scratchy blanket wrapped around me, crying like I hadn't done since my mom yelled at me when I was four for flushing my Superman action figure down the toilet.

Someone called my mom, and she came to take me home. I was barely aware she was there, even as she sat on the edge of the car doorframe and put her hand on my knee. "Jaime? James? It's okay, baby. Let's go home."

I stared at her hand, then slowly raised my head. "Mom?"

"Yes, honey. It's Mom."

I couldn't seem to stop crying. She climbed into the back seat and sat next to me. She wrapped her arms around me and gently pushed my head to her shoulder. Then I really let loose, crying so hard and so long my eyeballs ached for days.

When I was finally done, she led me over to the

Toyota, sat me inside, and fastened my seat belt. "Why, Mom?" I stared out the window as she climbed into the driver's seat. "Why did this have to happen?"

"I don't know. Sometimes, bad things happen and no one knows why. They just do."

But I knew why. Werewolf. For some reason, Wolf Creek was under some kind of spell. Maybe it was the name of the town, or maybe just bad luck. Whatever it was didn't matter, because I knew whose fault it really was. I knew who the killer was.

And I was going to see to it she never killed again.

$$\)$$

When we pulled up to the house, I threw open the car door, tossed the blanket off my shoulders and raced up the walk. Beth was home from her slumber party, watching out the window with the drapes pulled aside. I found out later that she waited for me for almost an hour, ever since Dad picked her up. But just then, I didn't care. All I cared about was that my best friend was dead.

As soon as she saw me get out of the car, she ran to meet me. "James. James! I heard what happened. Did you see the body?"

I didn't even slow down, just pushed her out of my way and ran into the house. "Aunt Judy, where are you? I know you're here somewhere."

Aunt Judy was calmly drying the mug she used for her morning Earl Grey. Like it was just another day. Like nothing was wrong. Like she hadn't murdered my best friend. Spying the tiny smirk on her face, I totally lost it.

"Murderer!" I screamed and lunged at her, wrapping my hands around her throat, squeezing tight. I wanted her dead. Hands grabbed at me, and for a second I lost my grip, but I was so full of rage I twisted out of their grasp and went for her throat again. She dropped the towel and the mug, which shattered when it hit the floor. She tried to back away, but I rushed forward. The blood-curdling scream that came out of her made me happy. I wanted her to feel as scared as she made Riff feel right before she killed him.

"Jaime." Dad tried to pull me off her. "What the hell are you doing?"

Mom beat at me with her fists. "Stop it, stop it!"

"She killed Riff. Murderer! Monster!" I screamed so loud it hurt my throat, but I didn't care. "You killed my best friend, you freak!" I lunged at her again.

The monster rubbed her throat where ugly purple bruises were already starting to show.

"I didn't touch him," she exclaimed. "I don't know what you're talking about."

"You're a werewolf, and you killed Riff. And Mary and those other people." The top of my head was ready to explode, I was screaming so hard. "And now, I'm going to kill you."

Dad tackled me around the knees, and I went down hard. We wrestled for a few seconds, until he was able to flip me onto my stomach and twist my arms behind my back. I tried to get away, but he sat on me, holding me down until I finally realized he wasn't going to let me up. My whole body went limp, and I laid there with my face jammed into the yellowed linoleum.

"Let him up, Robbie." I could see Mom's feet next to my head, and I think she placed her hand on Dad's shoulder to calm him. "You're hurting him."

"No, I'm not." He leaned down and whispered into my ear, "I don't know what this is all about, but I'm not going to let you up until you calm down. Do you understand?"

"Yesh," I mumbled. It was hard to talk with my mouth crammed against the floor. Not to mention difficult to breathe.

"Are you calm?"

I nodded.

"Okay. I'm going to let you up now. All right?"

"Yes."

He eased up, but still straddled me. Air flooded into my lungs and made me cough. He let go of my arms and helped me up. I rubbed my shoulder and hoped the blood would flow back into it. It hurt.

"Do you want to tell me what that was all about?" He looked at me funny, but I couldn't read his expression. He was puzzled, sure, but it was something else. Something deeper.

The women were huddled together as Mom tried to comfort Aunt Judy. She rubbed her throat and stared at me all wide-eyed and innocent. I glared at her and hoped it hurt a lot.

"Hey." Dad nudged me in the side. "We're waiting."

"She murdered Riff, and she killed all those people."

"What the hell are you talking about?"

"I never..." She shook her head, still rubbing her throat, and backed up a step.

"Don't believe anything she says, Dad. She's a murderer and a liar."

Mom put one arm around Aunt Judy's shoulders and her hand on her arm like she wanted to protect her from me.

"Okay, calm down." Dad grabbed my arm. "Why don't you fix us some tea?" he told Mom as he practically dragged me into the living room.

As they went into the kitchen, he walked me to the couch and pushed me into it by my shoulders. Then he stood there with his arms folded tightly across his chest.

"Well?"

"Well, what?"

"Explain yourself."

The whole story poured out of me. Everything. Including what Beth told me about her father's death not being an accident, about all the fights her parents had before Uncle Fred crashed, about the monster she saw that night outside her bedroom window. My dad stood there and listened quietly, until I finished with, "She's a werewolf, Dad."

"Oh, son." He flashed a quick look at Mom before sitting down next to me. "You're just upset about Riff."

Jerking away from him, I walked to the other side of the room. I would have tripped over Beth, wide-eyed and listening to everything, if she hadn't scooted out of the way at the last minute.

"I knew they wouldn't believe us," I said to her before turning to Dad. "I knew you wouldn't believe us."

He stood up and walked toward me with his arms outstretched. "Jaime, look."

"No." I backed away, my arms crossed.

"Son—" he started again.

Tears ran down my face, and I wiped the snot off my upper lip with the back of my hand. "Leave me alone!" I ran out the door, my sobs out of control now, and headed down the street. Didn't know where I was going, but it didn't matter. All that mattered was that no one believed there was a monster on the loose. Or that unless it was stopped it would kill again.

☽

Beth was surprised when James flew through the front door and attacked her mother. Until that point, she wasn't completely sure he believed the whole werewolf thing. But when he tried to strangle her mother, the whole thing became very real. Before, it was some vague story in the back of her mind, not exactly make-believe, but not exactly real, either. But now, there was no going back. Sometimes she wished she'd never found out that her mother was some kind of psycho freak. It would be so much easier to pretend everything was normal. That she was normal.

That was impossible now. It was all out in the open, and there was no going back. When he pounced on her mother, Beth couldn't believe it. It was scary because, by attacking her mother, he basically let her know that they knew what she was and what she was doing. Would she go after them next? Kill her nephew, maybe even her own daughter? It made Beth nervous and edgy, and it was bound to get worse. She needed to find him, and talk over their next move.

That bartender lady told him she would help them. At least, that's what she thought he'd said. She needed to find him, but didn't want anyone to know where she was going. She waited until the adults were settled in at the table with their tea before sneaking out the front door.

She wasn't sure, but she thought he had probably headed down the street towards Riff's house, but she didn't want to face Riff's parents, so she wandered over to Wolf Creek Road and started looking in all the stores. She checked the Rite-Aid, Circle K, PJ's, and The First Edition, before heading over to the town common to think about where to search next. Even though the sun was bright, it was a little cold and she could see her breath. She drew her hoodie closer and put up the hood against the chill breeze.

She sat there with her arms folded tightly against her body in an effort to keep warm. Where could he be? She checked just about everywhere she could think of. Eve-rywhere except...That's it! He had to be at the school playground, where James and Riff had spent hours and hours as little boys.

Hopping off the bench, she shoved her hands in her sweatshirt pockets to warm them, and hurried towards Wolf Creek Elementary. The playground was behind the school and jutted up to the wooded easement where Riff died.

She took the long way because the easement was roped off with crime tape. Even if it hadn't been, she wouldn't have gone that way anyway. It was way too spooky. In fact, she'd probably never go that way again.

Rounding the corner of the school, she had a clear shot of the elementary school playground. She scanned the yard, and as expected, spotted him sitting on top of the monkey bars. The sun was behind him, and for a sec-ond, he looked like a wolf, sitting on its haunches and howling up at the sky. Then she blinked, and he was just James again.

She walked over to the jungle gym and shaded her eyes against the sun. "Hey," she said quietly. She wasn't sure if he heard her or not because he didn't answer, so she said it again a little louder. "Hey."

He continued to gaze at the sky. "We spent so much time here as little kids. Did you know he was afraid of heights? Never wanted to come up here. Took me forever to get him to trust me enough to climb up here, and then when he did, he wouldn't even sit up here with me. Stood hanging on to the bars and kept his eyes closed the whole time. Finally got him up here in third grade."

She climbed up to sit next to him and appreciated how Riff felt. She didn't much like it up here either, but would do what she could to make her cousin feel better. "You guys went through a lot, didn't you?"

He nodded, tears staining his cheeks. "He wanted to be a storm chaser, you know? Loved thunderstorms, twisters, hail, stuff like that."

"Didn't know that."

"Remember that time he stood outside in the pouring rain? Started to hail golf balls, and we had to drag him inside kicking and screaming so he wouldn't get hurt."

She didn't remember, but she just nodded and let him talk.

"You were never in his room, but it's got all these pictures of lightning, really cool cloud formations. Even has a picture of this guy named Roger Jensen. Riff says he was the very first storm chaser. He has a CD with all the back issues of Storm Track magazine, and he's always making me look at something or other on the dumb thing." His voice started to crack, and he looked close to tears again. "Douche bag even has an awesome picture of a tornado as his computer wallpaper." He wiped his nose with the palm of his hand. "Had a picture."

She put her arm around him as he started to cry, huge sobs that shook them both so hard she was afraid they would fall. "It's okay," she murmured. "It's okay." She didn't know what else to say. When he laid his head on her shoulder, she squeezed him to her. Finally, when his sobs faded to sniffles, she tried to coax him down.

"Maybe we should get off this thing, go for some cocoa or something."

He wiped his eyes on her hoodie. "Riff loved hot chocolate. Especially with whipped cream."

"We could get whipped cream. Come on, let's go to PJs."

He wiped his nose on the tail of his flannel shirt. "'Kay."

After they climbed down, he turned and stared at the monkey bars. "Good bye, dude." He smiled so sadly it almost broke her heart. "You were the best friend I ever had."

She took his arm and gently pulled him around. He came willingly enough, and she was glad she'd been able to talk him down so easily. She'd been afraid he'd do something stupid.

She was right. He did. It just took a while.

Thursday, November 21, 2013

WANING GIBBOUS

Old moon
Growing smaller
87% Visible

Chapter 22

It was the day of Riff's funeral. He would've loved the weather: windy, cool, and overcast. I hadn't gone back to school because I was still numb. If it hadn't been for my mom, I would've spent the week in bed, but she got me up every morning, fixed breakfast and made sure I ate it, then parked me in front of the TV while she did her chores. At noon she would make me lunch and spend her afternoons trying to get me to play Yahtzee, checkers, Parcheesi, anything to keep my mind busy. On the third day, she offered to buy a Wii, but even that didn't hold any interest for me. It bothered me that she was taking time off just to be with me, but I didn't have the energy to tell her it wasn't working. What happened to Riff, and my guilt about not preventing it, was eating me up.

I was picking at my French toast that morning when she sat down across the table from me. "Jaime, I know this is difficult for you—"

"Difficult, Mom?"

What an understatement. It was the worst thing that ever happened to me, losing my friend to a werewolf, especially when I could have stopped it, somehow. I didn't know how, because Riff never listened to anybody, but I should have done something. Should have at least made him believe there was a werewolf. How could I explain all that to her?

She ignored my interruption and continued. "But you have to snap out of it. You can't go on like this, like some…I don't know…robot, shutting everyone down and closing yourself off. Do you think Riff would want you to do that?"

"No," I told her. "I suppose not."

"Okay, good. Now why don't you try and eat some of your breakfast? I'll go and lay out your suit for you."

"Never mind. I'm not hungry. I'll do it. I need to shine my shoes anyway."

"Are you sure?"

I nodded and headed for my old bedroom. When I got there, I closed the door and leaned against it. The last thing I wanted to do was go to my best friend's funeral. How could I get out of it? Then I sighed. I couldn't miss it, no matter what. Riff was gone, and there was nothing I could do to change that, but I could at least prevent it from happening to anyone else. I had to talk to Ms. Glass, whether she liked it or not. And I had to talk to her today. No more screwing around.

How could I approach her so she wouldn't run away again? I had to be careful, and not let anyone overhear us. Maybe we could meet somewhere after the service.

There was a knock at the door, and my mom poked her head inside the room, smiling when she saw I was shining my shoes. "Oh, good. You're getting ready." She seemed surprised as she walked over and handed me a shirt on a hanger. "I ironed your blue dress shirt for you."

"Thanks. Guess I'd better get dressed then."

"We'll be leaving for the church in about fifteen minutes."

On the way there, I leaned over to Beth. "If you see

Ms. Glass," I whispered, "try to get next to her, tell her we have to talk to her, and don't let her leave until she agrees to meet us."

"Okay, where?" she whispered back.

"Wherever she wants. Just make it today."

"What are you two whispering about?" Aunt Judy was in the front seat of Dad's old Buick, wedged in between my parents. Ever since the day I lost it, she stayed as far from me as possible, which was just fine with me.

"Nothing," Beth told her.

"Well, knock it off. It's rude."

"Sorry."

"Hey, Judy." Dad scratched his side absently. "Lighten up, will you? The boy just lost his best friend. Give the kids a break."

"I'll give them a break, all right," she muttered.

We pulled up at the church and Dad let us off in front while he went to park the car. Aunt Judy walked right on in, but Mom turned when she got to the top step. "Come inside, kids."

"We'll be right in, Mom. You go on ahead."

She started to say something, but I turned away so I could pretend not to hear her. When I looked back, she'd gone inside. We waited until right before the service started, but Ms. Glass never showed.

The church bells rang. We couldn't wait any longer. "Come on, let's go in," Beth said. "She'll be at the cemetery for sure. We'll see her then."

I hoped she was right. It might be our last chance.

☽

"The Lord is my shepherd..." Father Michael droned.

I wished I was like the rest of the town, totally oblivious to everything. I wanted to mourn my friend in peace, but my mind wouldn't let me. I kept thinking about what was going on, and wondering how to stop it.

"Surely goodness and mercy shall…"

The prayer was almost over. No sign of Ms. Glass. I glanced at Beth, and was surprised to see she was crying. I didn't think she even liked Riff, much less was sorry he was gone. Guess she wasn't such a pain after all. I looked over at Riff's family. His father was bawling his head off, his mother dabbed gently at her eyes, and his older sister shifted in the pew like she had to go to the bathroom. She didn't even seem upset.

It was all such a waste. There was no reason why Riff had to die. I watched my aunt, who sat there and pretended to be all upset. Like she really cared. My God, were those actual tears in her eyes? What a crock. Rage rose, and I didn't know how much longer I could sit there, in the same pew with the monster who murdered Riff and all those others, and not do anything.

"Amen."

Everyone watched Father Michael expectantly.

"The Wozniaks have asked me to say a few words of comfort." He gripped the sides of the Lectern and seemed to struggle for the right words. "We don't know why God chose to take Harold so young, but we must understand that he is with our Lord now and forever."

Yeah, no thanks to the hairy monster masquerading as my aunt. Someone sobbed loudly. It was Aunt Judy. That was it. I couldn't let her get away with pretending she cared.

I stood up and pointed at her. "Murderer!" I screamed. "You killed him. You killed Riff, and now I'm gonna kill you!"

I sprang toward her. Dad grabbed me and tried to

pull me back down into the pew. "What are you doing? Sit down."

Wrenching away from him, I climbed over Beth sitting on the end of the pew. Then I stumbled down the aisle and out the church doors. I almost fell down the steps but managed to catch myself at the last minute. I ran and ran until I couldn't breathe, then leaned against a tree in front of Lindy's old house. After a little while, I heard footsteps behind me and whirled around.

"Are you all right?" Beth's voice was low and soothing, and she approached me slowly, as if I were a wild animal she wanted to capture.

"Yeah, I'm okay. Pretty stupid thing to do, huh?"

"Probably not the smartest thing in the world," she agreed. "But they think you're just upset. Everyone knows how close you and Riff were."

"Yeah, but still, I shouldn't have said anything in public like that. It's just, well, I couldn't stand watching her cry like that, like she cared he was dead." I wiped my eyes on my sleeve and leaned against the tree.

She scanned the street.

"Wonder where Ms. Glass is."

"Yeah, me too. I'm dying to know what she has to say, if she's going to help us or not." I needed to find out how to kill the thing, no matter who it was. Hopefully Ms. Glass could tell me how, or help me, or something. If not, I was prepared to do it myself.

"Do you think she'll help us even if we tell her who we think it is?" Beth asked quietly.

"I don't know. Maybe we should keep that to ourselves."

"Yeah, maybe you're right. God, I wish it were somebody else."

"Me, too." I pulled on her sleeve. "Come on. We'd better get back."

"They were all heading over to the cemetery. I'm supposed to bring you over there."

We walked back toward the church, and then went around to the graveyard. Everyone was gathered around Riff's casket, and we wormed our way through the crowd until we stood next to my parents. I was super antsy, and it was hard for me to pay attention. I glanced over my shoulder several times. Where the hell was Ms. Glass?

Then I finally caught sight of her out of the corner of my eye. I nudged Beth and motioned with my head. She leaned forward slightly, saw Ms. Glass, and nodded. We slowly inched backward, trying to leave without anyone noticing.

We stood there for a minute or two to make sure no one did then turned and walked quickly away from the service and out the cemetery gate. Ms. Glass waited for us in her old beat-up Ford Ranger.

"Get in," she demanded and swung open the door on the passenger side.

We climbed in and she drove away, not slow but not fast. Just right, so as not to attract too much attention.

"It's good to see—" I started.

"Shhh," she commanded.

She turned left at the intersection and headed out of town. Beth and I looked at each other. Beth had a serious frown that brought back her unibrow.

I was concerned, too.

"Where are we—"

"Not yet." Ms. Glass didn't take her eyes off the road. "Wait."

We drove along in silence for a while. I was worried we'd be missed, but one look at our driver told me to keep my anxiety to myself. When we passed the town limits, Ms. Glass sighed audibly and her whole body seemed to relax. Even so, she drove until we reached the far side of Moonridge, the neighboring town. I almost laughed when she pulled into the parking lot at Douglas C. Wolfram Memorial Park and stopped behind a comfort station, out of sight of the road. The irony of the park's name wasn't lost on me.

"Okay, we're safe now."

"Ms. Glass, are you sure we needed to come way out here?" I glanced over at Beth. "Our parents will be wondering what happened to us."

"Of course we had to come out here. You want to be safe, don't you?" she snapped.

"Yeah, sure." I tried to calm her. "I'm just saying."

She turned and sat with her leg against the back of the seat, her arm slung over her knee. "Look, we don't have much time. Here's the scoop. Wolf Creek is full of werewolves. A whole pack of them. They've been around since right after my parents got married. Some of them are third and fourth generation."

Beth's eyes were huge as she scooted closer to me and wormed her way under my arm.

"But, how is that even possible?" I couldn't believe I'd spent my whole life surrounded by monsters and never knew.

"I'm not sure," she answered. "All's I know is that I'd hoped I'd never have to kill another one. That they'd keep their promise to my father and never go out on the hunt again."

"Another one?" Beth squeaked. "You—you mean you killed one before?"

"Never mind about all that now. You kids have access to a gun?"

"What?" I didn't like where this was going. "No."

"That's what I thought. Here." She pulled a scary-looking pistol out from behind her. It must have been tucked in her waistband.

Beth grabbed hold of my coat and pulled me away from it.

"Take it."

"No, I—I don't want it."

"Look, kid, you want to kill this thing or not?"

"Take it," Beth whispered, as white as I'd ever seen her, leaving her freckles dark against her skin, as if set in place with a black marker.

I frowned at the gun. Should I take it? Or should I forget the whole thing? Even as I questioned, I reached for the gun. No way I could forget it, if for no other reason than to make sure what happened to Riff never happened again.

I'd never touched a gun before. It was heavier than I expected. The grip was a little wide in my hand, but what did I know? I held it the same way I'd seen cops on TV do and aimed it out the windshield. I closed one eye and looked down the sight. I was just about to squeeze the trigger when a hand closed over mine and pushed the gun down onto the dashboard.

"This isn't a game," Ms. Glass warned. "Now, can you handle this thing, or not?"

I nodded.

"Good. Here's where the safety is, and this is how you release it." She showed me how it worked, then wanted me to do it. "You try."

After flipping it on and off a few times, I set it in my lap.

She pulled something out of her pocket. "Know what this is?" She handed the magazine to me, and I turned it over in my hand, then showed it to Beth.

"The bullets?" I reached for the magazine, but Ms. Glass just nodded and pushed my hand onto my lap.

"This magazine holds seven slugs. Seven very special bullets."

"Silver bullets."

"That's right." She nodded. "When I left town awhile back, I went to see someone who could make them for me and not ask questions."

"So how does this thing go in?" I tapped the magazine lightly against the bottom of the handle.

"Like this." She shoved it into the grip, then released it. "Now you."

I tried it a few times, until it felt comfortable. Then she handed me three more magazines. "Here, take these. Go out into the woods and practice somewhere where no one'll hear you. Use all twenty-one bullets in these mags. But you see the red 'X' on this one?"

I looked at what she pointed to and nodded.

"This is the one with the silver bullets. Hide it somewhere where no one will find it, or the gun."

"So how will we go after the werewolf?" Beth came out from under my coat and sat on the edge of the seat. "And when?"

"Okay, here's the deal." Ms. Glass peered out the windshield, pointing at the sky. "The next full moon cycle starts December seventeenth. A Tuesday. I'll have someone call your parents with some excuse to get them out of the house. After what you did at the funeral, it'll be coming for you."

"Oh." My throat was suddenly very dry. "You saw that?" How I wished I was kicking back in a booth at PJ's, slurping one of Diane's root beer floats, oblivious to the whole thing. "Guess it was a pretty stupid thing to do."

Beth patted my arm. "It's okay."

"Doesn't matter now. It would've come for you eventually anyway," Ms. Glass continued. "So, we'll sit up and wait for it. Then you'll get your chance to kill it."

With a really ugly chuckle, she pulled out the biggest

gun I'd ever seen and waved it back and forth in front of me. Her eyes had glazed over and it made me wonder what I'd gotten myself into, and with what kind of freak.

"Damn," Beth whispered.

"Meet my friend, Smitty. Smith and Wesson Magnum .500, the biggest, baddest gun on the planet. If this doesn't stop the damn thing, nothing will."

It reminded me of the old Looney Tune cartoons where the coyote chased the roadrunner and pulled a gun out of his pocket that was as big as he was. Before I realized what she was doing, she opened the cylinder and popped out some nasty-looking cartridges. She held one up for us to see. "Sucker's the most powerful cartridge out there. Fifty caliber. Explodes on impact."

"But," I said, puzzled. "That looks like a regular bullet. A really big bullet. But still. Don't you have any silver ones?"

She shoved them back into the cylinder and put the gun back into her pocket. "'Fraid not, kiddo."

"Why not?"

She eyeballed me a minute, as if deciding what she wanted to say. Then she reached out and put her hand on my shoulder. "This is something you have to do yourself. So that when you find another one, you'll know exactly what to do."

My throat burned. I swallowed, but there was no spit to soothe it. "Another one?" Sometimes my voice cracked at the worst times.

She started the Ranger and let it idle for a minute. Then she turned to me. "You're a born hunter, kid. Once you've found one, chances are you'll run into others. Just like I have." She put the truck in gear. "Now, we'd better get you two back before someone misses you."

How many monsters were out there? And how many would I have to kill before I felt safe again?

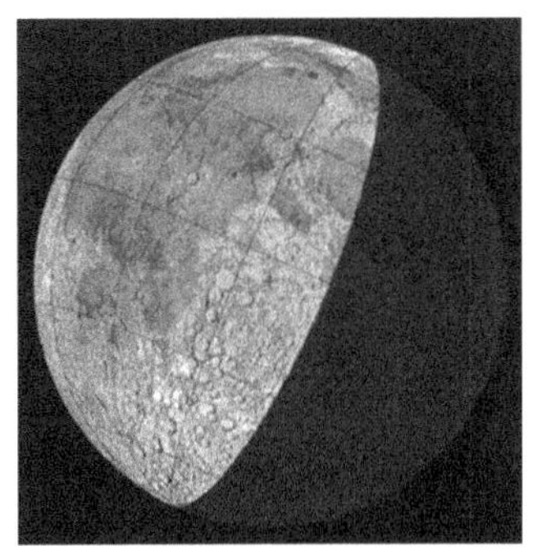

Saturday, November 23, 2013

WANING GIBBOUS
OLD MOON
GROWING SMALLER
72% VISIBLE

Chapter 23

Two days later, Beth bolted through the door, out of breath. "Guess what?"

"Hey, slow down." I didn't even bother to look up from the TV. "Catch your breath. Sit a spell."

"What are you, a Beverly Hillbilly?" She was still breathing hard. "Seriously. You'll never guess what Mom and I heard at the real estate lady's office." After my accusations, Aunt Judy decided to move, and she and my mom spent a lot of time hunting for a place.

"Let me guess. You found a place to move."

"No. Worse."

That caught my attention. We both regretted my stupidity at Riff's funeral. For a long time, I wanted nothing more than to be rid of my annoying cousin. Not now though, not when we were almost ready to go on the hunt. "Worse than moving out?"

She grabbed the remote and flipped off the television. "Much worse."

"Hey, what do you think you're doing?" I tried to grab the remote away, but she held it out of my reach.

"Will you shut up and listen to me? For once?"

"Okay." I was getting more than a little exasperated with her games. "Just tell me already."

She tossed the remote on the coffee table. "You'll never guess in a million years."

I was about a nanosecond away from punting her like a football. "Beth, I swear to God."

"Okay, okay." She waved her palms at me and took a deep breath. "Here goes. James, they fired him."

I sat up and took notice. I didn't like where this was heading. "Fired who?"

"The sheriff. They recalled the sheriff." She stuck her lower lip out so far it almost turned inside out.

"They what?" I couldn't believe it. Did he lose his job because of what we told him? Because he actually believed us?

"They canned him."

"Oh, my God. That's—"

"Wait," she interrupted. "That's not the worst of it."

"What? There's more?"

"Riggs is the new sheriff. At least until they elect someone else."

"Oh, that's just great." If he was unbearable before, I didn't want to think about how much more of a douche Riggs would be now that he actually had power to go with his arrogance.

"So what do we do now?"

"I have no idea."

Thursday, November 28, 2013
Thanksgiving

WANING CRESCENT

Old moon
Growing smaller
24% Visible

Chapter 24

It was Thanksgiving Day, but Beth didn't have much to be thankful for. Her mother was a monster, and as if that wasn't bad enough, her aunt found them a place all the way on the other side of town. They were moving there in the morning. Beth was scared to be alone with her mother, and she was supposed to up and leave the only place she felt safe and go move into a tiny room in some stranger's house where they'd have to sleep in the same bed? It wasn't fair.

She sat next to James and grimaced when he elbowed her in the side. "What?"

He pointed across the table, and she looked over at her uncle.

"I said, pass the taters, puppy." He was smiling at her, but his eyes were narrowed and dark, and there was a funny expression on his face. Was he trying to read her mind? If so, she doubted he'd like what was there.

"Sorry." She picked up the huge blue glass bowl with what was left of the mashed potatoes. After passing it over, she took the cloth napkin off her lap and wiped the corners of her mouth.

"May I please be excused?" She expected her mother to yell at her. "I'll clear the table when everyone's done."

"Don't worry about helping out tonight, honey," her mother told her. "You and Jaime go have some fun."

Beth almost fell out of her chair. Since when was her mother nice to her? She couldn't remember the last time she told Beth to have fun. Something was up, but she wasn't sure what. It might just be that she knew how much Beth didn't want to move and was actually sorry that they were, but she didn't think that was it. Maybe James would know.

"Hey, cuz, wait up." He pushed away from the table and stood up.

"I don't recall hearing you ask to be excused." Uncle Robbie's voice was stern but his eyes twinkled.

"Okay, can I be excused?"

"Fine. Just stick close to the house, and be back by four."

"Whatever. Come on," James said to Beth. "Let's go for a walk."

They walked in silence for about a block. She looked over her shoulder several times, half expecting her mother to follow them. "James." It was all she could do to keep from crying. "I'm scared. What if she kills me one night in my sleep?"

"Take it easy. She won't do anything to you at home. That'd be a little too obvious, don't you think?"

"I know, but still…"

"There's nothing to worry about."

"Did I tell you I found out that werewolves can control their transformation after a while, and change anytime they want to? Doesn't have to be a full moon. They just have to practice."

"I know. You told me, but so far as we know, she's only transformed during a full moon. Why would she change things now?"

She thought about it. "I don't know," she admitted.

"But just knowing she could scares the hell out of me."

They walked along in silence for a few minutes. She didn't realize where they were going until James suddenly stopped. She started to ask what was wrong, when she heard how hard he was breathing. He was staring straight ahead, and she turned to see what he was looking at. The electrical easement, the place where they found Riff, loomed ahead of them.

"Come on," she whined. "Let's go back."

"No." He took a deep breath. "Wait here."

She watched him trot across the street and up the hill. He stopped well before the piece of yellow police tape hanging off a tree branch and checked to see if anyone was watching, then plunged into the bushes. *What is he doing?* She swung her arms back and forth, occasionally banging her hands together, and scanned the street several times while she waited. Hopefully, no one would come by and ask questions.

After a few minutes, the bushes rustled. It made her nervous, but she wasn't going anywhere without James. He climbed out of the underbrush and waved.

"Where'd you go?" She bounced nervously on the balls of her feet. "What were you doing in there?"

He patted his jacket pocket. "Went to get Smitty's little brother."

"The gun?"

"Yep."

"What're you going to do with it? Shoot it?"

He nodded. "Come on, let's go over to Horseshoe Meadow. It's pretty secluded there. No one will ever hear anything. If we hurry, I'll have time to practice a bit before we have to get back."

As much as she wanted to hunt down and kill the werewolf, she was starting to have second thoughts about him shooting a gun at the thing. What if he missed and it killed him? Or worse, what if it bit him and turned him into one?

"I don't want to. Let's just forget it."

"Are you nuts? We might not get another chance to practice with this thing before the next full moon. It's now or never."

"No. I'm scared. Let's go back and have some pumpkin pie."

"Hey." He shook her hand off his arm. "If you want to chicken out, fine. Go home, you big baby, but I'm going to see this through to the end. She's going to pay for what she did to Riff."

"But—"

"I can't believe you." He walked away a few steps before turning back to her. He jabbed his finger at her. "You're the one who started this whole thing, convincing me there was a werewolf in town. You even made me believe it was your mother. Now you want to back out? Forget the whole thing? You're unbelievable, you know that?"

"Wait. Listen."

"No. I have nothing else to say to you. Leave me alone." He turned and walked quickly down the street.

She stood there and watched him go, wishing with all her heart none of this had ever happened. She sat down on the curb and cried.

When she finished, she wiped her eyes and headed down the street to where her cousin practiced killing a monster.

And whatever fate awaited her.

Tuesday, December 17, 2013

FULL MOON

Rises at midnight and
is the highest at dawn
100% Visible

Chapter 25

The day we were waiting for was cold and there were fluffy white clouds in the morning that grew darker as the day wore on. Right before three in the afternoon, it poured. Just in time for Beth and me to get soaked on our way home from school. We tried to fake stomachaches to stay home from school and get together at some point early in the day to plan exactly what we needed to do that night. Unfortunately, neither my mom, nor hers, fell for it. As soon as school was over, I ran to the elementary school to wait for Beth. Standing under a huge tree at the edge of the building, I pulled up my collar and tried to stay as dry as possible. *How come I never have a hood when I need one?* Secretly I hoped she remembered her umbrella.

It wasn't long before kids streamed out onto the sidewalk. I anxiously scanned the sea of umbrellas, finally spotting a pair of thick, brown Wendy's Hamburger girl braids underneath a red, polka dot umbrella, and called out. "Hey, Beth, over here."

She was obviously miserable, and the bags under her eyes were the color of a rotten banana skin. Her shoulders drooped and she walked like her feet weighed a ton. She wouldn't look at me.

What could I say to make her feel better? I was having a hard time with everything, too.

"Hey, James." She blew out a long, slow breath. "How you doing?" She held the umbrella up so I could duck under it.

For a second I hoped no one would see me, then decided I didn't really care.

"Thanks. I'm okay, I guess."

"Yeah, me too. Today's the big day, eh?" Her voice was low and monotone.

I shrugged, and we walked along in silence, something we'd done a lot lately. We were supposed to meet Ms. Glass at The Quiet Riot at three fifteen, and we made it to within a block of the bar when Beth stopped. Was she having second thoughts again?

"What's wrong?" I asked.

"We're really doing this, aren't we?"

"Unless you're too chicken, then I'll just do it myself."

Fire flashed behind her eyes. "I'm scared, but I'm not chickening out. I just wish things were different, that's all." She ran the toe of her boot along the edge of the sidewalk. "Plus, I don't know what'll happen to me after—you know. You know?"

It hit me then what she must be going through. God, to know you're about to lose your mother and be responsible for her death? What a horrible thing to have to deal with. I doubted I could do it. I put my arm around her shoulders. She was nothing but skin and bones. If we were lucky and managed to survive the night, it was my hope she could get past this and go back to being the cute little shit who annoyed me so much, like she used to be.

"I know. It'll be okay. You'll stay with us."

She smiled, even as tears welled, but looked fiercely determined to not let them spill out, and to do what needed to be done. "We'd better get going. Ms. Glass'll be wondering—"

Out of nowhere, Riggs appeared in front of us. "Where do you two think you're going?" He casually put one hand on his hip while the other gripped his holster. As usual, his bigheaded attitude practically oozed from his pores.

Shit. We didn't have time for this.

"We're just going to the Rite Aid for an ice cream cone."

He flashed his cheesy grin, lifted his chin to peer down his nose at us, and then jerked his head at something behind us. "Rite Aid's the other way."

"Come on, Deputy." I tried something my dad advised. I appealed to his so-called sense of fair play. Something I seriously doubted Riggs had, but it was worth a shot. "We're not hurting anyone, just minding our own business." I wanted to suggest he do the same, but bit my tongue instead.

"You're hurting me. I got to look at your ugly face. Now, I asked you a question. Where do you think you're going? Hmm?"

"None of your beeswax," Beth piped up and tried to get around him.

Big man grabbed her arm and squeezed. That did it. How dare he touch a little girl? Who did he think he was? Reacting, I pushed him as hard as I could. Since he was already off-balance, and I caught him off-guard, he went down. Hard. It happened so fast, neither Beth nor I had time to laugh before he sprang back and slammed me against the wall. He rammed my head into the stucco so hard it left dents in my face and hurt like hell. Riggs pulled my arms behind me and jammed his knee into the small of my back.

"Leave him alone. You're hurting him," she screamed and punched him.

Riggs snickered and pushed her down. He pulled out his handcuffs and closed them around my wrists before jerking me backward. I barely managed to stay on my feet as he shoved me up against the wall again and leaned in to whisper in my ear.

"Got you this time, you little maggot. Assaulting an officer. That's big time, baby. You're going down." His breath smelled like rotten meat, and I gagged, managing to swallow the bile without losing it. I wasn't about to give him the satisfaction.

"Let him go, Riggs."

Riggs whirled around but still kept me pinned to the wall.

"Sheriff, he tried to go for my gun when I asked him where he was going," Riggs lied. "Then he threw a punch."

"I said, let him go. I was standing right here. Saw the whole thing. Now, take off the cuffs."

Riggs glared at Sheriff Brazelton, started to say something but changed his mind. As he took off the cuffs, he growled softly, "This isn't over, punk. Not by a long shot."

I rubbed first one wrist, then the other. Beth wiped the mud from her jeans. Riggs put his handcuffs back on his duty belt.

Sheriff Brazelton took a step towards Riggs. "Go back to the office, Deputy."

"You have no authority anymore." Riggs adjusted his duty belt and sniffed. "I'm the acting sheriff now."

Sheriff Brazelton drew himself up to his full height and appeared to tower over Riggs, even though he was probably only a few inches taller. "You got it wrong,

Riggs. I'm still the sheriff of Wolf Creek. At least until the thirty-first."

Beth and I exchanged glances. I could tell by her face she was just as surprised to see him as I was. Maybe, if we managed to kill the werewolf, he could get his job back and the town wouldn't be stuck with the likes of Riggs as top cop.

"I suggest," the sheriff continued, "you do as you're told. We'll talk about this when I get back." When Riggs didn't respond, he added, "Now."

He watched Riggs strut down the street, like he was too important to use the sidewalk, and kept watching until the deputy disappeared inside the sheriff's office. Only then did the sheriff turn to me. "Are you okay?"

"Yeah." I rubbed my wrists. "I'm fine."

"Sure?"

"Yeah, I'm sure."

"How about you, little lady?" Without waiting for an answer, he squatted to wipe some mud off the toe of her boot. "Too bad you didn't get a chance to hit him over the head with your umbrella, eh?"

That broke the tension, and we all laughed. "You best be getting on home now."

I started to tell him that we had to see someone, but thought better of it. I didn't want to explain what we had planned only to have him try to stop us. Plus, we didn't have time anyway. We had to figure out some way to get to the bar without anyone else interfering.

Before it was too late.

☽

As it turned out, we didn't go to the bar, it came to us. Or rather, Ms. Glass did. We'd gone about three more blocks until we were far enough to double back so no one would notice us, when her ancient Ford Ranger pulled up and slowly paced us. The window on the passenger side rolled down and we heard her voice from within the depths of the cab. "There you are. Get in."

Beth and I exchanged glances. She shrugged. I opened the door and she climbed in. Getting in after her, I barely had time to shut the door before the tires squealed and we were off. This time, neither one of us spoke. We waited for Ms. Glass to start. Beth got antsy and shifted back and forth in her seat. I was nervous, too, and picked at a thread hanging from my backpack.

Finally, after what seemed like a week, she spoke.

"You guys ready?"

Beth nodded.

"What about you?" She studied me a few seconds before turning her attention back to the road.

"I'm ready, I guess. It's just—"

"Just nothing," she snapped. "Either we're doing this or we aren't. You have to be sure you can go through with it. Otherwise, one of us is gonna get hurt. As it is, we'll be lucky if we don't all die tonight."

"Ms. Glass?"

"Might as well call me Donna. I guess I should be on a first name basis with anyone I hunt werewolves with."

"Okay." I shrugged. "Donna. Why are you doing this?" It was something I wondered ever since the first day she dragged me into the crypt.

"Well, it's a long story. Suffice it to say, I've always known this day would come, ever since I was a kid just about your age." She jutted her head in Beth's direction. "My grandpa used to tell me stories about werewolves he knew, how some of them can go bad. Those are the ones we hunters take care of."

"Hunters? Plural? You mean there are others?"

"Not many, but enough to get the job done."

That there were actually people out there, like those guys on that show *Supernatural*—who not only knew werewolves were real, but hunted them down and killed them—blew me away. What kind of twisted world did we live in? Next thing you know, she'd tell me that vampires and the boogeyman were real, too.

"So what's the plan for tonight?" It was the first time Beth spoke.

I'd been so lost in thought I'd almost forgotten she was even there. "Yeah, have you figured out how to get my parents out of the house for the night?"

"They'll get a call about midnight telling them your aunt was in a bad accident and is dying in the hospital. It won't come for you until well after midnight, anyway."

Beth twirled a strand of hair between her fingers. "How are we going to get me to James's?"

"Your mom will get a similar call about his parents. Is your landlord still on that business trip?"

Beth nodded.

"Good." Donna studied her. "Your mom'll have no choice but to drop you off for him to watch. If she wants you to go anywhere else, you need to pitch a fit. Can you do that?"

"Oh, she can do that, all right."

Beth punched me in the arm.

I waved her off with my elbow. "Then what?"

Something ran across the road right in front of us, and Donna slammed on the brakes. The truck careened crazily all over the wet road. I threw my hands up and stopped myself before I banged into the dashboard.

"Everyone okay?" Donna stopped the car and shifted into park but left the engine running.

"I'm okay." I turned to Beth. "You all right?"

She wasn't. Blood dripped down her forehead as she

groaned and leaned forward. She raised her hand as if to touch her head, then it fell limply to her side.

"You're bleeding," I cried. "Oh my God, you're hurt!"

Donna calmly put one hand over the wound and the other on the back of Beth's head. "Reach into the glove box and get me the napkins."

"Shouldn't we take her to the hospital? I think we should take her to the hospital."

"First things first. We need to apply pressure to the wound, so it'll stop bleeding. Now get me the napkins."

I reached in and pulled out a wad of Dairy Queen napkins. "This enough?"

"That's fine." Donna was silent long enough for me to look over at her. An attempt to make sure she had my attention, I think. "Now, I'm going to take my hand away from her head. You take half the stack and put them right on the spot where she's bleeding. Then I want you to hold her head just like I am now. Hard. When the blood soaks through, I want you to toss the dirty napkins on the floor and put more clean ones on as quickly as you can. Can you do that for me?"

I nodded. We made the switch. At first, I was afraid I was hurting her, but then realized she passed out and wasn't feeling much of anything. It scared me and I forgot about everything else except for helping her.

Donna put the Ranger into gear and carefully checked the windows, first to the left, then the right, then back again, just like they teach you when you're six and crossing the street. She slowly let up on the brake and we rolled forward a few feet. "Look's like it's all clear."

Beth's blood had soaked through and I changed out the dirty napkins. Her breath was shallow and her face was deathly white.

"We'd better get her to the hospital." Donna accelerated and headed toward the hospital. "She may need a stitch or two." She probably needed more than two, but I was too busy praying she wouldn't die.

A loud crash ruptured the air around us. The truck fishtailed on the slick pavement again and I fought to keep Beth upright. Before the noise registered in my brain, there was another crash on the other side, and we spun out of control.

"What's happening?" I screamed.

The truck jumped the curb and slammed into a light pole. My elbow crashed through the window, hurting worse than anything I'd ever felt. When I looked over at Donna, I gasped. Her head must have hit the windshield because there was a great big hole in it and she was slumped over on her side.

"Donna?"

No answer. I couldn't tell how badly she was hurt. With Beth already unconscious and sprawled in the middle of the seat, I needed to get out and go around the other side to check on Donna. I laid Beth gently down on the seat and kissed her cheek. "I'll be right back, Beth. You'll be okay." I stumbled out of the cab. "Please don't be dead," I whispered. "Please don't be dead." I ran around the back, noting both sides of the bed were crumpled beyond repair. What hit us so hard? Grabbing the door handle on Donna's side, I pulled. It wouldn't budge. The doorframe was all out of whack, and there was no way the door would open.

Peeking through the window, I stared at Donna. Her scalp was torn open and there was blood everywhere. I didn't know what to do. My cousin was unconscious and the only adult nearby could be dead, for all I knew.

I reached through a hole in the broken window and gingerly shook Donna's shoulder.

"Donna? Donna, are you okay?"

There was no response. I had to get help. But how? Neither Beth nor I had a cell phone. Maybe Donna did? The thought of touching what might be a dead body again freaked me out, but I grimaced, closed my eyes, and reached into the pocket of her flannel shirt to see if she had one. No luck. Frantic by this time, I backed away from the Ranger and ran up the street.

"Help! Help!" After about half a block, I turned and ran the other way. "Help us! Someone, please!" It was no use. There wasn't anyone around. Running back to the truck, I heard moans coming from inside the cab. Maybe Donna wasn't dead after all. What did I know?

Turned out she was just shaken up. She'd regained consciousness and was trying to sit up. "Ow, that hurts," she said and leaned back in the seat.

"I thought you were dead." I didn't mean it to be an accusation, but that's the way it came out.

"No such luck. Takes more than a car wreck to take me out. Oh, man." She rubbed the back of her head. "Did you get the number of the moving van that hit us?"

"I'm not sure what hit us, but I don't think it was a moving van."

"That was a joke, kid."

"Oh. Sorry."

"'S'okay." A flap of torn scalp hung down over her left eye, and she tucked it back up on top of her head. "You can redeem yourself by helping me out of this thing."

"Well, that may be a problem. I can't get the door open."

She turned to look at Beth and groaned. Her hand flew to her neck as she grimaced. "How's your cousin doing?"

"Not so good."

"We better get her to the hospital. Fast." She plucked

several loose glass shards out of the weather-stripping and dropped them on the street. "I think we can get this sucker open if I push while you pull. You game?"

I nodded and grabbed the handle with both hands. It was really slippery from the rain. Donna leaned back and wedged both feet against the door. "On three. One. Two. Three!" We both nearly stroked out, we were straining so hard, but it didn't budge.

"Okay, stop. Stop." Blood ran down her forehead and she swiped at it with her sleeve. I leaned against the truck bed, exhausted, and rubbed my stinging elbow only to realize the sleeve of my jacket was soaked with blood. There wasn't time to worry about it.

Donna pulled herself out of the window and jumped lightly onto the street. She reached down and brushed off her pant leg. "More than one way to skin a cat."

Reaching back inside the cab, she pulled a small box out from somewhere. Who knew where she'd hidden it because I'd never seen it before. Maybe under her seat? Opening it, she pulled out a talkie and held it up for my inspection. "Just in case. We better call an ambulance for Beth, before it comes back to finish the job."

It? Did she think that the werewolf had caused the crash? Even more importantly, what would the accident do to our plans for tonight? It was crazy. Then again, the whole day had been crazy. Hell, this whole thing was crazy.

☽

Even though she was unconscious and we were all scared for her, Beth's being in the hospital made my life easier.

Not only did it give Donna and me a legitimate reason for everyone to be out of the house when things were set to go down, but now I wouldn't have to worry about Beth getting in the way.

We sat around her hospital bed. At least, my parents and I were there. No one knew where Aunt Judy was. Probably out doing whatever it was that werewolves did right before they transformed, but my parents were pissed. Especially my mom.

"How can she not be here?" Mom sat next to Beth and held her hand. Tears made her mascara run in dark streaks. "Her baby's in the hospital, and we can't even get a hold of her to let her know. What kind of mother goes off and doesn't tell anyone how she can be reached?"

"Oh, honey." Dad patted her shoulder. "How could she know something like this would happen?"

"And you." She whirled around in her chair and glared at me. "What in the world were you two doing with Donna Glass, anyway?"

I'd wracked my brain for an excuse because I'd known the question was coming. Nothing doable came to mind. I was stuck.

"Well?" she demanded.

There was no way she was going to give me a break on this one.

"I can't tell you."

"What do you mean, you can't tell me?"

"I'm sorry, Mom, I just can't." How could I explain we were supposed to team up with Donna to kill a werewolf? She'd have me committed to the psych ward for sure.

"James Robert Mannaro, you tell me right this minute what you were doing with her."

I shook my head and slumped down in my chair. Grounding was sure to be handed out, but I didn't care. I turned to my father. "Dad, you can understand why I can't tell you what's going on, can't you? You always taught me that a man's got to do what a man's got to do, right?"

She started to rise out of her chair, but Dad gently pushed her back down. What he was thinking? He sure wasn't saying anything.

So I pushed on.

"I don't mean to be rude, but I need you guys to back off on this one."

He crossed his arms and appeared to mull it over. "Why should we?"

"Because I'm asking you to trust me. There's something I need to do, and I have to do it with Donna Glass. I promise you, it's nothing bad."

Then I stopped talking. They were either going to stay out of it, or they were going to make it difficult. Either way, I was going to go through with it. It wasn't like I had a choice.

Dad studied me. I tried not to fidget. I wanted him to think I was entirely confident and at ease with what needed to be done, even if he didn't know what that was.

After forever, he turned back to Mom. "He's a pretty level-headed kid, Annette. I'm sure whatever he thinks is so important that he do is nothing like what happened with the windows." He turned to me. "Is it?"

"No. Like I said, it's nothing bad, I promise."

"Okay, then, we'll let it go this time." He couldn't help but see the daggers shooting from Mom's eyes. He wore a tiny smile, one I almost missed. "We're putting our trust in you, Jaime. Don't let us down."

"I won't." I swallowed, hard. "I have to do it now. Tonight."

Dad raised an eyebrow and Mom scowled, but neither one said anything.

I plunged ahead. "Donna's still waiting in the lobby. I'm going to have her drive me home."

Mom turned back to Beth and rubbed her arm.

Dad cocked his head to one side and studied me with the same funny expression he had on his face when I attacked Aunt Judy. It seemed to take forever before he answered. "Does this have anything to do with what you were doing when you crashed this afternoon?"

I nodded. Dad scrutinized my face. Would he understand once the truth came out? His stare made me uncomfortable, and I shifted nervously.

"Okay," he agreed. "We'll likely stay here all night, or at least until Judy shows up. Will you be okay?"

"Sure, Dad. I'm not a little kid, you know."

"No, I guess you're not, are you?"

He smiled, and I grinned back. Something passed between us, something unspoken, and I knew from then on, he would never again treat me like a kid. I was a man now, and I had to do what I could to protect my family, no matter the cost.

"So, I think I'll go now."

I came up behind my mom and kissed her on top of the head. She patted my cheek. Things would be okay between us. I took hold of my cousin's hand and squeezed it. "You get better, Beth, hear me?" The doctors said she probably couldn't hear us, but I could have sworn she squeezed me back. I leaned over and whispered in her ear. "When you wake up, it'll all be over. You'll see. Everything's going to be okay. I promise." I hoped it was one I could keep.

Taking the elevator down to the lobby, I was glad to be away from the smell of antiseptic and sickness. As soon as the elevator doors opened, I spotted Donna. Despite her small size, she was hard to miss, especially with the big bandage covering her scalp. She paced across one side of the room, kicking the wall when she came to it, then turned to pace back to the other wall, and kicked it as hard as she had the first one. I watched her with fascination. It was sort of like a tennis match, or one of those ancient Pong games.

When she saw me, she abandoned her march. "How's your cousin? How's Beth?"

"Still unconscious. The doctors say the next twenty-four hours are critical."

"How's her mother taking it?"

"Funny thing," I replied. "They can't seem to find her."

"They can't? Anyone know where she is? Work, maybe?"

"Aunt Judy doesn't work, just sits around watching talk shows all day." Should I tell her what Beth thought about her mother? Since we were in this thing to the end, I figured I might as well. Grabbing Donna's arm, I tried to take her outside so no one could hear us talking.

First she glared at me, then at my hand. "Get your hand off me. Now."

"Sor-ree." I pulled my hand away as quickly as I could, before she bit it off. "I just wanted to tell you something in private."

She shook her head and clicked her tongue. "Sorry, kid. I don't like to be touched, is all."

"Whatever. Come on, let's go." I walked out the automatic double doors and into the crisp night, heading straight for her falling-apart Ranger, amazed it was still drivable. The hospital doors opened behind me. I stuck my hands in my pockets and whistled a few notes. I knew she would follow me.

☽

Donna and I sat in my living room. The gun she gave me lay across my lap, loaded with the silver bullets. Smitty was tucked loosely into her jeans and a bottle of Ibuprofen sat on the coffee table in front of us. She'd dry-swallowed a couple to take the edge off the pain of the stitches in her scalp. The doctor gave her a prescription for painkillers, but she wouldn't take them, saying they'd make her too fuzzy. *It's a Wonderful Life* played low on the TV but neither one of us was actually watching it. It was after midnight, every light in the house was on, and we hadn't said a word for over an hour.

The silence was starting to get to me.

"Hey, Donna?"

"Yeah?"

"What did you mean back there?"

"Back where?" She yawned and stretched. "What're you talking about?"

"After we crashed. You know, before you called the paramedics? You said something about 'it' coming back to finish the job. What did you mean by that?"

She concentrated on the television and didn't answer my question.

"Donna?"

"Look, kid." Her eyes never left the TV. "Give it a rest, will you?"

"I can't. I have to know what you meant."

"I'm tired and don't want to talk about it."

This was so frustrating. We'd come all this way, and now she didn't want to share anything?

I couldn't let it go. "Beth said there doesn't have to be a full moon like everyone thinks. They can change any time they want to. Is that true?"

Donna glared then shook her head and sighed. "Not at first. It takes a while before they figure it out. Usually, by that time, they're a few years older than you."

"Huh?" That was confusing. She made it sound like a person was born a werewolf. But how was that possible?

"Let me tell you the facts of life, kid. You know how all the movies and books and stuff say that you have to be bitten by a werewolf to become one?"

I nodded.

"Not true. That's just what they want us to believe."

"Us? You mean people?"

"Human beings. It's a rumor they started after the first werewolf movie came out, before talkies. It was all about these people who used magic to turn themselves into wolves to avenge some wrong. They could become human whenever they wanted, and then switch back into a wolf at will."

"That's so lame."

"Actually, it's the truth. The Native Americans believe it and even have a legend about it."

"So, what you're saying is that we've been pretty lucky so far that it hasn't been able to change without a full moon?"

Donna shook her head and smiled sadly. "Don't kid yourself. It could've changed whenever it wanted to. It just chooses not to."

I gulped. Shivers crawled up and down my back and my arms broke out in goose bumps. We could've been wolf chow at any time. I couldn't wait for this night to be over. Let the monster come already.

After a few minutes, Donna turned to me again. "Ever heard of the Wolf Moon?"

I shook my head.

"It's next month," she said. "According to Indian lore, wolves howled at the moon every January and tried to get into the places where people huddled to stay warm."

I grabbed the remote and muted the television. "Why January?"

"Because January's the coldest month of the year. People typically become slow with the cold and the werewolf becomes stronger."

"Wait, what?" Something occurred to me when she mentioned the part about them being strong. "Does that mean—"

"It means," she interrupted, "that if we don't take this thing down now, tonight, then we might as well dig graves for everyone in town. It'll be unstoppable once the Wolf Moon rises."

"Oh, my God." If I thought I was sick before, I was almost terminal now.

"Exactly," she agreed. "But don't worry. You won't miss."

"How can you be so sure?"

"Because you have heart, and because you're smart. And, most importantly, because you don't have a choice."

"Oh, great." That was a real confidence booster. The fate of the entire town rested in the hands of a scared fourteen-year-old. They say a hero is someone with the courage to act the way they have to no matter how scared they are. I didn't want to be a hero. I just wanted to make it through the night.

$$\mathbb{D}$$

It ran from its human lair in wolf form, then transformed back into a human in order to fully comprehend what was being said inside. Did they know who it was? They knew tonight was the night, but what fun it was having eavesdropping on their pathetic chatter. The stupid humans actually thought they would prevail, that they would be able to kill it.

Let them think that all they want. As a human, it was smarter than people gave it credit for. As a werewolf, it was nearly invincible. Crouched beneath the window, it listened to the boy and the hunter as the hunter explained about the power of the Wolf Moon. That made it sneer. There was so much they didn't understand about it, about its strength, its power.

Its hunger for human flesh.

☽

I must have fallen asleep, because when the gun nearly slipped off my lap I woke with a start. Images from the muted television flickered, and, for a minute, I wasn't sure where I was. It all came back to me in a rush. "Shit. All we need is for me to accidentally shoot this thing off before the werewolf even gets here."

"I'm beginning to think it's not coming." Donna yawned and stretched for what seemed like the thirty-seventh time that night. "It's after four in the morning."

"But it has to come tonight. It just has to." I sniffed and wiped my nose with my sleeve.

"Don't get all weepy on me, kid."

"Damn it, my name is James." It was all I could take. We'd wasted a whole night waiting for the stupid thing to come when it was probably curled up in bed, sound asleep like I wanted to be. And I was really tired of being called kid. "Call me James or don't call me at all."

"Okay, okay. Crap. I'm just saying there's roughly two hours left until sunrise, so it's probably toying with us, trying to catch us off-guard. It's probably waiting for the Wolf Moon."

"No, it'll come." I hoped I sounded more sure than I felt.

"Look, kid—I mean James. I'm going to call it a night." She stood up, jammed her gun into her waistband, stretched, and then headed for the front door.

"But, you can't leave. The moon isn't even down yet."

She checked her watch, a big black thing dwarfing her wrist. "It's nearly four-thirty. I'm telling you, it's not coming."

"Just look out the window, at the moon. Please?" Over the years, I'd found that when nothing else worked, a whine was a good last resort.

"Are you serious?"

I nodded.

She sighed, shook her head, and went to the window. She pulled the blinds apart and peered outside. "There. See? I'm looking. Nothing there. As far as the moon still being up, so what? It'll be morning soon, and the sun will be up."

"But the moon's still there, right?"

"Yes, it's still up." She turned from the window to face me. "But it's almost down."

"Just another fifteen minutes?" I begged. "Please?"

"Fine." She leaned against the windowsill. "But not a minute longer."

☽

You won't have to wait even that long. Barely able to contain its laughter, it triumphantly transformed into its true self. The werewolf snarled as bloodlust coursed through its veins.

Twice as strong as a human, it was nearly inde-structible now. Instinct kicked in and took control. It couldn't wait to get to the humans on the other side of the window.

The werewolf's humanity was completely gone.

☽

"This is ridiculous. I've had it." Donna walked away from the window after about ten minutes scowling so hard I was afraid she would hit me. Instead, she put her hands on my shoulders and leaned into my face. "I'm going to go home, pour myself a beer, and then pass out on my bed. My nice, soft bed. You should do the same."

"But you said—"

"I know what I said, but I was wrong. It's not coming. Not tonight anyway." She headed for the front door.

I scrambled after her and blocked her way. "What if I say no? What if I don't let you go?" It was all bravado. True, I was two or three inches taller than her, but I'd never be able to stop her if she really wanted to go through me.

"Then I'll be forced to kick your ass." She stood there with her arms crossed, Smitty peeking out from underneath her flannel shirt. Would she use it on me? She followed my gaze and chuckled. "What, this?" She gestured at the gun.

I stood my ground, even as I sensed this wouldn't have a happy ending if I kept pushing.

"Don't look so worried." She tossed the gun onto the couch and pushed her sleeves up her arms. "I don't need a weapon to take down a little creep like you. Now, move out of my way."

I moved away. She headed for the couch. When she bent down to pick up the gun, a dark shape passed in front of the window.

"Shit," I yelled. "It's here. I saw it. I saw it!"

"Hold on." She turned toward me, gun in hand. "What exactly did you see?"

"The werewolf. I saw the werewolf."

She pushed me out of the way and carefully pulled the blinds apart, studying the street. "I don't see anything."

The lights went out. I think I screamed. It was so dark, and I couldn't see anything except the window. When I backed away from it, I bumped into the entry table, knocking over the family portrait we took when I was about five. The glass shattered. I squinted to see through the gloom when a hand grabbed my shoulder. I screamed and tried to wriggle away.

"Don't panic," Donna whispered into my ear, sounding as scared as I was. "It could just be a fuse."

"No, it's here." I was positive, even if I'd only seen its shadow. Somehow, I could sense it close by. "It's right outside."

As if to prove me right, there was a loud scratch on the window. Then a howl. It was the most terrifying thing I'd ever heard.

"Shit." Now Donna sounded scared, which freaked me out. "Run!"

The window exploded. Shards of glass flew at me as the werewolf burst through the wall, landing on all fours. It glanced at me, then charged directly at Donna. It was so incredibly fast that Donna didn't even have time to draw her gun before it caught her and threw her across the room. She hit the wall and crumpled to the floor.

"Donna!" I was afraid she was dead. I fumbled in my waistband for my gun. It wasn't there. I was crying. Where had I left it? The coffee table. It was on the coffee table. I ran toward it and hooked my foot on the leg of the couch. Tripped. Fell.

Then it was on me. I could feel its hot breath on the back of my neck. Burning saliva dripped into my ears. I somehow managed to turn over and came face-to-face with its glowing red eyes. I slapped at its head. Grabbing handfuls of thick, wiry hair, slick from the rain, I tried to get a hold, but my hands kept slipping off. It sat on my chest, and I couldn't move, couldn't even breathe. Its nails gouged my cheek. The pain was intense. I screamed then screamed again. I wondered if I'd ever stop.

Only when I realized it wasn't on me anymore did I stop. It could have easily killed me. Why hadn't it? There was a high, piercing screech, full of pain and rage. Scrambling back on hands and heel, I saw the werewolf pin Donna to the floor. She thrashed, but it bit her shoulder. Blood splattered the walls and soaked the carpet as Donna began to lose the fight. Blood was everywhere. I scrambled to my gun, and silently thanked God I'd loaded it the minute we'd walked in the door.

Grabbing it, I rolled over and jumped up. When I turned to aim, an enormous paw sliced through the air and slammed into my face. I twisted and crashed into Mom's entry table. Dazed, I crumpled to the floor. Sounds filled the room and assaulted me. Snarls. Growls. Screams. Pounding. Thumping. My cheek throbbed. My ears rang. My head spun. Everything was a blur.

Blinking several times, I tried to clear my vision. Donna was dying. My hands shook. When I glanced down, I realized the gun was still in my grasp. I aimed. Fired. Missed. Tried a second time, then a third. The bullets went wild until a primitive scream indicated I actually hit the werewolf. It grabbed its shoulder, then pulled its bloody paw away. It stared at it, surprised, and roared. The sound filled my mind.

Before I could think, it hurled itself forward, rushing so fast I almost couldn't see it. Somehow, I got the gun up, closed my eyes, and pulled the trigger. Again. And again. The shots echoed through the room. Then there was a blood-curdling scream.

Coming out of me.

☽

"Jaime? Son, wake up."

I didn't want to. I didn't want to see anything or find out what had happened. But when my dad lightly slapped my face, I had no choice but to open my eyes.

"What—" Then I remembered and started swinging. I think I clipped my father on the side of the head before he grabbed my wrists and held me down until I stopped fighting. He wasn't the werewolf. I shot the werewolf. Didn't I? Straining under Dad's weight, I tried to see past him, to where the monster was.

"It's okay." He hovered over me. "It's dead."

"Dead? Are you sure?"

He nodded. "You shot it. Don't you remember?"

Unfortunately, I did. He eased off me and I pushed myself upright. When my knees crumpled, he grabbed me under the arms, hefted me up, and leaned me against the wall.

As if from far away, a voice floated into my consciousness, faint and distant. "Robbie, for heaven's sake, sit him down on the couch before he passes out again."

Hands dragged me over and sat me next to Mom. Her arm came across my shoulders and I leaned against her, enjoying the warmth of her embrace. Once the room stopped spinning and the urge to puke disappeared, I opened my eyes.

Donna lay in a dark puddle. I must have whimpered, because Dad turned and looked over his shoulder.

He turned back to me, his eyes hooded and dull. "I'm sorry, son. She's gone."

"Did I—"

"No. The werewolf killed her."

"It's okay, sweetie." Mom assured me with a pat on the knee. "You killed it. See?"

She pointed to the other side of the room.

It lay there, several bloody holes in its chest. It didn't look like anything I'd ever seen, or even imagined. Half way between human and beast, but not resembling either. We watched it slowly take on more human features. Within a few minutes, it was no longer a monster at all. Nor was it who I assumed it was, not by a long shot. I gasped as a small strawberry-colored birthmark appeared on her forehead.

It was PJ, the diner owner.

Thursday, December 19, 2013

WANING CRESCENT

Old moon
Growing smaller
41% Visible

Chapter 26

It was early evening when I finally woke, exhausted—emotionally as well as physically. Murmured voices came from the kitchen, so I swung my feet off the bed and onto the floor. My whole body felt like it'd been run over by Donna's make-believe moving van. I groaned, rubbed the back of my neck, and slowly stood, testing my arms, legs, and body to make sure all the parts were still there. Satisfied that I was still in one piece, I left my bedroom and walked into the kitchen.

The adults sat at the table with a pot of tea in front of them. There was also a full plate of Christmas cookies that hadn't been touched. Standing in the doorway for a minute, I enjoyed the fact my family was mostly intact. The only thing missing was Beth.

When my mom saw me, she smiled like the Cheshire cat from that Disney cartoon. "There you are, sleepy head. We've been waiting for you." She pulled out the chair next to her and patted the seat. "Come and sit here next to me."

I ran my fingers through my hair, mustered up something resembling a smile, and went and sat down.

"Do you want some tea?" Aunt Judy offered and picked up the teapot. "It's blueberry."

Oh, God, Aunt Judy. How could I ever face her again?

"Auntie, I—"

"We'll talk about it later, sweetie." She stood, kissed me on the cheek, then wiped the lipstick mark off with her thumb. "Would you rather I fix you a pot of Earl Grey? Get some caffeine going to help you wake up?"

I nodded, unable to speak. My throat closed as tears welled and threatened to spill. I didn't care. I'd made a terrible mistake, but it seemed like she'd forgiven me anyway. Even though I didn't deserve it.

When she set a huge mug in front of me, I cupped my hands around it and inhaled. I didn't care for tea, especially Earl Grey, but if I dumped a ton of sugar into it, I could handle it. Anything to make it up to my aunt.

I dumped about a cup and a half of sugar into my mug, blew on it, and took a sip. It did taste better than it smelled. I took another sip before realizing no one was looking at me. Mom was chewing her nails, Dad was scratching his side under his arm, and Aunt Judy was staring at a point on the wall somewhere behind me.

"What?" I put down my mug. "Is it Beth? Is she okay?"

"She's going to be just fine," Dad began. "She woke up this morning about four-fifteen, and asked for you."

"She did?"

He nodded. It was so weird that she'd regained consciousness about the same time the werewolf attacked. But I didn't get a chance to think about that until later.

"We have something to tell you." He licked his lips, something he only did when he was really, really nervous. "Something we should've told you a while ago, before all this started." He glanced at Mom, who nodded, and he continued. "A long time ago, right after your mother and I graduated from high school, actually, we decided we'd leave the town where we grew up and find a place where we could live in peace.

"You see, son, we were once part of a very violent society. We came to Wolf Creek with a bunch of our friends to start over in a new place. To start a new life." He paused and reached out to put his hand on top of mine.

"I don't understand."

"I know you don't, but I hope you will after we show you something."

"We wanted, no, we *needed,* to live in harmony with humans," Mom added.

"Live—in harmony—with humans?" That made no sense at all. Was I missing something?

That's when Dad's face began to distort. At first, I thought I'd been knocked on the head too hard, so I blinked and rubbed a hand across my eyes. It didn't help, because his face was really changing. It got bigger, broader, somehow, and began to flicker, like a heat shimmer on the horizon. Squinting, I cocked my head in an attempt to focus. When he remained fuzzy, I turned to Mom, only to find that she was fuzzy, too. Then it hit me that this had nothing to do with my eyes.

I was sitting in the kitchen I'd grown up and eaten all my meals in, the one I felt safe in, but what I was seeing would change my life forever. Pieces clicked into place, and I stood up so fast my chair flew into the wall behind me, gouging a deep hole that Dad would have to repair in a few days.

"No," I shouted. "It's not possible."

"Yes, son. It is."

I looked into the face of the monster.

Tuesday, June 2, 2015

FULL MOON

100% Visible

Chapter 27

Two years later:

Today was my sixteenth birthday. Never thought I'd make it, after what happened when I was fourteen. Especially finding out I was a werewolf. That was worse than watching Donna Glass die, accusing my aunt of being a psychopathic monster, and losing my best friend all put together. I still miss Riff every day. We were supposed to get our driver's licenses together. Go to the prom together. Get our first jobs together. I'll never have another friend like Riff.

I talk to Donna sometimes. Ask her for advice on how to handle things. Once in a while, I can almost hear her talking to me. It's how I knew where to find the stash of silver bullets she'd hidden in the storeroom behind the bar. Every December ninth, I put one on her grave. I'll do it every year for the rest of my life.

It turned out that PJ had caught a virus. Moonspell. It's where a werewolf loses control over herself—or himself, because we males can catch it, too—and can't stop their transformation during the full moon, no matter how much they might want to. And because a victim of Moonspell can't control their actions, poor PJ couldn't help but do what came naturally. It's kind of how humans could slowly go insane. It happened a little at a time, and the victim usually didn't even realize it.

The whole town turned out for PJ's funeral. That was the day I started to tell who was one of us and who wasn't. You'd be surprised. I was.

Beth's thirteen now, a straight A student, but still a little smart-ass. She just finished seventh grade and has her first boyfriend. I do miss the Wendy's hair, though.

Aunt Judy got a job with the Defense Department and they moved to Colorado. It took a while, but Beth finally accepted the fact that her father really did have a heart attack, which was why he drove his Audi into a tree. She spends a month with us every summer and I look forward to seeing her. She's actually excited about being a werewolf and can't wait for her time to come, no matter how bad I tell her it is.

It took me a long time to wrap my head around everything that happened. I was brought up with all the same myths and legends about werewolves as my human friends, so it took me time to adjust to the fact that I was one, especially after transforming last year. Hurt like hell at first, what with your bones elongating, your head doubling in size, and all that hair you have to deal with. Your skin burns, your teeth hurt, and, to be honest, running around with no clothes on doesn't do much for me.

But it's the bloodlust that's hardest to control. It's a werewolf's nature to eat human flesh, but the very idea turns my stomach. The urge is almost overwhelming.

Imagine if someone you loved, your mother or sister or aunt, were tortured and murdered. Then the loser who did it bragged about it all over town but was never punished. The rage you'd feel, the insane fury, would make it difficult, if not impossible, not to hunt the psycho down and do the same thing to him.

That's exactly what our bloodlust is like.

Kind of like the way my whole body itches, just under the skin where I can't get to it.

My parents tell me that it takes time, but sometimes I worry. Now that I'm in high school, I've made a few new friends. It's been hard, but so far I'm doing okay. I've learned to take it one lunar cycle at a time. I guess my parents are right.

Only time will tell.

About the Author

After sixteen years as a paralegal, Lisanne Harrington staged a coup and left the straight-laced corporate world behind forever. Now she panders to her muse, a sarcastic little so-and-so who delights in getting the voices in her head to either all speak at once in a cacophony of noise or to remain completely silent. Only copious hamburgers and Diet Cherry Dr. Peppers will ensure their complicity in filling her head with stories of serial killers, werewolves, and the things that live under your bed.

When not writing, she watches reruns of *Gilmore Girls*, horror movies like *Sharknado* and *Fido*, and Investigation Discovery crime shows. She likes scary clowns, coffee with flavored creamer, and French fries. Lots and lots of French fries. She lives in SoCal, in the small town she fashioned *Moonspell's* Wolf Creek after, with her beloved husband and persistently rowdy but sweet miniature pinscher, Fiona.

9 781626 945258